TWICE UPON A LIE

TWICE UPON A LIE

Once Upon A Crime Trilogy: Book Two

NOLON KING

STERLING & STONE

Chapter One

IT WAS ALMOST WITCHING HOUR, the time of night when superstitious fools thought the denizens of hell wielded the most power.

He didn't fear the supernatural. Not when there was so much evil in the world wrought by human hands. And various other body parts.

A warm breeze caressed his chin, his cheeks. The bill of his baseball cap, pulled low, blocked the air from reaching higher. Sweat dampened his hair, but he couldn't remove the hat on the off chance someone might pass by. It wouldn't do to be recognized. That's why he'd rented a generic sedan. Why he'd smeared dirt on the license plate. Why he'd already popped the hood and prepared the equipment.

A random passerby just glancing his way would see

1

nothing but a guy waiting on a jump. Unless they took a closer look. But anyone who got that near to him wouldn't survive the inspection.

He had a plan. A carefully crafted, every-contingency-accounted-for plan. It had required countless hours of research and application, well worth the time and effort. There was no way to know the number of criminals who'd been caught because they believed a Hollywood myth, but he was determined not to add to that number.

Contrary to what movies would like people to believe, the likelihood of someone dying from live jumper cables touching their skin was incredibly small. But the likelihood of someone dying from a properly calibrated picana was practically a foregone conclusion.

He knew first-hand how painful a shock from a wand could be. Had endured hours of high-voltage, low-current jolts over the years at the hands of a number of sadists.

Sadists like Caleb Yates, whose favorite implement of torture was a cattle prod.

No, his plan required planning. Precision. Perfection.

And he was ready. He'd thought of everything.

The rental.

The hat.

The elaborate assembly guaranteeing a high-voltage, *high*-current shock.

The jumper cable ruse.

Now, all he had to do was wait.

That was the hardest part. Time slowed with each passing second. Anticipation built in proportion. His heart rate climbed until his pulse thudded in his ears, drowning out the dirge of the crickets and the rumble of thunder.

When he didn't think he could wait a moment more, the harsh beam of headlights cut through the gloom of darkness.

Finally.

A shiver of excitement shuddered through him.

It was the perfect night to enact his plan. He'd waited weeks for stormy weather. Roiling clouds now cloaked the moon and stars. The threat of rain was the perfect lure … no one could resist helping a "friend" whose battery died when a torrential downpour was imminent. Not when he was in the middle of nowhere, so there'd be no Good Samaritans passing by. The only thing better would be if the rain was actually falling, but he'd planned for that, too. Had a pail of water ready and waiting.

A flash of lightning illuminated the road and the car driving toward him, which was almost definitely a silver Jaguar — and Caleb Yates.

When the vehicle crossed lanes to pull nose-to-nose with his rental, even the tiniest niggle of doubt fled. It was the Jag. It was Yates.

It was time.

He wiped his clammy hands on his thighs. If sweat-slicked fingers compromised his grip, it could all be over.

Caleb turned off his engine, then climbed out of his car. Even though it was the middle of the night, he'd taken the time to change out of pajamas — if he'd even been wearing any — and dressed in pressed khaki slacks and a pristine white golf shirt. His damp hair had been combed back from his face. He'd even donned his watch. The only indication that he'd been roused from slumber was a slight shadow of stubble on his face.

Surprised he hadn't dealt with that, too.

What kind of self-important asshole found out his friend was stranded and about to get caught in a storm, then took the time to shower and root through his closet before rendering aid?

Unbelievable.

A fresh wave of anger surged through him, tinging his vision red in the otherwise black of night.

"Hey, man." Caleb leaned down to pop his hood while speaking. "I can't believe you aren't a member of an auto club. Not that I mind helping."

Though he very clearly did.

"I mean, I couldn't leave you stranded in a storm, right?" He gave a mirthless chuckle as he slammed his door closed, then he strutted to the front of his car, preening like some kind of superhero wannabe. While fumbling for the release, he said, "What the hell are you doing out here in the middle of the night, anyway?"

"There was something I had to take care of." He fought to hold in a burst of maniacal laughter. What would Yates say if he blurted out the truth? It would be so satisfying to see the look on his face when realization dawned.

But it would be even more satisfying at the culmination of his plan. He'd have his moment. Any second now …

Cables in hand, he stepped forward. Stood right behind the bastard. His hands trembled with rapturous anticipation. And this time, he couldn't hold back a snigger.

Yates raised the hood, turned around. "Hand me the— Oh, good. You've got them ready. No, not like that. You have to connect the dead battery first." He flicked one of the red clamps. "Only the positive. Not the negative yet. Once you do yours, I'll connect both of mine. Then you connect the black one last. Got it?"

"Got it." He turned back to his car. But instead of attaching the clamp to the battery, he cranked up the power feeding his homemade picana.

"Ready on your end?" Caleb asked.

"Oh, yeah. Been waiting for this for longer than you can possibly imagine."

"Really? How long were you out here before you called me?"

He spun around, flung the water all over Caleb.

"What the—"

Clutching the rod tightly, he jabbed it into the asshole's chest, cutting off the petulant whines and vulgar exhortations he was undoubtedly about to utter.

Time slowed to continental-drift speed.

Caleb's eyes widened. His face contorted, equal parts electric shock and abject horror. His knuckles turned white as his fingers tightened around the useless handles of the unattached jumper cables. As the current coursed through his veins, his body went rigid. Grew taller. Stretched until he flew off his feet, backward into the inner workings of his car. He slid onto his bumper then slumped to the ground.

The Jaguar's headlamps reflected off the sides of his face, his tanned skin a sickly blue in the artificial light. When he pitched forward, the back of his designer shirt was marred with streaks of grease and grime.

Muscles no longer contracting, his face fell slack. The cables fell from his flaccid grip. Absent was the rise and fall of his chest, the flutter of his eyelids … anything indicating life.

But it wasn't enough.

He stepped closer. Straddled the heap of blood and bone and body formerly known as Caleb Yates. As he had no interest in touching the man — he didn't deserve the courtesy, and it would be a grave mistake to leave behind DNA evidence — he used his foot to nudge him back. Unable to stop himself, he put all his weight behind that leg, grinding the sole of his shoe into the soft flesh of Caleb's pectoral muscle.

Even that wasn't enough.

So he backed up, made sure he wasn't touching so much as a hair on Caleb's head, then plunged the rod into his chest once more.

Would have been so much more satisfying if it was a sword. Or if Yates had been alive to suffer the assault again.

But neither was the case and time was of the essence, so he returned to his rental. Dismantled his picana device, stowed the items in a duffle in the back seat. Properly attached the jumper cables, carefully aligned the clamps with the marks he'd already left on Caleb's body, then delivered a pointless shock to the inanimate corpse, the smell of singeing fabric and burning flesh an assault on his nostrils. It was an odor he knew too well — one he gagged on in his nightmares and woke choking on, the memories as visceral as reality.

He hoped never to experience such a reek again. That was the whole point of this night — to exorcise that particular ghost from his past.

After adding the cables to his bag, he climbed behind the wheel.

It had taken Yates fifteen minutes longer to get there than he'd expected, so he'd already been there a quarter hour more than he'd budgeted for. But he couldn't resist taking one last moment to revel in the beauty of his triumph. To celebrate the victory, long overdue but immensely cathartic. To swim in the rush of endorphins flooding his system until he was dizzy with euphoria and languorous with gratification.

Caleb Yates had finally paid for his crimes. And, as was fitting, his sentence had been carried out at the hand of his victim. It didn't get better than that. Justice had been meted, and in fairer fashion than any court in the land could demand.

Yet the pleasure was short-lived. The satisfaction fleeting. He couldn't let it go. It wasn't enough to pay back shock for shock.

He needed to pay back humiliation for humiliation, too.

Earlier, time had crawled. Now, it raced. He'd already been there too long. But he had one last punishment to dole out. One Yates deserved, just as much if not more than the electrocution.

After quickly donning gloves, he popped the trunk. Found the spare tire, but more importantly, the lug wrench that went with it. Walked back to Caleb.

"Shame about those pants. No one's ever going to know how nicely they were pressed when they find them bunched around your ankles."

Unfastening the belt, button, and zipper was more difficult than he expected, and the seconds flew by. Perspiration dripped down his temples, ran down his back. His fingers trembled so much, they were nearly useless, and the latex covering them made it difficult for him to feel what he was attempting to do. Finally, though, he had the waistband loosened.

The first drops of rain started to fall, then the skies opened. He was soaked in an instant. A flash of lightning brightened the night, chased immediately by a roar of thunder.

It took even more effort to slide down the sopping wet slacks. He was panting with exertion by the time he managed it.

Holding a metal rod in the middle of a storm was the last thing he wanted to do. But he paused, finding it difficult to finish. Maybe because it was a spur of the moment decision rather than something he'd carefully planned.

More likely because it was too intimate. Deserved, to be sure. But still … did anyone deserve such a violation?

Yes. Hell, yes. Yates did.

He'd never been the one on this side of the assault before. His stomach nearly revolted at the thought of what he was about to do. But it was nothing that hadn't been done to him hundreds of times. Maybe thousands.

Deep breath in, deep breath out.

Tire iron in position, grip firm.

Another inhale. Another flash of lightning. Another roar of thunder, right on its tail.

He jolted. Jerked his arm. Shoved — maybe harder than necessary.

The force awakened something inside him. Something … feral. Something that wasn't satisfied with one deep plunge. He repeated the motion over and over and over again, jamming the tire iron farther each time until he was utterly spent.

But unlike when it was done to him, there was no pleading, no crying, no screaming.

There was nothing.

And he felt hollow. Because one degradation didn't make up for dozens. Just like one electric jolt didn't cancel out countless others.

He wouldn't be satisfied until they'd all paid. And even then, it might not be enough. It might never be enough.

Drenched and drained of energy, he trudged back to his rental. He started the engine, turned on his headlights. Took a final look at the fruits of his labor. Then he drove away. Tomorrow, he would replace the lug wrench, return the car, then start working on his next plan for retribution. But tonight, he would sleep. He'd earned the rest.

It was the witching hour. And he'd just slayed one of his demons.

Chapter Two

JIM TRUDGED up the precinct's back stairs to the bullpen, rubbing sleep from his eyes. He stumbled on the last step and nearly took a header into the door. That trip and recovery should have jolted him awake, but it only made him alert for an instant. Then exhaustion settled on him like a shroud again. When he started to yawn, he didn't even bother stifling it.

If he had to be up all night, it would be nice if it was because he was doing something pleasurable. Something worth the bleary vision and lethargy. But no, he'd stayed up staring at the ceiling, the ghost of crimes past haunting his thoughts.

Had been that way on and off for the better part of the year. Since his last partner had died, actually. First, it was a night here or there. Then it was once, maybe twice a month. Now it was once or twice a week.

Pretty soon, it would be every fucking night.

He made a mental note to buy some melatonin before going home. In the meantime, he needed to slog through the next eight or nine hours. With any luck, he and

Sullivan wouldn't catch any new cases, so he could ride the desk and catch up on paperwork. Boring, but just what his weary body needed today. Assuming he could stay awake.

"Hey, Jim.

"Morning, McPherson."

"Charlie. Norm." He nodded at the detectives as he shuffled past them. They were standing at a case board covered with photos, papers, and almost illegible words scrawled in dry-erase marker. A few words popped out at him as he ambled by. Wine. Poison. Easton Burgess.

Easton Burgess? That name was familiar.

"When'd you land the Burgess case?"

"We've had it since the beginning," Norm said.

"What's it been, now?" Charlie asked. "Three weeks?"

"Give or take," his partner confirmed. "Why?"

Jim shook his head. "Didn't know you had that one. Wasn't on your board."

"Solved the Schumaker case yesterday," Norm said. "It was the nanny."

"You always thought it was. Nice work."

"Thanks."

"Took that info down this morning. Put this stuff up." Charlie nodded toward the board.

"Any leads?"

They both shook their heads.

"Something'll turn up."

Each muttered something he couldn't make out as they returned their gazes to their evidence.

Jim walked to the back table, where the box of donuts held only crumbs and the coffee pot was empty. Should have stopped for breakfast like he usually did, but he'd been running late. And of course, he was also too late for the meager offerings here. Sighing, he rinsed out the carafe, filled up the reservoir, put a filter and grounds in the basket, then hit the "on" button. The station wouldn't pay for a gourmet brand, so it wasn't going to be good. But it would at least be fresh. And he made sure it would be strong.

While he waited, he went to the vending machine. Zingers weren't exactly the breakfast of champions, but he told himself the raspberry coating was technically fruit and coconut was healthy in its natural form, so he bought two packages. If nothing else, he might get a sugar high for an hour or two.

Chelsea was glaring at him across the room. Early. The woman was perpetually early. And perpetually irritated with him when he wasn't. To her, on time was late. Today, he was officially late.

As a peace offering, he pointed to the coffee then to her. She held up an insulated cup. Probably brought hot milk or something equally wholesome from home. He ate two Zingers while the pot finished brewing, then he poured himself a cup — hot, strong, and not nearly as robust as the Italian roast he favored at the coffee shop.

What he wouldn't do for an espresso right about now.

Jim wove around the desks in the bullpen, ignoring the whispers and stares from a few uniforms passing through. When he sat at his desk across from his partner, he held up his unopened package of snack cakes. "Have breakfast yet? Want one?"

"That's not breakfast." Sullivan wrinkled her nose. "Honestly, you have the palate of a child."

"You know better than that. I've cooked for you plenty of times." He covered his mouth, doing a poor job of hiding another yawn.

"Is this ever going to stop?"

"What? Me being tired? Insomnia is temporary. I'll pass out eventually."

"Hopefully not behind the wheel of a car. But that's not what I meant."

"Junk for breakfast? I didn't have time to make eggs. Or stop at the cafe."

"I'm talking about your animosity toward the unis."

He ate half a snack cake in one bite then chased it with some scalding hot java. That woke him up. After he coughed on an errant crumb or coconut flake, he said, "Let's get something straight. I don't have any animosity toward any of the uniforms downstairs. Well, Thompson's not my favorite guy on the force. And his buddies Miller and Berger are cut from a similar cloth." He thought back six months to the fight they'd started with him in the locker room. The one he was more than happy to finish. Even if the captain hadn't been overjoyed about it. "But that's it. Any so-called animosity you're sensing between me and other officers is all their damage, not mine."

"You could make more of an effort."

"How? They're the ones who hate me. Tell them to make the effort."

"Why must you always be difficult?"

"I prefer to think of myself as uncompromising."

"Of course you do." Chelsea turned up the volume on her computer.

She was listening to the *Steel City Special* podcast. Again. Today, the too-charming-to-be-genuine host, Kingston Kane, was interviewing a local doctor instead of his usual silver screen celebrity.

Jim couldn't stand the guy. He saw right through the facade. But then, he had a perspective Chelsea didn't.

"I thought you only listened to that crap when someone famous was on."

"Dr. Van Covington is famous. He wrote the definitive book on couples therapy."

"That's a movie starring Vince Vaughn. Not his best work, not his worst. Decent cast, all told. A few pretty funny moments. There's this scene where—"

"I'm not talking about the movie. I'm talking about a well-respected psychiatrist and his work with failing relationships. He's even had sessions with movie stars."

"Why would someone from Hollywood come to Steel City for marriage counseling?"

"Because he's that good. Now, shh." She batted her hand at him.

But Davenport's door flew open with a bang. He stood at the threshold and bellowed, "McPherson. Sullivan. Get in here."

She sighed. "This was going to be a good one, too."

"It's not a network show, Chels." Jim pushed to his feet. "It's a podcast. Play it later."

"It's not the same as listening live."

He rolled his eyes at her back as he followed her to the captain's office.

The "Captain Lou Davenport" nameplate at the front of the desk was the only thing remotely in its proper place in the office. He had a drawer pulled out to hold his phone because his desk was littered with files and papers. His laptop was balanced precariously on his windowsill. A suit jacket and tie hung off a U-shaped handle of an umbrella that he'd wedged inside a half-open filing cabinet.

"Sit," he barked.

One of the chairs was over by the bookcase. Hopefully the captain hadn't tried standing on it to reach something on the top shelf. It was highly unlikely the sagging seat would support his ample girth. Jim wasn't sure it would hold his weight. But Chelsea had gone for the other chair, so this one was his only option. He dragged it back to the front of the desk.

Meanwhile, his partner took a pile of papers off the other one. She looked around for a place to put it, and as the desk was overflowing and Davenport didn't reach for the pages or suggest where she could put them, she chose to stack them neatly on the floor. Just before she sat, she looked at the broken chair Jim had carried over then cocked her head toward the one she'd cleared.

Nice of her to switch with him. She didn't weigh enough to fall through the sagging seat. Even so, she perched on the edge instead of sitting back comfortably. He sat back in the chair she'd relinquished and stifled another yawn.

"Am I keeping you from your beauty sleep, McPherson?"

"Sorry, Captain. I didn't sleep last night."

Sullivan scowled and muttered, "Now's not the time to discuss your extracurricular activities."

He sighed. "Insomnia is hardly an extracurricular activity."

"Children, no bickering in the backseat." Davenport grabbed his coffee, took a large gulp, winced. When he put the cup down, he missed the tiny clear spot on his desk where it would fit. It tipped over, spilling the last few sips onto a folder. "Son of a—"

"I got it." Chelsea jumped to her feet and pulled a wad of tissues from her pocket. She blotted the small puddle until just a small brown stain remained.

"Thanks, Sullivan." The captain sighed and leaned back in his chair. "I swear, the files multiply every time I look away."

"Something we can do to help?" she asked.

"Budgets. Interdepartmental disciplinary actions." He glanced at Jim. "Close rates down. Caseloads up. Undercover ops crossing zones. Public approval ratings at a record low." He sighed again. "I'm getting too old for this."

"What can we do?" Jim asked.

"Solve a high-profile case. Quickly. Give the department a win."

"We solved the Grimm Reaper case. That got us some good press."

"That was six months ago."

"Sir." Chelsea shifted her weight. When the chair creaked, she froze. "All our cases are important. We put the same effort into each of them."

"This isn't a press conference, Sullivan. You don't have to be politically correct. Yes, all our cases are important, but there's no denying some are more publicly scrutinized than others."

"Captain," Jim said, "none of us has any high-profile cases right now. The most notable unsolved murder Zone Four has is the Burgess case, and Charlie and Norm have that one."

Davenport picked up the folder with the fresh coffee stain then passed it across his desk to Jim. "You've got one now. Some muckety-muck from the Hill. Just came in this morning."

"How do you already have a file on him? Her?"

"Him. The boys in white collar crimes sent it down. Potential money launderer."

"Uh, Captain?" Chelsea said. "We're homicide."

"You don't say." He grabbed his empty cup, scowled, then set it down again. "This info landed on my desk because the guy just turned up dead."

"He cheat the people he was in bed with?" Jim asked.

"Funny you should put it that way."

"What do you mean?"

"The murderer was clearly trying to send a message. And it doesn't look money-related."

"How does it look?" Chelsea asked.

Jim frowned. "Was the guy found in his lover's bed or something?"

Davenport shook his head. "Or something."

"What?"

"No. Beaver Hollow Road. Right out in the open."

"Beaver Hollow Road is hardly in the open," Jim said. "No one uses it except the occasional college kid on the way to class."

"I didn't say well-traveled. I said out in the open. Now, get going. With any luck, you can get the body out of there before the press gets wind of what happened."

"What did happen?" Chelsea asked.

Jim finally opened the folder and looked at the name at the top of the first page.

Caleb Yates.

His stomach soured. That's why Easton Burgess's name was familiar to him. Both Yates and Burgess were friends with his parents.

Was it just coincidence, or was someone targeting the wealthy of the city?

He had a feeling the latter was the case. No proof yet. Just a hunch. But his hunches were almost always right. And if he was right, he was, for the first time in his professional life, terrified.

Because it might mean his mom and dad were now in danger.

Chapter Three

THE DRIVE to Beaver Hollow Road was short, but Chelsea had to take the opportunity to discuss her concerns with her partner. She hadn't been sure she should until he told her to drive.

He *never* let her drive.

"Jim?"

His eyes were closed. "Hmm?"

"Look, I don't mean to cross a line, but—"

"We're partners. Very little you could say to me would be crossing a line."

"Your dating life is starting to impact our work, and I'm concerned."

He opened his eyes and turned toward her. "I'm curious, Sullivan. When, exactly, did you decide I was a serial dater? Day one or did you wait until day two?"

"I … I never said you were a serial dater." She didn't say it, but she did imply it. And now she needed to defend it. "What you do on your off hours is none of my business—"

"Damn straight."

"Until it is. You do go out a lot."

"Says who?"

"The day we met you made a lewd comment about the … date you'd had the night before. You have an on-again/off-again relationship with that woman at that restaurant."

"If you mean Alessa, there's nothing 'on' about it."

"You've been out on quite a few dates since I met you, and I'm pretty sure they've all been with different women."

"It's a crime to date different people?"

"No, but it is a problem if it's making you tired at work."

He sighed. "I am sorry if I said something crass the day we met. I honestly don't remember what it was, but I'm sure it was a joke. Obviously a bad one, but there was nothing malicious about it. I treat the women I date with respect, and I should do better about being respectful to you, too."

"Well, I mean, we're cops. And partners. We should be more casual and comfortable with each other than random coworkers."

"Regardless, if it bothers you, I'll be more careful. But it might interest you to know that since we met six months ago, I think I've had three dates. And none of them were all-nighters. So I don't know why you're under the impression that I'm in a different bed every night, but I'd really like the judgment to stop. I clearly offended you with something I said six months ago, but it was an accident. And I don't think I've done it since. If I did, I apologize again. But you make snide comments daily about me and my sex life, and you're not only doing it on purpose, you're wrong. It gets old, Sullivan."

Why was she so judgmental of his private life? And why did she think it was a lot more active than it was?

"If I misjudged you, then I'm sorry. But you've been dragging yourself to work for months, practically asleep on your feet. I just assumed—"

"That's right. You assumed. You never asked."

"Then I'm asking now. If you weren't … out with someone, why are you so tired?"

"Because I'm not sleeping."

"Obviously. But why?"

"Oh, look. We're here." He jumped out of the car while she was still rolling to a stop.

Chelsea sighed and parked the car. As she donned gloves, she headed over to where he was already talking with the medical examiner.

Nia Washington had been with the department for almost six months, and she was doing a great job. But one look at the ME's expression, and it was clear this case was a first for her. One look at the victim, and Chelsea knew it was a first for her, as well. She couldn't contain her gasp of horror.

"I know," Nia said. "I was stunned, too."

Stunned? Try horrified.

The man had been partially stripped then sodomized with a tire iron. He'd been left with the offending implement still inserted, and given how little of the handle was visible, she feared it had ruptured one — or all — of his internal organs. The thought of dying that way made her gag. She whirled around. Took a few deep breaths until she was certain she wouldn't contaminate the crime scene. Turned slowly back toward the victim, though she kept her gaze averted from the lower half of his body. "What a horrible way to go."

"This isn't what killed him," Nia said.

"You're kidding. It's so … the depth is … how did it not …" Chelsea sighed. "If not that, then what was the cause of death?"

"It looks like he was electrocuted."

She glanced at the sky, where dark clouds rolled fat and low toward the horizon. It would start raining again any minute. "It stormed last night."

McPherson shook his head. "Wasn't lightning that did this. It was intentional."

"How can you tell?"

"Well, for one thing, the weather couldn't shove a lug wrench up someone's—"

"Jim!" Nia's eyes were wide.

He rolled his.

"Before you got here, I did a cursory exam. The front of his shirt has two burn marks on it. My guess is that's where the current entered his body, and that's the COD. I'll know more once I have him back at the morgue."

"Aren't you going to …" Chelsea gestured at the tire iron.

"No. If at all possible, it's best remove it in a controlled environment. Sorry. The techs and I will figure out how to best transport the vic. I'm about ready to load him now, if that's okay with you."

"I've seen enough." She'd seen way more than enough. "Jim?"

"Are you and the techs done documenting everything?" he asked Nia.

"Yes." She gestured for a technician to join her then slipped a bag over one of the victim's hands. "I was here an hour before you guys. What took you so long? You usually beat me to a scene."

"We headed out as soon as Davenport assigned us the

case," Chelsea said. "Might have taken him a while to give it to us, though. He had a file for us already, so he could have been waiting on that. Could have been there for months, though. Hard to tell. I don't know how he can find anything in that mess."

"Well, I got the call practically the second I got to the morgue. I hadn't even put away my car keys." Nia turned the vic onto his side then slid a bag over his other hand. "Since I hadn't started work yet, it was easy for me to head out right away." She started giving instructions to the two crime scene technicians who came to help her.

Chelsea concentrated on the victim's shirt, keeping her focus away from his exposed genitalia as well as from the expression of agony frozen on his face. And that's when she saw it. "Nia? Did you document that?"

"What? The burn holes?"

"No. That smudge." She pointed to his chest then all three of them leaned closer to get a better look. "Kind of looks like the sole of a shoe, doesn't it?"

"Maybe." Nia grabbed her camera. "I already have pics of the shirt, but let me get a few more of this mark, just to be sure."

"And see if you can get trace off it. Probably just road grit from here, but we could get lucky and find some weird dirt from somewhere exclusive. And if we can identify the shoe make and size—"

"I know how to do my job, Chelsea. So do the techs."

"Right. Of course. Sorry."

Nia smiled. "It's okay. I want to catch the person who did this as much as you do."

"I'll leave you to it, then." She turned away. The last thing she wanted was to watch them try to move the decedent with the tire iron still in place.

Times like these, she wondered if she'd picked the right

profession. She loved putting away criminals, but cleaning up the streets required her to become mired in the muck first, and she didn't always have the stomach for it.

Chelsea took a few steps back to survey the whole scene. No houses. No businesses. No cameras. Nothing but overgrown weeds on the side of the road. They weren't going to find video evidence or witnesses. Even if they did, it had been storming the night before. It would have been too dark for anyone to see anything if they'd tried to, and a recording would have been useless. The rain probably washed away any DNA.

Great. The captain wanted a slam-dunk on a high-profile case, and they had practically nothing to go on.

Jim walked over to her. "See anything?"

"No. Nothing. We aren't going to have any witnesses or any video evidence. We desperately needed the rain, but it didn't do us any favors."

"Want to speculate?"

"Guessing isn't police work."

"No, but like you said, we've got precious little to go on. At least until the autopsy is done. I've got a working theory."

"Based on what? We have no evidence."

"We have a dead rich guy who was on the side of the road. Looks like he had car trouble, right?"

"Why would a rich guy be on this road in the middle of the night?"

"I can think of plenty of reasons. Buying drugs? On the way home from a date?"

Of course he'd think about a date. Chelsea shook her head at herself. She needed to stop jumping to conclusions about him and his social life. "He looks like he's in his fifties, maybe sixties. Based on the clothes and car, and what Davenport said, he's clearly well-off. If he was using drugs, I'd think he had a better source than someone who would want to meet here. As for your other theory, who would he be dating around here? Some random sorority girl he had to sneak to be with? Surely, he'd be more discriminating that that."

"That's not my theory. I just said it was possible. So, to answer your question, a lot of older men prefer younger women. And the rich ones often find them willing."

"I know. But … I don't know. Seems like a quick ticket to a paternity suit and having to pay out a lot of that all-important money he's so obviously rolling in."

"I never said it was smart. I said it happens. Regardless, that's not what I'm thinking."

"Then why'd you bring it up?"

"Trying to get your mind going."

Chelsea sighed and rolled her eyes. "Stop worrying about my mind. What is your theory?"

"No. Keep going. What do you think?"

"I'm not thinking anything yet."

"Then what do you think I think?"

"Seriously?"

"Yeah, Sullivan. Seriously. Either guess, or guess about what I think. But stretch your mind a little and see if you don't stumble on a new idea or twelve. This isn't going to be our usual case, and we're probably going to have to be mentally nimble. Maybe downright creative."

She averted her gaze from the body being loaded into the coroner's van. "He's on his way back to his wife after cheating with his little chippy—"

"Chippy?"

"Call her whatever you want. Anyway, he breaks down. Someone happens to come by, sees the helpless rich guy, then takes advantage of the situation. Things get out of hand, and he gets killed. And if that wasn't enough, sodomized." She shook her head. "No. I don't buy it."

"You're not going outside your comfort zone. Your focus is too narrow."

"I think we should wait until we have more evidence to look at."

"Well, we don't right now. So, I'll tell you what I'm thinking. No wife. No sorority girl. And not even broken down out here."

"How do you know he wasn't married? Oh, no ring? Not everyone wears a ring, though."

He didn't say anything.

"Why don't you think he was seeing a college girl? And of course he was broken down. His car is on the side of the road, and the hood is up."

"For someone not willing to guess, you're already locked into one scenario — one the evidence doesn't even support. Broaden your mind a bit."

They'd been partners for six months, and they had an impressive close rate. His record was legendary before they were paired up. But in all that time, he still hadn't realized that she didn't guess. She let the evidence guide her. His way of speculating might land him on a theory that eventually panned out, but it was even more likely that it wouldn't. Some of his ideas were completely outlandish. Maybe they made a good team because they were opposites in that regard. But that didn't make him easy to keep up with. Or even work with, at times. "Okay, Jim. Since we've got no real leads and you're determined to make wild guesses, what was your single rich guy doing out here?"

"Definitely not dating a college girl." Jim tapped his

chin as he stared at the silver Jaguar. "I don't think it was a crime of opportunity. His wallet and phone were still on him. Sound system was still in the car. Clearly wasn't a carjacking."

"So, a sexual deviant happened upon him when he was broken down? And that still doesn't explain why he was out in the middle of nowhere."

"I don't think he was broken down, either."

Chelsea pushed her hair out of her face. It was starting to drizzle. If the techs had any hope of recovering anything useful from last night, they were down to minutes, maybe only seconds. She turned to Jim. "Why? If he wasn't seeing a co-ed and wasn't broken down, how did he end up dead and violated on the side of a deserted road?"

"The burn marks on his shirt. They're about the size of jumper cable clamps, right?"

"Yeah."

"And this happened in the rain. Before last night, we were in the middle of a drought. Now, all of a sudden, there's rain and the guy gets electrocuted. Seems way too coincidental. I think it was planned."

"Someone planned to electrocute him when he broke down on the side of a deserted road in the middle of the night? How? How could anyone possibly plan that?"

"Because our vic didn't break down. He came out here to help out someone who was broken down. Someone who called him for assistance."

Chelsea looked up at him. "Someone he knew."

"Exactly. The storm was a lure. Couldn't wait for an auto club or a ride share because of the rain. Might have been stuck for hours, just waiting. Besides, water conducts electricity. Would have made the jumper cables more dangerous."

"Our vic knew his killer well enough to render aid in a storm. That seriously narrows our suspect list."

Jim smiled and nodded.

Maybe speculation wasn't such a bad idea, after all. "We need to pull his phone records."

"And narrow our small list down to one."

Chapter Four

Jim stifled a yawn as he walked up to his parents' door. Didn't even feel bad about leaving work an hour early. He'd had a sleepless night followed by a hellacious day — lousy weather, sadistic murder, very little evidence, phone records a bust, no autopsy report until the morning.

Yeah, the day was a total shit-show. And it wasn't over yet.

All he wanted to do was go home and sleep. Didn't even care if he had dinner.

Instead, he shook rainwater out of his hair, sloughed it off his arms, and wiped his feet on their welcome mat. The juxtaposition of such a warm and cheery greeting — even as he scraped the soles of his shoes on it — with the sad and somber message he was about to deliver struck him as painful and cruel. He usually tried not to think about such things, but he also usually delivered this kind of news to strangers, and while he was genuinely compassionate and empathized with them, he was also able to maintain a professional distance.

That wasn't the case today.

The door swung open before he could reach for the handle.

"What are you standing out there for?" Dad said. "You've been there for more than a minute."

"How do you know?" Jim stepped inside, trying not to brush against his father on his way past. He didn't quite manage it.

Dad held up his phone while wiping off his elbow. "New security system. We can see anyone anywhere in or around the house."

It gave him a little peace of mind to know his parents were safe — relatively speaking — at home. At the same time, it tore at him to think such measures were necessary.

Now, perhaps more than ever.

"Mom home?"

"In the kitchen. Come on. I'll get us towels and maybe she can be persuaded to make us a snack."

Jim followed him down the hall. "You'll be eating dinner in a couple hours."

"That's right. A couple hours. So … snack."

"If you eat now, you'll ruin your dinner." Mom's voice came from the kitchen, but she met them at the end of the hall, towels in hand. She tossed one at Dad but started dabbing at Jim's arm with the other.

He took it from her, kissed her cheek, then scrubbed himself dry.

"I hope you're hungry. We're having carnitas for dinner. I have a four-pound roast in the oven."

"Four pounds? For the two of you?"

"Three, now. You will stay, won't you?"

"I really just want to go home."

"Nonsense. There's plenty, and you're already here."

"Plenty? You made enough for an army."

"If there's any left—"

"There won't be," Dad said.

"There better be." Mom shot him a look. "I'll pack the leftovers for you to take home. Are you okay? You look like you've lost weight."

"I haven't."

"Have you been eating? That's it, you're definitely staying. I'll make rice, too."

"Mom, I'm not staying. And you don't need to make rice."

"Look at you. You're peaked. And too thin."

"I'm not too thin. I'm just tired. It's been a long day. I just want to go home, get a shower, and go to bed."

"And not eat? Don't be silly. You're staying for dinner."

"Mother!" His voice was a little louder than he intended.

Her eyes widened, and she took a slight step back.

"James." Dad scowled at him.

"I'm sorry. I didn't mean to yell. Like I said, it's been a long day, and it's not quite over yet. Can we sit?" He motioned to the table.

"I'll get us something to drink. Iced tea?" Mom headed toward the refrigerator, stopped mid-way, then turned around. "Wine? Something stronger?"

"I really don't want anything. But I do need to talk to you both. Can we please just sit?" He dropped into his usual chair at the table.

She opened the refrigerator door. "Brant, will you help me for a moment?"

Dad joined her. He returned with plates, napkins, and a platter of olives and cheeses. Mom was on his heels with a bottle of wine and three glasses.

Jim rubbed his head. Should have just asked for something stronger and been done with it. It was so much easier to accept his mother's offer of one thing — anything —

than it was to try to decline. She'd empty her entire kitchen before letting him leave without eating or drinking something. And didn't bourbon sound good right about now?

While she poured, Dad popped an olive in his mouth. "These are the good ones. Where'd you get these, Vivian?"

"That little shop at the Warehouse District. The one that sells the Mediterranean foods and spices."

Jim drained half his wine in one gulp.

Mom finished pouring her glass, then she emptied the bottle into his. "You know, I have—"

"Really, this is more than enough. I came here because …" But he didn't have the words.

"What is it, Jim?" She placed her hand over his.

He squeezed her fingers. Looked across the table at his dad. Shook his head. "I have some bad news."

Mom's palm grew noticeably colder. Her grip tightened even though she was trembling. "You're scaring me. Are you sick?"

His dad's complexion took on a pale, greenish tinge under his tan.

Jim shook his head. "No. It's not me. I'm fine."

"Are you sure?" She touched his forehead. "You don't look well."

He took another long sip. "I told you, I'm just tired. Chelsea and I are on a case that …"

"What?" Dad asked.

"It's hitting too close to home. I'm worried about you two. And I have bad news."

"Your case might impact us?" Dad took a long draw from his own glass.

"Two of the detectives in my precinct are investigating Easton Burgess's death."

"Easton?" Mom put down her drink. "He had a heart attack."

Jim shook his head. "It's looking like he was poisoned. Something in the wine. I don't have the details."

Both his parents pushed their glasses away from them.

Finally, Dad sighed. "That's tragic, and I'm — we're — sorry to hear it. But I don't understand what it has to do with us. You don't think we had something to do with it, do you?"

Mom gasped.

Jim shook his head. "No, nothing like that." He tipped his head side to side and rolled his shoulders, trying to alleviate the tension that seemed to have taken up permanent residence in his neck and back.

"Then, what?" Dad slipped his arm around Mom. They scooted closer to each other in such a seamless way, it looked less like an awkward shifting of chairs and more like a long-practiced choreographed dance. And in many ways, it was.

He envied them their ease together. Their innate sense of their partner's needs and the comfort they provided each other.

Jim didn't have that with anyone. Closest he'd come was with his first partner on the force. Certainly didn't have it in his dating life.

Wouldn't mind a little of that comfort now.

"Chelsea and I caught a case this morning. A murder." Obviously. He was a homicide detective, what else would it be? Jaywalking?

"Someone associated with Easton?" Mom asked.

"It was Caleb Yates."

Tears welled in her eyes, rolled down her cheeks. Dad's face somehow grew even paler as he pulled her into a tight embrace. She nestled against him and cried softly into his chest.

"Are you sure?" Dad whispered, voice hoarse.

Jim nodded. "I'm sorry to break the news like this. I just needed to be sure you knew. So you could take precautions."

"Precautions?" Mom's head whipped up. "Why?"

"I'm not trying to scare you."

"Well, what are you trying to do? Look how you've upset your mother."

"Between Yates last night and Burgess a few weeks ago, I—"

"Easton was a heart attack!" Mom's eyes were wild, her breathing rapid. "That's what everyone said!"

"It's not, Mom. Or at least, it's not being treated like natural causes. Not anymore. It's been labeled suspicious and is under investigation."

"Who would want to hurt Easton? Or Caleb?"

Dad rubbed her arm as he continued to hold and comfort her. "Jim, are you sure about this? Maybe there's been a mistake. Who identified Caleb's bod—" His voice broke. He cleared his throat. "Who identified the remains?"

"I was there, Dad. I saw him. Saw his car. There's no mistake."

"Then maybe it was an accident. Maybe both were accidents and the police are investigating for nothing."

Jim shook his head. "I wish that were true, but no. This was no accident. That's why I wanted to tell you myself. Check in on you. Make sure you're being cautious and not taking unnecessary risks. Not answering the door to strangers. Staying in unless you absolutely have to go somewhere."

"What about the funeral tomorrow?" Mom asked.

"What funeral?"

"Alex's."

"Who?"

"Alexander Kensington," Dad said.

The name tickled something in Jim's brain, but he couldn't put his finger on it and shook his head.

"Average height. Bald on top. Resting frown face but he's almost always laughing at something."

"Kind of looks like a peanut," Mom added.

That was helpful.

"One of the founders of X-Cellcior Biotech?" Dad's eyebrows arched. "Surely you recognize that."

At the mention of the company name, realization dawned. Jim had seen Kensington at a few of his parents' holiday parties and every now and then at the country club, but he'd never said so much as a syllable to the man. He always seemed too busy boasting about himself to bother with a peon like a police detective — even if that detective was the son of Brant and Vivian McPherson.

And Mom was right. He did look like a peanut.

"Kensington's dead?"

Dad shook his head. "For a cop, you're woefully uninformed about the goings-on in this city."

"In my defense, he doesn't live in the zone I cover."

"There's this marvelous invention called the news. Perhaps you've heard of it? I'm given to understand it's available in a wide range of media and is accessible twenty-four hours a day."

"Thanks, Dad. I'll look into that." He popped a piece of cheese in his mouth. Shouldn't have done that. It only made him realize he was hungry.

"You really hadn't heard?" Mom asked.

"I've been a little busy. When I'm not working, I'm trying to sleep."

"Trying? That's why you look so dreadful."

"Thanks."

She continued like he hadn't spoken. "You're working too much, and you're not sleeping."

"I'm working the same amount as every other detective in the city."

"When was the last time you went on a date?"

"I'm not discussing my love life with you."

"Alessa still isn't seeing anyone. Why don't you give her a call?"

"Not going to happen." He pushed away from the table, stood, then bent down for an olive.

"You two were so good together."

"I need to leave now, Mom."

"Why won't you even consider a reconciliation? I'm certain she'd say yes if you asked her out. Even just to talk."

"What are the details of the funeral tomorrow? Is it at Kuruc's Funeral Home? Which cemetery? I need to make plans with Sullivan."

"Jim, just because you ignore what I'm saying doesn't change the truth of it. The two of you are perfect for each other. If you're so adamant on rejecting her—"

"I didn't reject her, Mom."

"Then why did you break up?"

He looked at his father for help.

Dad merely shrugged, clearly aware once his wife started meddling, she wouldn't be stopped.

Jim snatched one last olive from the tray before walking around to the other side of the table. "Never mind. I'll look up the details online. See you both tomorrow." He planted a kiss on the top of his mom's head, squeezed his dad's shoulder, then headed for the hall.

No surprise, his parents followed him.

As soon as he passed through the front door, he turned around. "Keep all your doors locked and the security system activated. Make sure your cell phones are always charged. And don't turn off the cameras."

Dad frowned but nodded.

Mom shook her head. "You don't really think we're in danger, do you?"

"I don't know. But three of your friends seem to have been."

"More like acquaintances," Dad said. "We're seldom in the same circles. Sort of circle-adjacent."

"Just be careful." The three of them stood there for a moment, staring at each other. Then he pointed at the door. "I'm not leaving until I hear you lock up."

Mom rolled her eyes as she started walking back toward the kitchen.

"You do realize we're the parents, right? We're the ones who are supposed to take care of you."

"Not this time."

"Be careful, Jim. If these deaths are related, you're talking about a killer who apparently can get to anybody. I don't know all the ins and outs of a situation like that — certainly not like you, anyway — but I do know that kind of killer, that kind of mind. It's not to be taken lightly."

"I know, Dad. That's why I'm so worried about you and Mom."

"And that's why we worry about you." He gave his son a rueful smile before closing the door.

Jim stayed there until he heard the lock engage, then he headed to his car.

His dad wasn't wrong. If these murders were connected, the killer had both a keen mind and access to the most elite citizens of the city. That made them extremely dangerous. Especially to the people Jim loved.

Chapter Five

CHELSEA TOOK from her pocket a vial of essential oils, a strong homemade blend of some of her favorite scents — lavender, tea tree, eucalyptus, lemon, and peppermint. It wasn't the simplest or cheapest of the aromas she mixed, but nothing she'd experimented with worked as well as this blend when finding a ripe corpse or attending an autopsy.

She dabbed some under her nose then slipped on a mask before opening the door to the morgue.

The oils and facial covering helped, but they didn't block everything. Hopefully, her revulsion didn't show.

Nia looked up and smiled. "Still not used to it, huh?"

"I don't know what you mean."

"Yeah, you do. But if you want to play it cool, fine by me." She looked down again and continued working. "What are you all dressed up for?"

Chelsea looked down at her black pantsuit, a choice she regretted after her second cup of coffee. Chances were she'd be changing into something more practical — and comfortable — at lunch. "McPherson and I are going to a funeral this morning."

Nia's head snapped up. "A cop? I didn't hear anything."

"Not one of us." Thank God. "Alexander Kensington's. Jim has a hunch his murder and our case are related. Easton Burgess, too, if you can believe that."

"Well, yeah. I can see where that's possible." She bent over her work again.

Chelsea inched forward, but not far enough to see the gory details of Nia's autopsy. The stench was bad enough. "Really? The MOs are entirely different."

"But the vics are all similar, right? Pillars of the community. Titans of industry."

"Friends, Jim says. Or at least acquaintances. But they don't live near each other. Don't work in the same fields. Best he could tell me was he'd seen them at the same functions before."

"Most people who reach the pinnacle of their careers run in the same circles, I would think. At least, when they all live and work in the same city."

"That's a tenuous thread. Just as likely to break as it is to tie all the murders together."

"So? Investigate until you prove the connection or rule it out."

"That's why we're going to the funeral."

"Then, hopefully you have an answer soon enough."

"Speaking of answers …"

"Sorry, Chelsea. I only have a preliminary report so far. I have to finish this one and conduct another before I get to your guy. Probably won't be able to start him until tomorrow."

"Tomorrow?"

"It's first-come, first-served. Unless the brass tells me otherwise."

"Didn't Davenport tell you this was important?"

Nia laughed. "He tells me they're all important." She sobered. "And they are. Just because Caleb Yates was wealthy doesn't mean he gets moved to the front of the line. Not in my morgue, anyway."

"Sorry. I'm just anxious to get as much information as I can. I want to get this guy before he strikes again. Or woman, I guess."

"You were right the first time, I think."

"Oh?"

"It would have taken a lot of strength to do what the killer did with the tire iron. I suppose it could have been an extraordinarily powerful woman, or one fueled by an excess of adrenaline or something synthetic, but if I had to guess, I'd say it was a man who did it. I'll know more after the autopsy, but that's in my initial report, which I've already emailed you and Jim."

Chelsea wrinkled her nose — partly against the smell, partly against the image Nia's words painted. "Crime of passion, then? Because we didn't think it was a spontaneous event. We thought circumstances suggested a lot of forethought and planning."

"Can't it be both? A crime of passion doesn't necessarily mean a crime of opportunity, does it? I think you're right regarding the preplanning. The murder was definitely premeditated. But that doesn't mean the killer wasn't impassioned. In fact, I'd guess his anger with the victim was why he planned and executed the murder to begin with."

"You're right. I'm being too narrow with my word choices and definitions. I just want answers."

"You'll get them. But not from me. Not today, anyway. Read the preliminary report. If you have any questions, let me know. Otherwise, I'll probably start the autopsy first thing tomorrow and then compile my findings for you."

"Thanks, Nia."

"Sure. I hope you find something useful at the funeral."

"Me, too. I'll take any lead at this point, no matter how small." She waved on her way out the door. It wasn't until she was halfway down the hall that she took off her mask. The cloying reek of decay and the metallic odor of blood lingered in her nose. Or the thought of the corpse's stench did. Only with a deep breath could she detect her essential oil blend, and she had to suffer more unpleasant smells if she did so.

Breathing shallowly — and through her mouth — she stopped in the restroom. After freshening up, she sprayed her clothes with a fabric refresher and even spritzed some in her hair. She reapplied lipstick and the essential oils, then she returned to her desk.

Jim was already there. And he'd cleaned up for the occasion. Gone was the casually tousled hair, the ever-present stubble, and the clothes that barely met departmental dress code standards. His hair was carefully combed, his face clean shaven, and he wore a gorgeous — and probably custom-tailored — black suit with a crisp, blindingly white shirt and a gray tie.

Her jaw dropped, and she had to make a determined effort to close her mouth. She had wondered if she'd over-dressed for the occasion. Now she feared the opposite was the case.

Chelsea slipped into her seat across from him. The fronts of their desks were butted together, making for one large work surface between them. Yet hers was always tidy and his always … not. Today was no exception, and he rifled through papers looking for God knew what. "Morning, Jim. What'd you lose today?"

"I printed us both a copy of Nia's preliminary report. I don't know where I put them, though."

Neil walked up behind him, cup of coffee in one hand, sheaf of papers in the other. He dropped the pages on Jim's desk and bumped him with his elbow. "You left these back by the coffee maker. And I just brought a box of donuts up, if you want to grab one before they're all picked over."

"Thanks, Rafferty." McPherson give him a weak smile but didn't make eye contact. He separated the two reports, passed one across the desks, then plopped into his chair.

Chelsea, however, smiled up at her long-time friend and former patrol partner. "Returned paperwork and donuts? You've outdone yourself, Neil."

He shook his head. "Not me. You did. You look incredible today, Chels."

"This old thing?" She laughed. If he had been anyone else, she'd have taken it as a come-on. But Neil was … Neil. He wouldn't have felt more like her brother if they'd shared DNA.

Jim glanced over at her then went back to his reading.

"You got a hot date?" Neil asked.

"In the middle of a workday?"

He shrugged. "After work."

"If I did, I wouldn't be dressed for it now. We're checking out a funeral this morning."

"Kensington's?"

"Yeah. Why?"

"Had drinks with Morrison last night." The three of them plus Danny Sherick had been inseparable in the academy, but only she and Neil had been assigned to Zone Four after graduating. Morrison was in Zone Three and Sherick had gone to the State Police. Of the three city cops, she was the only one who had already made detective. "He's working traffic over there today. Between you and me, he's not happy about it."

"It's a crappy detail. Directing traffic in this heat."

Neil shrugged. "Wouldn't have to do it if Kensington wasn't connected."

"Connected? To the mob? I didn't think we had that kind of problem here."

"It's not like the 1930s, but the mafia will never truly go away. Anyhow, that's not what I meant."

Chelsea glanced at Jim, who couldn't look more interested in his papers if they'd had naked ladies on them. He was clearly eavesdropping, not that the conversation was confidential. She returned her attention to Neil, who had propped his hip on her desk and was starting to settle in and get comfortable. "Then what do you mean?"

"Come on, Sullivan. You haven't been off the streets that long that you've forgotten how things work. We might wear the badges, but we don't keep order in this city. And we might report to the mayor, but he sure as hell doesn't run it. The power players in this city — hell, in any metropolis — are the people who get the mayor elected. They're the ones who call the shots. Government and democracy are nothing but an illusion."

"You can't be that gullible, Neil. You don't really believe that."

"If you don't, you're the naive one." He looked toward the main door and popped to his feet. "Davenport's coming. Gotta go." Neil started walking toward the back stairs. As he left, he spoke over his shoulder. "You really do look hot today, Sullivan."

Chelsea waved him off and picked up her copy of the preliminary autopsy report. As Davenport passed, he muttered hello. At least, she hoped that's what it was, as she offered a chipper greeting of her own. "Good morning, Captain."

He paused on his way to his office, looked at them

both. A puzzled expression crossed his face, then he nodded and continued on.

She met Jim's gaze. "You didn't even say hello."

After staring at her a long moment, he said, "You do look really good today."

Her face flamed, and she ran her hands through her hair. "No ponytail today. Seemed too casual. I'm kind of regretting the decision, though. It's going to be so hot at the cemetery."

"Yeah. I'm not looking forward to putting this jacket back on."

"It's a beautiful suit. You look quite handsome today."

"Is that your way of saying I don't look handsome any other time?"

She scowled. "Why do you have to be so difficult?"

He laughed. "Because it makes you react like that."

"Point taken."

Jim glanced at his watch. "We need to go. I'll drive."

"Of course you will."

"The funeral home and cemetery are thirty minutes away, and that's without traffic."

"I'm surprised he didn't choose someplace in the city. Or near where he lives." She preceded him down the stairs and pitched her voice so he could hear over her clomping heels. "Why all the way to Upper Bristol?"

"That's where he grew up. Probably wanted to be with the rest of his family. I looked up the cemetery last night. Over a hundred acres of rolling hills and mature trees. Twenty-one different … gardens, I think they called them. Looks like a beautiful place. If you care about that sort of thing."

"You don't?"

"When I'm gone, I'm gone. I doubt I'll really care

where they put my body at that point. Probably have more pressing concerns, seeing as I'll be dead and all."

Chelsea was quiet as they crossed the parking lot. But after they were both in the SUV and he was backing out, she turned toward him. "You're not really worried about that, are you?"

"About what?"

"The afterlife. Where you end up."

"Looking for an existential debate? Or a theological one?"

"Neither. I … I just don't want you thinking badly of yourself. Or worrying about anything."

"Trying to save my soul, Sullivan? You know, now that you mention it, you do remind me of Sister Sarah."

"I didn't mention anything." She was silent for a moment while she tried to figure out what he meant. After a long while, she gave up. "Who's Sister Sarah?"

Jim glanced at her. "*Guys and Dolls*? Save-a-Soul Mission? Sarah Brown and Sky Masterson?"

She shook her head.

"Jean Simmons and Marlon Brando? No?"

"Sorry."

"Come on, Chels. It's a classic."

"If it didn't take place on the ice and involve a stick and a puck, my dad didn't watch it."

"That's no excuse. You haven't lived with your dad in ages."

"When I do turn on the television, it's usually crime shows. Sometimes one of the home improvement channels."

"I'm going to look and see which streaming service airs it. Then we're watching it. I'll get pizza and beer—"

"I don't—"

"I know. Soda for you. We have to do it soon. Maybe

this weekend. I'm going to make it my mission to school you on old movies."

"I've done all right so far in my life without watching any."

"You haven't seen *any* of the classics?"

She sighed. "I don't know. I'm sure I've seen something you call 'classic' at some point."

"You've led a sad life."

He wasn't wrong. "I'm doing okay."

"I don't know how you can call yourself an adult and not have seen *Guys and Dolls*."

"I don't know any grown men of our generation who have seen it."

He pressed his hand to his chest and splayed his fingers wide. "You wound me."

"Who'd have thought Big Bad Detective McPherson had a soft spot for old musicals?"

"At least you know *of* the movie. And if you're trying to tease me, you should know I'll never apologize for being a fan of Brando. Or Sinatra."

"I think you were born in the wrong decade, Jim."

"Funny. I often think that of you."

She frowned and looked out the window.

"Hey." He nudged her arm. "That's not a bad thing."

Wasn't it? It was so hard to tell anymore. She was never certain if he was joking or serious, so she usually assumed he was serious.

He cleared his throat. "So, while I'm driving, why don't you go over that report. See if there's anything we should take note of before we get to the funeral."

Chelsea read through the pages Nia had sent them, but there was nothing that they hadn't discussed in person. Nothing that Jim was apparently hoping for. "Pretty standard stuff at this point. Cause of death was electrocution, not … the assault with the tire iron." The memory made her stomach roil. "The initial tox screen didn't turn up anything of note, but she collected a blood sample for a more thorough analysis. She'll know more after the autopsy."

"I was afraid of that. Would have been nice to have a hair, a fiber … anything that would get us closer to ID-ing his killer. As it is, we're just looking for someone acting odd at a funeral. And everyone acts odd at a funeral."

"Well, maybe we're not totally in the dark."

"You find something in the report?"

"No. I was thinking about what Neil said."

"Rafferty?"

"Yeah. He said the mayor isn't in charge. Lawmakers make the laws to suit those in power, and cops enforce said laws the same way."

"So?"

"So, do you think that's true?"

Jim sighed. "Sullivan, that's been true since laws existed, more or less. That's hardly a new lead to chase down."

"It seems so cynical. Why become a cop if the system's so corrupt?"

"Because it's not always corrupt. The movers and shakers only throw their weight around if they need something. And most of the time, they don't because they already have a lot or are getting what they want somewhere else. So we can help most victims and their loved ones. We don't often encounter road blocks like this. When we do, though, it makes our job twice as difficult."

"I don't believe that. That's not how the world works."

"Life's not the box of chocolates Forest Gump proclaimed it to be. Sure, it's almost always a surprise. But it's seldom a sweet one."

46

"You're wrong."

He glanced her way.

"Well, I hope it's not that bad. Our society is based on equality."

"On paper, maybe. But ask any woman, any person of color, anyone who doesn't practice a Judeo-Christian religion or has an alternative lifestyle of any kind if everything is equal."

"Well, it's better here than anywhere else."

"So they say."

"You don't think so?"

"I think most people go around paying no attention to the man behind the curtain. The illusion of equality only works if you're willing to believe the big floating head. Surely you've seen that old movie."

She sighed. "Yes. Of course. But in Oz, everyone was equal."

"Oz was an injury-induced delusion. In reality, Almira Gulch had all the money and power in Dorothy's little corner of Kansas, and she was going to have Toto killed simply because he jumped her fence."

"Now who's the movie buff? It was because Toto bit her."

"Because he was always jumping her fence. Or digging under it. I don't remember which."

"Your view of life is so dark."

"You asked. I'm just calling it like I see it. So, what did you see in Rafferty's off-the-cuff statement that got past your rose-colored glasses?"

"If our theory is true, Caleb Yates knew his killer. And if your theory is true and our case is linked to Burgess and Kensington, then we're seriously narrowing the suspect pool."

"How? They all travel in the same circles."

"Yes. But we can eliminate family members. Or at least put them in the B column."

"Maybe."

"Humor me."

"Fine. Go on."

"So, if it's someone who has access to all three men and it's not family, that takes us to friends and acquaintances."

His jaw ticked.

She raised her eyebrows at that, but he didn't elaborate. Or maybe he didn't see her questioning look. In any event, she continued her train of thought. "We can probably safely exclude work associates, too, as they're all in different fields."

"Okay. What's this have to do with Rafferty?"

"If what he — and apparently you — thinks is true, then there's going to be someone who knows all three victims *and* who knows the mayor. Probably also the chief of police and the district attorney."

"And?"

"This person — the guy who knows the mayor, the chief, and the DA, maybe a few influential judges — thinks he's untouchable. We find him, then we'll have found our suspect."

"So close, Sullivan. But no dice."

"What do you mean?"

"You're right about someone pulling strings way above our pay grade. But you're wrong about who. Our suspect isn't the guy at the top. He's *taking out* the guys at the top."

"What? But we agreed the killer is someone Kensington, Burgess, and Yates knew. Someone who can get close to them. That means someone in the same high-powered circle as they are. That hardly screams 'vigilante' to me."

"Could be. Could also be a disgruntled former employee."

"They all work in different industries."

"Someone who feels he was swindled in a deal."

"By all of them? Three different deals?"

"I don't know, Sullivan. What I do know is your profile is just as likely to be of our current or future victims as it is of the killer. Maybe more."

"So, what do we look for at the cemetery?"

"Someone behaving strangely."

"But like you said, it's a funeral. No one's going to be acting normal."

"And now you see the problem."

Chapter Six

PRESENT DAY
Memorial Grove Cemetery
10:02 a.m.

OH, my God. Would the service never end? How could a man of the cloth lie so convincingly for so long? Just give the "ashes to ashes, dust to dust" speech and get on with it already.

Seeking peace and serenity, he tuned out and took a few deep breaths. In through his nose, out through pursed lips. Centering. Calming.

Composed.

His heart rate decreased as his patience increased.

He inhaled again, enjoying the perfume of freshly mowed grass and dozens — no, hundreds — of blooms. And just like that, his pleasure fled.

Too many for Alexander Kensington. The man deserved no flowers at all. Maybe black roses. Perhaps petals that had withered and died and would crumble to

51

dust at the softest touch, or the shriveled husks of dead botanical pods whose dried seeds inside emitted a death rattle when moved.

But fresh bouquets? Not for him. Not by today's standards of flowers at funerals. Now, floral sprays were designed to honor the deceased, to express sympathy for his passing.

He didn't deserve the sentiment.

Oh, for yesteryear, when flower arrangements were placed around a casket to ward off the stench of decomposing organs and rotting flesh. That was the fate Kensington deserved. Thanks to modern methods of internment, he would cheat that fate, too. Embalmed, preserved. Viewed by thousands of mourners over the last two days. Laid to rest surrounded by family and friends. Proceedings televised so the world could mark the passing of a titan of industry.

It was so much more than he deserved. It wasn't fair.

At least it had been a closed casket. He'd made sure the man wasn't fit for display.

His heart tripped at the memory. The rush of adrenaline pumping through his veins now was a shallow echo of the flood of endorphins that had once lifted him on a wave of exhilaration and unbridled rage then brought him crashing down on Kensington.

On his body.

On his head.

On his *face*.

Oh, it had been glorious retribution. That first impact reminded him of the fat slap of a home run hitter connecting with a slider, right on the sweet spot of the bat — a satisfying *crack* that echoed and lingered long after the damage was done.

And he'd done damage. Though one strike was nowhere near enough.

Kensington had invited him over for a game of billiards. Only asked because his family wasn't home and it was a game he thought he could win. Wasn't the bald bastard surprised at the way *he* played the game? Why shoot one ball with a cue stick when he could shove three into a sock and swing them like a military flail?

And swing them he did.

Yes, the first strike was the most gratifying. The reverberation up his arm was as spiritually fulfilling as the sound of the crack of Kensington's skull, but neither elicited a rapturous thrill equal to the man's expressions morphing rapidly from shock to pain to fear.

Ah, fear. Sweet as the smell of the flowers surrounding them now. Exciting as a first kiss. Titillating as the promise of sex. Just thinking about Alex's terror rising stirred something deep inside him. The more the bastard's life force ebbed, the more excitement flowed through him until, at last, Kensington was no more.

Didn't stop him from another swing or two, but the satisfaction had stopped when the prick's heart did.

Now, he stood with the other mourners under a giant maple tree, affecting a look of personal grief and sympathy for the family. With perverse satisfaction, he noted that not a single "loved one" shed a tear. They could try to claim Kennedy-level decorum and say they had to remain stoic in public for the sake of etiquette, but he knew better.

They were as glad as he was to see the asshole dead.

His only regret was that he didn't think to use the cue stick on Kensington the way he'd used the lug wrench on Yates. But he hadn't had that epiphany yet.

Wonder what the family would have thought of that …

walking in and seeing a piece of wood shoved up that fat bastard's miserable ass.

Far less than was his due.

A summer breeze shook the tree limbs, and dappled sunlight danced over the gleaming mahogany of the coffin — another luxury Kensington didn't deserve.

The officiant finally stopped droning on and directed them to disperse before the casket was installed in the mausoleum. He stood off to the side, making small talk with people who passed. When only the immediate family remained, he made himself leave. He still had plans to carry out, and if he drew suspicion on himself now, he might not get to see them all through. That would be the final insult, and he couldn't bear that.

Memorial Grove had acres of land and miles of road winding through it. He rolled down his windows and drove around the property for a while, surprisingly at peace in his surroundings. Giant statues of angels and saints smiled down on him, almost as though they condoned what he'd done. What he intended to keep doing.

If they'd ever been there for him in years past, he might give a flying fuck.

Fifteen minutes later, he made his way back toward Kensington's tomb, prepared to claim he was lost if anyone was still there.

But no mourners remained. The dead man was alone, as he should be.

He watched from a small distance as the gravediggers brought in a rig to haul the coffin inside the crypt. It was anticlimactic without a cascade of dirt pouring into a hole and burying the odious man with other vile creatures that would feast on his flesh.

While he'd enjoyed reliving Kensington's murder, he found no solace at his internment. It was a disappointment, a letdown. An end far too noble for the kind of man — the kind of monster — Alex was.

What he yearned for was the rush of meting out punishment, of administering justice for years of wrong doings.

What he craved — and would have — was his next victim.

Chapter Seven

JIM WAVED at his parents from the archway leading into the Kensington's dining room. They started weaving through the guests on their way to him.

"This is weird," Chelsea said. "It was one thing standing outside a mausoleum during his burial service. But coming to the reception after? That's for family and friends."

"We are family and friends. Well, acquaintances, anyway."

"Uh, no. We're not. I've never met any of these people in my life."

"I have."

"Good for you. The only place I've seen any of these people is on the news."

"Not true. You've met my parents."

"Once. At the hospital. When they had more pressing concerns on their minds."

"Well, this will give you a chance to get better acquainted."

"What?"

But he didn't have time to explain to her. His parents had cleared the gauntlet and his mom already had him in a hug. "Hey, Mom. Dad."

She stepped back. "Darling. Glad you could make it."

"You remember Chelsea."

Mom smiled. "Of course. So nice to see you again. Though the circumstances could be better."

"Mrs. McPherson. Mr. McPherson. Hello."

"Brant and Vivian, please." Dad shook her hand and gave a slight bow.

Jim rolled his eyes.

Mom handed him her plate. "You need to eat."

"We just got here. I'll get something in a bit."

"Well, start with this. You're looking peaked."

"You always say that."

"Then stop looking that way. Chelsea, dear, come with me. They have a wait staff passing trays of food, but there are also a few buffet tables set up."

"I'm fine, thanks, Mrs. McPherson."

"Vivian."

"Vivian."

"Nonsense. You're even thinner than Jimmy."

"I'd hope so!"

Mom laughed. "I meant proportionally speaking, of course. You two don't take proper care of yourselves. Did you even have breakfast today?"

"Coffee."

"That's it. Come with me. We're going to load you up." She took Chelsea's hand, pulled her forward, then started walking away. "I've used this caterer before. Their food is quite good, but you have got to try the crab cakes. They're exceptional." Her voice trailed off.

Chelsea looked desperately over her shoulder before they rounded the corner.

Dad held up his own plate. "Shrimp cocktail?"

"No, thanks. I'll get something in a bit. I want to look around first."

"Haven't found what you're looking for?"

"Not yet."

"Do you even know what you're looking for?"

"Honestly, no."

"How can you look for something when you don't know what that something is?"

"I'll know it when I see it, Dad."

"Well, how about we head back to the buffet? You can rescue your lovely partner from your mother, and I can get more shrimp. Maybe you'll find what you want on your way there."

As they started walking, Jim said, "God, you're as bad as Mom. Don't do that anymore."

"Do what?"

"Call her lovely. Or anything else inappropriate."

"How is it inappropriate to give her a compliment?"

"For starters, you didn't give her one. You said it to me. And second, I don't want you saying it to her, either. It's not like that with us. It can't be like that. We have to work together."

"Well, if you'd rekindle things with Alessa, your mother and I wouldn't have to intervene."

"You don't have to intervene now."

"If we're ever going to have grandchildren, I think we do."

They were nearing a buffet table. His mother had Chelsea cornered between a wall and a statue. He could only hope she was keeping her opinions about his love life to herself.

"My work partner is off limits, Dad."

"We'll put a pin in this discussion for now."

"We won't have it again, period."

"Have what again, darling?" Mom asked.

"Nothing. How's the food?" He nodded at Chelsea's nearly overflowing plate.

"Delicious. Want to help me eat some?" She held it out toward him.

"How would you know, dear? You haven't had any yet."

Chelsea gave his mother a wan smile then nibbled the corner of a canapé. "Yum."

"God, Mom. You put more calories on this one plate than she eats in a week."

"That just proves my point. The two of you aren't taking care of yourselves."

Jim reached over for Chelsea's dish — for which she mouthed a silent thank you out of view of his parents — then handed it to his dad. "Here. You said you were hungry. Have at it. We need to work." Then he took his partner by the elbow and guided her away.

"Thanks." This time, she gave voice to her appreciation. "Your mother is a force of nature."

"Dad's right on her heels."

"I don't think I would have gotten away from her without your intervention."

"Consider yourself rescued. But now, we need to work. Or do you want to eat first?"

"My stomach's too upset. I started the day in the morgue, and now I'm hobnobbing above my station. I couldn't eat if I tried."

"What are you talking about, above your station? There's no such thing as a station."

"There absolutely is, and I'm well out of mine. More to the point, that's why we're here, right? To figure out why the cream of the local crop is being targeted?"

"It is. But I don't like the way you put it."

"Doesn't matter how I put it. It is what it is. And right now, we have a job to do."

They rounded the corner from the main hallway into a formal parlor. Jim scanned the room for familiar faces. Then he stopped in his tracks.

"What is it?" Chelsea murmured.

"Not what," he managed through clenched teeth. "Who."

"Who?"

But he didn't have time to prepare her. From across the room, a woman locked onto him then sauntered over. "Jim McPherson. Fancy meeting you here. Or did you finally get booted off the force and now you're openly associating with the people who protected you?"

"Marcela Soto. Chelsea Sullivan."

His partner politely held out her hand, though her brow was wrinkled with confusion.

Soto ignored it, choosing instead to sneer as she looked Chelsea head to toe and back. "Flavor of the week, McPherson? Odd to start slumming it when you're at a social event."

Chelsea lowered her hand. Though she glared at Soto, her face turned scarlet.

"I'd thank you to show some respect to my partner, *Detective* Sullivan."

"Partner, huh?" She turned to Chelsea. "You know what he did? What he's capable of?"

"I know well and good what he's capable of. And I count myself lucky to have him watch my back. As for what he did, I do know. It's a shame you're too short-sighted to see the truth."

Soto laughed and turned back to Jim. "This one's

spunky. I like her. Assuming she doesn't turn out to be as dirty as you."

Chelsea lunged forward.

He pulled her back.

Soto only laughed harder. "What are you doing here, anyway? If she's not your date, then you're here in an official capacity. And I know this isn't your case because it's mine."

Jim had hoped to work in cooperation with the lead on the Kensington case, but now that he knew who the detective was, it was a nonstarter. "What do you care why I'm here?"

"Because I don't want you getting in my way. Can't have my case thrown out because a dirty cop tainted my evidence."

"Wow." Chelsea shook her head. "You're really something."

"Damn right, I am. And don't you forget it." She turned from Sullivan and skewered Jim with a glare that would make many suspects wither. "You don't want to tell me why you're here, fine. I can't make you. And I don't have cause to throw you out. Yet. But if you impede my investigation in even the most tangential way, I'll rain hellfire down on you until you drown in it. Do I make myself clear?"

"Have a lovely day, Marcela. Hope I don't see you around."

Soto intentionally bumped into each of them as she strode between them. Then she stormed off in the direction they'd just come from.

Chelsea stared after her. "So, she's delightful."

"Yeah. A little ray of sunshine to brighten our day."

"But she was right about one thing."

He cocked an eyebrow.

"I don't fit in here."

"Not this again."

"It's a fact. I think you might learn more if I leave. Or at least if we split up. People will be more likely to talk to one of their own than they are a stranger."

"I'm not one of them."

"No, you are. You just don't want to be. But you belong. Your parents socialize with these people, and you probably do, too. Or did at one point. While I'm with you, we look like cops. I stand out because I don't belong, and that draws attention to you, too. But when you're on your own, you look like a guest. So, go be a guest. Find out what we need to know. I'll wait outside." She turned to leave.

He grabbed her elbow. "Oh, no you don't. You're trying to get out of an uncomfortable situation by putting it all on me. But I'm uncomfortable, too. Just in a different way. You said I have your back. If you meant that, then you'll stay. And you'll cover mine, too."

"I hate it when you're logical."

"I hate it when you're not."

"I'm logical. Usually." Her lips twitched as she fought a chuckle. And finally lost the battle.

"Agree to disagree."

She rolled her eyes.

"Listen. For every dowager here who's going to want to flirt with me, there's a dirty old man who'd get his kicks out of chatting you up. Why don't we divide and conquer, then meet back at the buffet table in thirty? By then, I'll probably be ready to eat them out of food."

"I don't like it, but all right."

"You'll look more approachable if you smile."

"I don't want to be approachable."

"Chelsea …"

"Fine." She sighed.

"You look nervous. Carry a drink so you have something to do with your hands."

"You do your thing. Let me do mine." Then she wandered off toward the dining room.

They'd just been in the parlor. He found it distasteful to go into the billiard room. So, he meandered through the foyer toward a less formal living room. As he was passing the closed double doors of what was likely an office, a crash sounded from inside. Instinct kicked in, and he burst into the room.

Mrs. Kensington stood near the window, shards of broken crystal and a puddle of amber liquid at her feet. She slowly looked up at him. Her eyes held a vacant look, and her face was oddly expressionless. "I seem to have broken the cognac decanter."

"I'll go find a towel."

Her hand fluttered dismissively in the air. "Leave it be. Now I'll have an excuse to get the floors refinished." Her words slurred. "I never liked this stain color. So dark. Everything in this room, dark. Everything about Alex, dark."

That was a thread he wanted to pull. But first, he had to get her off her feet before her legs refused to support her weight. He crossed her room and slipped his arm around her waist. "Let's get you to the chair."

"Do you?"

"Do I what?" Jim helped her sit behind her husband's desk.

"Like this stain color? It's dark, righ? Evrythin's dark."

"Are you okay, Mrs. Kensington?"

She squinted at him. "You're Vizvian's boy, aren't you? Tim?"

"Jim."

"Tha's wha I said."

"How much did you have to drink, Mrs. Kensington?"

"Ophelia."

"How much, Ophelia."

"Jus a few nips."

"And by a few nips, you mean …"

"Four. Glasses." She put her finger to her lips. Or tried to. She hit her cheek, chin, and nose before finally succeeding. "Shhhh. Don't tell Dr. Conving … Dr. Covintone …" Her face scrunched as she considered what she wanted to say. "Dr. Cov-nin-none … wha'nenver."

The fact that she had to speak so deliberately and still couldn't get out a few syllables concerned him more than the broken bottle or even the four glasses. Though she was thin enough that four glasses might get her drunk, he remembered her as always being generous with her pours and perpetually having a glass in hand, so he expected she had a decent tolerance. Which meant more was at play. "Did this doctor give you a shot or a pill, Ophelia?"

She sprawled back in the chair and laughed. "Like a lil ol' pill was gonna help. You know who found 'im that way? Me. You know who that bitch of a cop thinks did it? Me. Why would I kill my meal ticket? Hmmm? Alex had 'is faults, same's nan-nyone. Worse'n most, truth be told. And sure, we had poblemens. Probemblems. Plobums?"

"Problems?"

She snapped her fingers. Kind of. "Yass. Tha's the word. We had probemens. But he paid for all this." She waved at the room. "Kind of fool would I be to kiss all this g'bye?"

"What kind of problems? Were you separated?"

"Only a smidge. He tol' me to move out, but it was jus' for a lil while. I know he was gonna take me back. But Detective Bitchface didn' believe me. Thinks I'd kill Alex over money. Hmph. If I 'as gonna off 'im, it'd be fer far worse 'en 'at."

"For what, then?"

This time, her finger didn't come close to her lips. "Shh. It wa' 'is secret ta tell. Not mine. I was'n even s'posed ta know."

Her words were getting harder to decipher. Her eyelids drooped, and her head lolled.

"Ophelia, is your doctor here now?"

The way her body twitched might have been a shrug. Might have been the first stirrings of a seizure. He had no way of knowing. But he couldn't risk another second without getting a professional opinion. She'd spiraled out of control — and out of consciousness — fast.

Jim darted from the room in search of anyone who could help. In the groups of people milling about, he didn't see a single doctor he recognized. So, he started asking each cluster of people if any of them was a medical professional, and each time he was answered with variants of "no." Finally, he stood in the middle of the main hallway and yelled over the din of the guests and catering staff. "Excuse me! Is there a doctor here? A nurse? An EMT?"

His shouted questions were met with a quiet hum of hushed discussion, but no affirmative replies, so he fished in his pocket for his phone to call 911. Chelsea scurried toward him from the kitchen as his parents approached from the dining room. He'd already pressed the three numbers and was about to connect the call when he noticed his mother was pulling a woman along with her. Everyone converged on him at the same time, and they moved as a unit, him in the lead, back toward the study without him issuing directions.

"Jim, this is Dr. Daly," Mom said. "Catherine and I play tennis at the club a few times a month."

"Pleasure." He held one of the office doors for her then followed her inside.

"Do you know what she took?"

"She said she had four glasses of cognac. I didn't see how much was still in the bottle before it shattered on the floor. She also implied a doctor gave her something. A pill. But she never said what kind."

"Call 911. Someone help me get her onto the floor. We need to lay her on her side."

Chelsea was already speaking softly into her phone, so Jim helped with Ophelia. "Should we induce vomiting?"

"Not if she took some form of benzodiazepine, which would be my guess for a grieving widow." She lifted each of Ophelia's eyelids and shone the beam of her cell phone's light directly onto her pupils. Then she looked at her wrist watch while taking checking her pulse. "If we can rouse her, great. Otherwise, we'll just monitor her vitals until the EMTs get here. Do CPR if necessary. Make sure she doesn't choke if she does throw up."

Chelsea ended her call. "Dispatcher said probably five minutes, maybe ten."

"Certainly don't need another death on top of Alex's," Dr. Daly muttered.

"Do you know the Kensingtons well?" Jim asked.

His mother glared at him.

"Alex more than Ophelia. X-Cellcior awarded me grant money last year, and he kept in touch to see how my research was coming."

"You're not a medical doctor?"

"No, I am. I don't practice, though. I have a lab by the river. But I promise you, I know what I'm doing. Inducing vomiting is the wrong call in this case."

Before he could question her further, the EMTs

arrived. Dr. Daly chose to ride with Ophelia in the ambulance.

When they were gone, Dad said, "I'll see if the caterers or any of the guests have the kids' numbers. They should know their mother is on the way to the hospital." He hurried out of the room.

Mom smacked his arm. "How could you embarrass me like that?"

"Like what?"

Chelsea walked over to the window then started picking up the broken crystal pieces.

"Catherine is my friend. And you were interrogating her like she's a common criminal."

"I was merely making polite conversation."

"Oh, don't give me that. You're seldom polite, and certainly not in a crisis."

"Gee, thanks, Mom."

Soto burst into the room. Her cheeks were flushed, and she huffed for breath. "Why didn't you call me, McPherson?"

"Oh, right. Because when I'm busy saving someone's life, I always think about calling you."

"That's why you're here today. You waited until I was out at the pool house." Her eyes were wide, wild. Her chest heaved as she sucked in large lungfuls of air. "Then, when the coast was clear, you poisoned her."

"Why?"

"What?" Mom asked, gaze darting back and forth between Jim and Soto.

"Because … because you and Ophelia were having an affair! That's why you killed Alexander, to get him out of the way. She couldn't leave him because she'd walk away with nothing. But if he died, she'd get it all."

"That's ridiculous!" Mom stepped toward.

Jim pulled her back. "If we were having an affair, why would I kill her when she was coming into a fortune?"

Soto paused, frowned, then her eyebrows arched. "She jilted you. It all makes sense. You bump off her husband so the two of you can live off her inheritance, but then she decides she'd rather not share. She threatened to turn you in, so you tried to kill her, too."

"How dare you accuse my son of—"

"Your son? Then I've got some questions for you, Mrs. McPherson."

"Marcela, give it a rest. You're bent out of shape because your prime suspect almost died and you weren't here but I was."

"And just why were you, Jim?"

"If you're so sure you're right — though we all know you're not — maybe you should go to the hospital. I have every confidence the doctors will save her, and you'll want to be there when she comes to so you can get her statement."

"If she points the finger your way, I'll throw every charge in the book at you."

"She's old enough to be my mother, Marcela. I wasn't sleeping with her. Or doing anything else. I barely even know her."

"I'll be in touch, McPherson."

"Can't wait."

Soto stormed from the room.

"Jim—"

"Not now, Mom. Please."

She stared at him for a pregnant moment, then her shoulders slumped. "I guess I'll go find your father, then."

"Before you go, one question."

"What?"

"Why's Dad looking for the Kensington kids?"

"Because they should know their mother overdosed. What's wrong with you today?"

"No, I mean …" He ran his hand through his hair. It had already been too long a day, and it was barely lunchtime. "This is the reception following their father's burial. Why aren't they here?"

"Oh. Um … I think the youngest boy said something about catching a flight back to Phoenix. The eldest got into a heated discussion with one of the board members, then both of them left for the office. And Gina went back to her house to lie down. She doesn't have a very strong constitution, and I'm sure this was a difficult day for her."

"How do you know all this?"

"Because I'm a considerate conversationalist and actually listen when I talk to people."

"I listen. It's my job to pay attention and read a room."

"Yes, darling, but you don't actually like to talk to people. So you don't chat with them. You interrogate them. People are far less likely to open up if they feel like they're under suspicion. Or will be." She patted him on the cheek then left the room.

"I know how to talk to people," he muttered.

Chelsea walked over. "Your mom is something else."

"You should see her when she's angry."

She chuckled. "Well, this day didn't go exactly as planned. What now? Head to the hospital to get a few moments with Mrs. Kensington when she comes to?"

"With Soto there? No thanks. I'm starving. Why don't we grab a bite to eat and sort through everything we learned today?"

"This place is too depressing. Can we leave?"

"Pizza?"

"Burgers?"

"Sure."

They exited the office. Jim turned toward the front door while Chelsea headed the other way. She grabbed his elbow. "Where are you going?"

"We agreed on burgers. Where are you going?"

"To say goodbye to your parents."

"If we try, we'll never get out of here."

"It's rude not to."

"They're used to it. Let's go."

She shook her head but walked with him through the foyer. "This was the craziest funeral I've ever been to."

He scoffed. "This wasn't even in my top ten."

"You're joking?"

Jim unlocked the car then opened his door. "Did I never tell you about my Uncle Edgar's funeral?"

"Tell me on the way to lunch. Unless you want to start talking about the case now." She climbed into the passenger seat.

He folded himself behind the wheel. "I guess we really do have a lot to talk about. I think there's more than meets the eye when it comes to the Kensingtons."

Chapter Eight

As Chelsea finished changing into something more practical, she reviewed all the events of that morning, from the autopsy to the funeral to the reception. She and Jim had gone over everything at lunch, and after a lengthy discussion over burgers — interrupted by a brief argument over whether zucchini fries were better than regular, which despite his vehement insistence to the contrary, they definitely were — they'd agreed on one thing.

The only case that was officially theirs to work on was Caleb Yates's murder, and they had no idea who was behind it.

She dropped onto a bench to rub the soreness out of her toes before slipping into more comfortable shoes. Heels might complete an outfit, but they weren't designed for all-day wear. Or her feet weren't. Maybe both.

Jim was waiting for her, probably impatiently. He always took their work seriously, but maybe because he was loosely acquainted with the victims in this case, he was particularly driven to solve it. Together, they were going to talk to Charlie and Norm. If they could definitively link victims Yates and Burgess, the captain would be more tolerant of them expanding their investigation. Provided he didn't take Jim off the case because of his connection to it.

Who was she kidding? Her partner would just work it in private if he was removed from it. And Davenport had to know that. It was better for all of them to keep Jim officially involved. That way, he still had to answer to someone for all his actions. At least, for the time being.

Her phone dinged. She didn't even glance at the screen. It would be a text from him, nagging her to hurry. He really had no patience. It was a minor miracle he hadn't left her there and sought out Norm and Charlie on his own.

On her way out of the locker room, Chelsea started to tie her hair into a ponytail. She almost bumped into Jim when she opened the door. "You couldn't give me five minutes?"

"Wasn't me." As they walked back to the bullpen, he held up his phone, the text app open. "It was Davenport."

She squinted at his message, then once her hair was secured, pulled out her own device to read the text. "Someone confessed to killing Yates? Nice. It'll be the easiest arrest we ever make."

"Don't you think we should hear him out before throwing the book at him?"

"It's not like we're looking at evidence and following a hunch, Jim. He's *confessing*. Why would he lie?"

"I don't know. But you said it yourself — we're not going off the evidence here. At the very least, we need to question him and see what he has to say before processing him."

"That's why we're going to go talk to him." She stopped beside her desk for a tablet and pen. "And making him write down his statement. In fact, I want to take lead on this one. You're too close to this to be objective."

A snuffly sort of snort was his only response. She took his lack of verbal argument as consent.

He continued walking toward the interrogation rooms. Chelsea hurried to catch him then maintained that pace to keep up with his long strides.

Jim glanced down at her notepad. "I just feel like you're jumping the gun."

"It's like you don't want to put this case to bed."

"No, I do. Nobody would be happier than me if this turns out to be legit. But it seems odd that we were reaching for leads, then all of a sudden, someone comes forward with a confession. It's too tidy."

"Or maybe we got lucky."

He stopped and stared at her. "If we arrest the wrong person, that means there's still a killer walking free."

"And if we do have our guy, we take a killer off the streets."

"What about Burgess and Kensington?"

Chelsea shrugged. "What about them? If our guy murdered all of them, then everyone puts a case to bed. And if he's only responsible for Yates, the other cases aren't ours to fret over."

"You're awfully detached on this one. Your bleeding heart usually makes everything more complicated."

"And you're often too dispassionate. Why is this one suddenly eating at you?"

He ran his hand through his hair and started walking again.

She didn't get him. Every time she thought they were on the same page, she discovered they weren't even in the same book.

By the time she reached the interrogation room, he was

already seated. She slipped into the lone vacant chair — across from the man who could make her job easy, beside the man who seemed determined to complicate things.

Chelsea put down the tablet and pen, reviewed the text she'd received from Davenport, then stared at the self-confessed murderer on the other side of the table. No harm letting him stew for a bit while she studied him and considered the best tactic to take.

"Mr. Speikman," Jim said. "Donald. Mind if we call you Donald? Or do you prefer Don?"

So much for her getting to take the lead.

"Don, I guess."

"You guess? You don't know how you prefer to be addressed?"

"Don. I prefer Don."

"Don, I'm puzzled. A murderer typically goes to great lengths to avoid being caught. You, on the other hand, have walked right into our precinct and confessed to a brutal crime. Mind explaining that?"

He shrugged. "What's to say? I did it. I felt bad after. Here I am, ready to atone. That's how the justice system works, right?"

"Not in my experience," Jim muttered.

"Mr. Speikman." Chelsea offered him the most empathetic smile she could muster. "Donald. Can you tell us how you knew the victim?"

"I didn't."

"Then why did you kill him?"

"It was a spur of the moment thing. Like road rage, but without the wheels."

Everything they'd uncovered so far suggested it was anything but a crime of opportunity. She began to deflate, fearing Jim might be right. But they needed more. So much more. "Could you please explain that?"

He shrugged. "Storm had rolled in. It was the first rain we'd had in a long time, so the ground couldn't drink in the water fast enough. Made the swales rush like a river, overflow onto the road. I was running past the Sportsplex. It was really dark and hard to find a place to cut through the tree line to the Vietnam Veterans Pavilion. Figured the cops wouldn't be through there in a storm, so it would be safe to take shelter there without being kicked out like we usually are."

"'Like we usually are.' Who and what do you mean by that?"

"There are a few of us who more often than not crash for the night around Beaver Hollow Park. You cops always kick us out of there. Sometimes university security does, if we get too close to Friar Street and the school buildings, especially if there are students or staff around. Believe it or not, it's easier to tuck into a nook right on campus than it is to stay on the fringes of their property. People notice you less if you just act like you belong there. But my on-campus hiding places were already taken, and the student ID I'd … found had been deactivated, so I couldn't get into a building. With a storm coming, I wanted a roof over my head. Closest one was the pavilion. So, I headed there. Don't know where the other guys were."

"What other guys?" Jim asked.

"Like I said, there are a few of us who usually meet up at night. Safety in numbers, you know. Nice to have someone there to watch your six."

"We need their info."

"Don't know their names. One answers to Columbus, I think because he came from Italy. He's got a foreign accent. That's all I know about him. The other goes by Imperial. No idea why."

77

"And you're usually with them, but not that night. Why?"

"I don't know why. Because I never saw them. It's not like we're family and check in every hour. All I know is I was on my own that night. And, like I said, I wanted to get out of the rain. So I headed to the park. Skies opened part way there."

Chelsea picked up the pen, twirled it through her fingers like a tiny baton. "You were alone?"

"Yeah. Told you, I don't know where the guys were."

"I mean, no one other than your usual companions? A lady friend? A" — she sought for a delicate way to ask about a drug dealer or buyer — "business associate?"

Jim stared at her.

Speikman snorted. "Business associate? No. After I left the board room, I was on my own."

She scowled. "I meant someone buying or selling drugs."

His jaw ticked. "Not my scene."

"What about someone buying or selling sexual favors?" Jim asked.

Speikman just rolled his eyes.

"I'll take that as a no," Chelsea said.

"What time did you typically meet your … friends?" Jim said.

"Do I look like I got a watch? I don't know. Why?"

She rested her forearms on the table and leaned a little closer to him. "It can help us understand the events of the evening if we understand your routine and if or how you deviated from it."

"Me and the guys don't have a set time to meet. Sometimes before sunset, sometimes well after. Depended on who tried their luck on campus or at a shelter and whether they found a place to bunk or not. There were nights we weren't together at all, so not meeting up that night wasn't odd. Kind of hard to break a routine when you don't have one to begin with."

"Okay," Jim said. "You couldn't find your friends and couldn't stay on campus, so you headed for the pavilion. Then what?"

"Like I said, I was double-timing it down Beaver Hollow Road. Was already soaked, but it was a warm night. Still, didn't mean I wanted to get wetter. My mood was already foul when this silver Jag comes zooming past. Barely missed running me over. Tires sprayed me with a wall of muck from the overspill. I flipped him off and screamed at him. Never thought Yates would actually stop and confront me."

Chelsea interlaced her fingers and squeezed them. This was another troubling detail. How'd he know the victim's name was Yates? Granted, the victim's name had been all over the news, but Donald Speikman was a self-confessed homeless man. He wasn't reading the *Steel City Tribune* on his smartphone, and he certainly wasn't watching the news over morning coffee from the comfort of his living room.

She cleared her throat. "Did you and Mr. Yates have a history?"

"You mean before he carelessly drenched me then came at me with a tire iron for complaining about it? No. Can't say as I ever met him before that. Which is odd, don't you think, considering we clearly run in the same circles?"

Jim sucked in a very loud breath and cracked his neck by tipping his head side to side.

Speikman sighed. "No. We didn't have a history. So, you want me to sign something, or what?"

"We're not done yet, Donald. You still haven't given us a clear picture of what happened that night." She scooted her chair back a few inches to more easily lean farther forward. "Why did Caleb Yates come after you with a tire iron?"

"Told you. I pissed him off when I gave him the finger and yelled at him."

"So, you're telling me he nearly hit you with his car and accidentally doused you with water, but instead of ignoring you or waving an apology, he stopped the car in the middle of a storm to take exception with your displeasure?"

"I wouldn't phrase it that way, but yeah."

"How would you phrase it?"

"Am I going to have to say everything five times? If so, we're going to be here a well into the night, maybe the next morning."

"We'll be here as long as it takes to get a clear picture of what happened."

"Then could you could order a pizza? I'm starved."

"Let's finish this first."

He slumped in his chair.

She picked up the pen again. Tapped it on the tablet. "So, back to your statement. Caleb Yates stopped when you flipped him off. He got out of his car and came at you with a tire iron."

"Yes."

"And you just stood there — waiting — while he went to the back of his car, opened the trunk, lifted the spare tire cover, then rooted around for the lug wrench?"

Speikman shoved back his seat and jumped up. The only things keeping him from lunging or running or whatever he wanted to do were the wrist restraints securing him to the table.

The outburst happened fast. Chelsea had grown a little too relaxed and didn't respond quickly enough. In fact, she barely reacted at all. But Jim was ready. He leaped to his feet and drew his weapon.

Speikman closed his eyes, took a deep breath, then met her gaze.

Chelsea placed her hand on her partner's arm and felt the slight tremor running through him. "It's okay," she whispered. "It's over. Stand down."

He stared across the table while Speikman assumed a docile posture. Even then, Jim waited a few more seconds before holstering his gun. He rounded the table, righted the overturned chair, then returned to Chelsea's side. Only after Speikman sat did he also take a seat. "You can see how well that little outburst worked."

"Yeah." The chains clinked as he held up his hands, his wrists now red from the friction of his exertion.

"Don't try anything like that again."

"It was a reflex. Won't happen again."

Chelsea took a deep breath. "Donald, can you please explain what happened after Caleb Yates exited his vehicle?"

Speikman sighed, closed his eyes, and hung his head. "I told you." His voice was soft, his tone resigned. "He came at me with a tire iron. Exited the car with it, so he must have had it up front with him for some reason."

"Uh-huh." That made absolutely no sense. "And then?"

He looked up at her. "What do you think? We fought. I took it from him. Beat him with it. When I realized I'd taken it too far, I ran."

She and Jim exchanged looks.

"What did you do with the tire iron after?"

"Threw it in the river. It had my prints on it, so I didn't want to leave it behind."

"I'm sorry." Chelsea shook her head. "You were out of

your mind with rage when the two of you fought, so much so that you took things too far and killed him. But then you immediately calmed enough to have the presence of mind to take the weapon with you and dispose of it?"

"I did a stupid thing, but I'm not stupid. Big difference."

Jim pushed to his feet. "Sullivan, the hall."

She led him out of the room.

After he pulled the door closed behind them, he leaned against the wall and crossed his arms. "We've wasted enough time on this glory hound. Time to cut him loose."

"Not yet."

"Oh, come on. You were so convinced this would be the end of the case that even with all the holes in his statement, you refuse to admit he's not our guy."

"No, that's not it."

"What is it, then? Because I see zero benefit to entertaining his delusions any longer."

"He doesn't have the details of the case right — obviously — but he knows more than the media has reported. Yates's name, the fact that a tire iron was involved."

"But not where the damn thing came from. He said it came from the Jag, but the techs said Yates's lug wrench was right where it belonged in the trunk."

"That's not the point."

"Then what is?"

"It's obvious he's not the killer. But he might be a witness."

Jim closed his eyes and banged the back of his head softly off the wall. "Great. Our best lead is a nut job who wants to take credit for a crime he didn't commit."

"Huh."

He looked at her. "What?"

"Delusional. Nut job. Those were your words."

"So?"

"So, maybe he does have something mentally wrong with him."

"You think?" Jim scoffed. "Good lead or not, that just means he's not going to be credible on the stand. It hardly helps us."

"But if we can talk to his doctor, maybe we can find out why he's lying."

"And what good will that do us?"

"Before we talked to Speikman, we were operating under the assumption that Yates, Burgess, and Kensington were all victims of the same killer. A killer they all knew. And they'd all been targeted because of their position in society. Their wealth, their power."

"Yeah. What about it?"

"If our murderer has access to these people, it stands to reason he's one of them. Maybe the richest, most powerful of them all. Don't you think someone with those kinds of resources could entice a vagrant to take the blame for a crime he didn't commit? Pay him to take the fall?"

"Why? If the DA believed him, he'd be going to jail. Money wouldn't do him any good."

"But not for long. A decent attorney would get the charge reduced to manslaughter, and because he confessed, he wouldn't get the maximum sentence. And a great attorney — one he could afford with his new wealth — could get the charge lowered to self-defense."

He shook his head. "If that's the case, we need to look into his financials. It wouldn't make him a witness. He'd be an accessory."

"Maybe he's a witness who became an accessory after the fact."

"Either way, we follow the money."

"I agree that's our next step. But I still think we need to

look into his mental health record. I'm not sure what it is that's bugging me about him, but something's not gelling."

"Yeah, he's a liar."

"It's more than that, Jim. You can see it in his eyes. He needs help."

"No. Our victims' families need justice. Other innocent families out there need protection."

"We still only have one case. One victim. One family we need to help."

"Until the killer strikes again. Then who will we have to avenge?" He pushed off the wall then strode down the hall.

"Avenge? We don't avenge people."

But he didn't even slow his stride.

"Jim!"

What the heck was wrong with him? And what was she going to do about it?

Would she even have a chance before he did something he couldn't come back from?

Chapter Nine

Jim BOUNCED his legs as he waited for the receptionist to find a doctor willing to speak with them. He already knew it was a wasted trip and only went because Chelsea wouldn't drop it. Whatever hunch she had wasn't going to pan out here. Not without a warrant or a signed HIPAA form, and they had neither. He was surprised Don Speikman had told them which free clinic he went to.

Chelsea nudged him. "Do you have to shake your legs like that?"

"No."

A few seconds later, she elbowed him harder. "You said you'd stop."

"No. I said I didn't have to do this. You didn't ask me to stop."

"Fine. I'm asking now. Would you please stop that?"

"No."

She huffed. "It's making me motion sick."

"You're not the one moving."

The receptionist returned to her desk.

Jim cleared his throat. Twice. When she looked at him,

he cocked an eyebrow. And when she still didn't volunteer any information, he said, "Well?"

"Dr. Aikens will be with you shortly." She started typing at her workstation, avoiding eye contact with him. "But she is very busy, so be considerate of her time."

He never understood why receptionists were often the grumpiest employees. They were hired to welcome people and help direct them. Did they not read the job description? Was the screening process poorly handled? They couldn't all be nepotism hires who didn't care about their jobs or fear losing them.

The door out of the waiting room opened. A woman in a lab coat stood there, a polite but wary look on her face. "Detectives?"

All his impatient rants evaporated from his brain. Time to get down to business. He climbed to his feet in a second then crossed the room in three long strides, Chelsea at his heels. When he reached her, he shook her hand and smiled to try to put her at ease. "Thanks for seeing us, Dr. Aikens."

"I'm really not sure what I can do for you."

"Just a moment of your time, please?" Chelsea tipped her head toward the door.

Dr. Aikens frowned but led them to a small office in the back of the building that looked more like an on-call doctor's room rather than her personal space, as there were no personal effects on the desk or walls. It was sparsely furnished, with only a bank of filing cabinets, a bookshelf full of medical reference tomes, and a desk separating two visitor chairs from the doctor's seat.

Jim and Chelsea sat across from Dr. Aikens, who laid her hands on top of a folder. "As I was saying in reception, there's really nothing I can tell you about any of our patients. Not without a warrant or the patient's consent."

"Well, that's not entirely true." Sullivan also leaned forward onto the desk. "When a patient is an imminent threat to himself or others, you're obligated to report it."

"I'm not a psychiatrist, Detective, and as such do not typically treat people in psychological distress. The Tarasoff law doesn't apply to me."

"Typically?"

"In the case of this free clinic, I don't see them at all. So, I'm afraid you've wasted your time."

"Not necessarily." She tapped her finger on the desk, starting to infringe on the doctor's personal space. "HIPAA privacy rules state you are obligated to give us information on any patient implicated in a crime, victim or perpetrator."

"Technically, it says I'm permitted to, not obligated to. And there is only certain information — very general information — I can give in order to help you protect a victim or catch a perpetrator."

Jim had heard enough. There were other threads he wanted to pull, and this was taking too long. "Ladies, please. We're getting way off topic. This doesn't have to be contentious."

"It's not your medical license at stake."

"No," Chelsea countered, "it's our ability to take a killer off the streets before he strikes again."

Dr. Aikens sighed and rubbed her forehead. Then she opened the folder in front of her. "There's actually very little in here about Mr. Speikman."

"Well, what is in there?" She reached for the file.

The doctor pulled it out of Sullivan's reach. "Do you mind? There is still information in here I can't give you."

"What can you tell us?" Jim asked.

She grabbed a pen and a notepad, jotted a few lines, tore off the top page, then handed him the paper. "His address, or at least what we have on file for him. Many people who come here lie about that."

That was practically a given, seeing as their guy was homeless.

"Also, the name of the psychiatrist who treated him and his contact information."

"So, Speikman did seek help for a mental disorder?" Chelsea's voice held traces of triumph and accusation.

Neither was going to convince the doctor to cooperate further.

"I've told you all I can. Now, if you'll excuse me, I have patients to see." Dr. Aikens rose and gestured to the door.

Jim pushed to his feet. "Thank you, Doctor."

She nodded.

He pulled his partner out of her chair, half-expecting her to dig in her heels. Thankfully, she didn't resist. Then he led her to the door.

Neither of them spoke until they were back in the car. He cranked the air conditioning and waited for her to pounce on the paper like a panther on its prey.

Instead, she turned toward him, calm and collected. "Well?"

"You need to work on your schmoozing skills."

"Not me. The paper."

He passed it over, barely interested. His money was on the actual money, and he wanted to get back to the precinct to go through Speikman's financials. Wouldn't be a bad idea to go over all the accounts of each of the three victims. Might help link them and point to their killer. And despite different locales and MOs, Jim was convinced there was just one murderer.

She gasped. "Speikman was treated by a Dr. Covington. You don't think … no. It couldn't be."

"What?"

"Do you think it's really *the* Dr. Covington?"

"Why is that name familiar?"

"Dr. Covington." She stared at him like that would clear up his confusion.

He shrugged.

"Dr. *Van* Covington."

"Repeating his name a million times isn't going to jog my memory."

"He was just on *Steel City Special*!"

"Oh. That guy."

"Don't say it like that. He's brilliant. If this Dr. Covington is Dr. Van Covington, we're in luck."

"I want to get back to the station and start going through financials."

"You promised we'd run down the therapist lead first, if we got one."

Jim sighed. "Fine. Call and see if this doctor will see us."

Chelsea dug her phone from her pocket. "I hope it's—"

"I know. Just call."

She held her breath as she pushed send.

Crazy. He shook his head and let his thoughts wander as she spoke to whomever answered her call. The name Covington was striking a chord with him, though for a far different reason than it resonated with his partner. He just couldn't grasp why. He'd been too worried about his parents lately to focus on his job, which was a problem in and of itself, but even more so because he needed to do his job in order to protect them.

A squeal from the passenger seat pulled him from his worries.

"It *is* Dr. Van Covington. And he'll see us now."

"Great." He put the car in gear then pulled out of the

parking space. Chelsea clearly thought it was great and totally missed his sarcasm. All he wanted to do was get back to work and start running down real leads. The only reason he didn't suggest dividing and conquering was because he didn't want her over-exaggerating the importance of anything she learned from Covington just because she was star-struck.

"I can't believe you aren't more excited."

"I can't believe you're as excited as you are. Sorry, Sullivan, but you're going to see what a waste of time this is."

"How can you say that?"

"Because we already know Speikman isn't our killer."

"But he might know who the killer is. Could be a witness, could be an accessory. We need to know what's going on in his head if we want to know his motivations."

"That's what interrogation is for."

"This can save us hours of wasted time asking questions that won't lead anywhere."

"You just want to meet this guy."

"I do. But we didn't know Dr. Van Covington was his doctor when I first suggested meeting his therapist. In fact, we didn't even know that he had a therapist at that point. This is still the right call."

"Would you please stop saying his full name and title like that?"

"You're being awfully snippy."

"And you're being awfully short-sighted. This guy is going to stall us like Dr. Aikens tried to. And even if he's willing to talk, we're not going to learn anything useful."

"We could learn any number of things. Childhood trauma. Workplace harassment."

"He doesn't have a job. He doesn't have a fucking home."

"Well, you can be a Negative Nellie all you want. I firmly believe we're going to learn valuable information about Speikman from Covington. He's a genius. A pioneer in interpersonal relationships."

At least she'd dropped the full name shit. "Interpersonal relationships. Doesn't mean he knows anything about the motivations of a homeless man."

"You act like he got his degree from the bottom of a cereal box. Even if his specialty is couples, he's trained to treat anyone. And don't you think it's magnanimous of him to volunteer at a free clinic?"

"Yeah. He makes the fine folks at Doctors Without Borders look like slackers."

She sighed. "I'm telling you, Covington is going to tell us something that will give us insight into Speikman's mental state. And that is going to tell us whether he's a witness or accomplice. Then we'll get to the bottom of this murder. Maybe all the murders."

"I hope you're right, Sullivan. Otherwise, we're wasting valuable time on nothing." Time that would be better spent protecting his parents.

"I know I'm right. Wait until you see how brilliant this man is. He's going to be the key to breaking this case wide open."

Jim stopped the car in front of a two-story brick home in Barlow Park. "This can't be right. It's a house, not an office park."

"His office is in Birch Hill. But Covington often sees couples at his house. And their own houses, too. Makes people more comfortable."

"Whatever. Made good time. I've never seen the Lincoln Tubes move so well at rush hour. I'm usually stuck in the tunnel for at least two red lights."

"You think we have time to run to a store before going in? A grocery store? A pharmacy?"

"Why?"

She bit her lip and avoided eye contact. "I thought I'd buy a hardcover copy of his book then ask him to sign it."

"We're here on duty. You're not asking for an autograph." He got out of the car.

Chelsea shrugged and followed him. "His book was brilliant. There's nothing wrong with me showing a little appreciation for his research. Most people would be flattered to know their work was so well received."

"We're not here as … fans. We're here in a professional capacity."

"Don't see why it can't be both."

Jim rung the bell. "Really?"

She rolled her eyes. "Of course I get it. It's just … I'm impressed by him. Dr. Covington is the first famous person I've ever had the opportunity to meet."

"One of these days, I'll introduce you to some of our local sports heroes. How's that?"

"You know—" But the door swung wide, cutting her off.

The doctor stood there, grinning. "The door to happiness opens outward."

"Your door opens inward," Jim said. "What's that say about you?"

And Covington burst into laughter.

Chapter Ten

CHELSEA STOOD THERE, mouth agape. *This* was the doctor she idolized? He seemed less like a psychiatrist and more like someone in need of one.

Covington calmed himself and waved away the last vestiges of his mirth. "I do apologize. I was just reading Kierkegaard when you rang the bell. That very quote, actually. It was inappropriate, to be sure, but I couldn't help myself. Never would have done that to a patient, of course, but I'm just tickled that you recognized it." He shook his head. "Where are my manners? Please, come in."

Chelsea stepped into an opulent foyer, followed by Jim. Then Covington led them to a posh living room, where he had a tray of appetizers and beverages waiting for them. The spread looked every bit as good as that at the funeral reception, and as lunchtime's burger and zucchini fries were a fond but distant memory, she pressed her hand to her stomach and prayed it wouldn't betray her by growling.

After they were seated, Jim nodded to the book on the table. "*Either/Or*. That's not exactly light reading."

"Kierkegaard is my favorite philosopher. He's always fascinated me. I tried reading the original Danish, but I don't have quite the grasp of the language necessary, so I have to stick with the English editions. But I have to assume a little something is lost in translation, so I read and reread, hoping repetition will open my eyes to a truth I can't access in his native tongue."

"You speak Danish?" Chelsea asked.

"Not well enough, I'm afraid. Yet. But I'll get there." He smiled and gestured to the table. "Please, help yourselves."

She was about to reach for a tiny triangle of avocado toast when Jim declined for both of them. Instead of a quick nosh to silence the gurgling, she sat back, stewed, and tried to focus on the purpose of their meeting while her partner continued to direct the conversation.

"Thank you for squeezing us in so close to quitting time."

Dr. Covington crossed the room. "I should apologize for keeping you so late. It's never really quitting time for me. I offer concierge services for many of my clients, which means I'm available on their schedule, not mine. And seldom do they request appointments during conventional working hours, as they're too busy working themselves." After closing the blinds, he returned to the sofa. "I hate to lose the view, but if I don't block the afternoon sun, the house gets too warm for even the AC too cool it. It's been so hot lately."

"Steel City summers," Jim said.

"I know my home is rather far from your precinct, but I'm only in my office once a week these days, and you said this was urgent, so I didn't want to put you off until I was in Birch Hill again."

"We appreciate you seeing us now. The time isn't a problem. We're never really off the clock, either, when it comes to active cases."

Covington looked at his watch. "Well, I do have an appointment soon, so perhaps we should get down to business. How can I help you?"

"We're here about one of your patients," Chelsea said.

"Then I'm afraid you came all this way for nothing. You know I can't discuss patients without a warrant."

"And you know that's not true."

Covington gave her a cool, appraising look. "Tell me, Detective. Why did you join the force? Are you following in someone's footsteps? Feel you have something to prove?"

Her jaw dropped. The instant she realized it, she snapped her mouth shut.

Jim cleared his throat. "Dr. Covington, we're not asking you to violate HIPAA rules or American Medical Association mandates. Your license is safe. We're just trying to get some insight on a patient of yours who may be a danger to himself or others."

Covington stared at him for a long time before he finally spoke. "Who? And what kind of danger? Specifically."

"Donald Speikman. We know he's seen you at the free clinic. We're just looking for … well, anything you can tell us, really."

"Why? What prompted you to seek me out? To fear he's a danger to himself or others?"

"We can't share the details of an ongoing investigation," Chelsea said.

"Then I can't share the details of a patient's file. You should know that, Detective."

"It could be a matter of life or death."

"A scenario for which you've offered no proof. It's up to me to determine if he's a danger to himself or society. Not you."

Was that true? She wasn't really sure. "Doctor, this man is trying to take the blame for a crime he didn't commit. And he's refusing to tell us why. We need some insight into his psyche so we can determine why he might be lying and also how best to get past his defenses and have him tell us what we want to know."

"But what you want to know might not be best for Mr. Speikman."

"But it is what's best for society as a collective entity." Jim pointed at the book on the table. "You like philosophy. Doesn't Kierkegaard orate about ethics?"

"Have you studied his work?"

"Not since Philosophy 101 in college."

"Then you've either missed or forgotten his premise. He is widely considered the father of existentialism. What does that tell you?"

"Is there going to be a test later?"

Covington laughed. "You do have a sharp tongue." His gaze lingered on Jim's mouth for a moment, then he nodded at his copy of *Either/Or*. "This is one of Kierkegaard's most famous works. In it, he suggests an ethical person puts the good of the society above personal desires."

"Well, yeah. That's the definition of ethics, right?"

"But that's not the end of it. He goes on to say that always acting for the good of others can lead to boredom."

"There's a reason people say rules were made to be broken."

Covington wagged his finger and clucked his tongue. "Ah, but therein lies the problem. Following the rules makes for a healthy collective but a damaged individual. And if everyone behaves that way, we're left with a collection of damaged individuals. So, if you have a society of unhappy people, how can the collective be healthy?"

"But you assume following the rules and being happy are mutually exclusive. I don't think they have to be."

"Tell that to a married couple."

"What?"

Covington shook his head. "Sorry. My specialty is, after all, relationships. But we're getting off topic. My earlier point was that Mr. Speikman has rights, and I can't violate them because you have a hunch. Do you have any solid evidence that proves he's a danger to himself or others?"

"Well, no. That's what we needed you for."

"Then you can see my dilemma."

Chelsea leaned forward and rested her elbows on her knees. "Doctor, this man either was complicit in the murder of a respected member of society, or he is a witness to the crime. We don't know if he confessed to assuage his guilt, to try to hide from a threat, or because he's deluded, but we do have to get to the truth of the matter. His statement doesn't make any sense. And without answers, we have to set him free. If he is involved, we're putting someone dangerous on the streets. If he's a witness, we could be putting him at risk."

"If he was a witness, his story should make sense."

"In theory, sure. But eyewitness accounts are notoriously unreliable. As I'm sure someone with your credentials would know."

Covington crossed his foot over his knee then tapped his fingers on his leg. His gaze traveled from Chelsea to her partner, where it lingered for a long moment.

Jim shifted in his seat. "Doctor, we really could use your help on this. Though we're only working one case, there are other detectives seeking justice for other victims, and we suspect they're related. Any insight you can give us could be instrumental in getting a killer off the streets."

"You didn't mention multiple victims."

"Speikman confessed to knowing something about *one* victim. We need to see if he's connected to the others. Or even if the others are connected at all."

"What do you think is the killer's MO? What links the crimes, in your opinion?"

"We aren't there yet."

Chelsea faked a cough. When Jim glanced at her, she arched her brow. What was he thinking? They didn't discuss open investigations with outsiders.

"Tell you what, Detective. I'll look through Speikman's file. If I see any red flags, I'll let you know." He took a beautiful leather wallet from his pocket, retrieved a business card, then handed it over. "That has my personal cell number on it. Text me so I have your information, and once I've reviewed my notes, I'll report what I've uncovered." He rose. "But now, if you'll excuse me, my next appointment will be arriving shortly."

"Of course." Jim pushed to his feet, pocketed the card, then shook the doctor's hand. "We appreciate your help."

Chelsea led the way to the foyer, where they said their farewells then stepped outside. She had just folded herself into the passenger seat when Covington started to walk toward them. "Detective!"

Jim, who had only just rounded the bumper and hadn't yet opened his door, stopped and looked back at him. "Yeah?"

"It occurs to me your precinct probably doesn't have a profiling department like the FBI does."

"Well, no." He gave a mirthless chuckle. "That's part of our job."

"If you give me some information on the other victims, I may be able to help you piece the puzzle together. Find some commonality you missed. Possibly determine what might have made these people targets in the first place, which could lead to your killer and his or her motivations. We could discuss it over drinks, perhaps?"

Chelsea was grateful she was already in her seat and behind darkened windows. She'd always thought of Jim as a bit of a womanizer and couldn't imagine how he'd react to being hit on by a man. A very attractive, very accomplished, very suave man. She stared at him, waiting to see what he'd say or do, fully expecting his face to turn red and his words to come out in stutters and stammers.

But he was as smooth as the doctor. He merely took his phone and the business card from his pocket, typed out a text, then hit send. "Thanks, Doc. We appreciate anything you might turn up."

Covington smiled and nodded. "I'll be in touch."

Jim waved then climbed into the car. He tossed his phone into the cupholder between them.

The doctor stood at his door until they'd pulled away.

Once they were out of his line of sight, she turned toward her partner. "Are we going to discuss this?"

"There's nothing to discuss."

"You gave your new boyfriend the names of victims. In an active investigation."

"He's not my boyfriend. And it's not like these cases weren't heavily covered in the news already."

"But he didn't know we were trying to link them. No one's supposed to know that. Davenport hasn't even given us the okay to do that."

"He doesn't have to. We let the evidence dictate the direction of the investigation, not the captain."

"And not some random guy, either."

Jim sighed. "Dr. Covington is not some random guy. He's an accomplished psychiatrist who's well regarded in his field. Which you well know."

"Before we went to see him, you couldn't care less about him. You didn't even want to go."

"And you practically hero-worshipped him. So, what changed? Are you angry because he didn't take to you? Jealous because he was nicer to me?"

"Nicer to you? Jim, he was *hitting* on you. Barely even acknowledged I was there. He doesn't want to help us. He just wanted your number. And he got it. Along with a date."

"It's not a date. We agreed to meet to discuss the case."

"Then why wasn't I invited?"

He sighed. "What does it matter how we get the information you want? You wanted Speikman's motivation, and this is how we'll get it."

"But you shouldn't have given him the other names."

"Chelsea, the guy reads Kierkegaard for fun. Sometimes in *Danish*. Clearly, he's well educated and very intelligent. Wouldn't be a stretch to assume he suspected a connection between the victims before we did."

His phone dinged, alerting him to an incoming text. She snatched it out of the cupholder before he could grab it.

"Give me that. It could be a private message."

"This is your work phone. I'm entitled to see anything that comes across."

He groped for the device with one hand while steering with the other. "No, you're not. What if it's about a disciplinary review?"

"If you didn't get written up for your fight with Thompson, you're not getting written up for anything."

"Give me my damn phone."

"It's not safe to read a text while driving, anyway." She batted away his hand while she looked at the screen. "It's from Covington. 'I'll start researching after my session. Looking forward to discussing my findings with you. Were you thinking a club, or would you prefer dinner here?'"

Jim scowled.

"Well? Where do you want your date? I'll reply for you."

"Put down my phone, Sullivan."

She returned it to the cupholder. As much as she was enjoying teasing him, she was concerned. "I don't trust him."

"Twenty minutes ago, you were angry because I wouldn't let you buy his book and ask for his autograph."

"They say never meet your idols."

"He's your idol?"

"No. You know what I mean. People always let you down when you get to know them. They're never who they claim to be."

"And who did he claim to be?"

"Smart. Insightful. Someone genuinely interested in helping people."

"You got all that from a self-help book and a fifteen-minute podcast?"

"What more do I need?"

"Maybe actually meeting him in person and talking to him would be a better indication of who he is."

"I did meet him. Just now."

"Yeah, but you'd already formed an opinion first. You put him on a pedestal he didn't ask to be on, then you got upset because you think he fell off it."

"That's a bit of an exaggeration."

"Besides, nothing he did warrants your disappointment. He opened his home to us. Offered us food. Agreed to look into our cases, possibly at the risk of his career."

She crossed her arms. "HIPAA allows doctors to disclose information to prevent crimes or self-harm. He's at no professional risk."

"Your dislike and mistrust are irrational. You said yourself, the guy is brilliant. And now that we met him, I agree. You're just miffed because he wasn't interested in you."

"That's crazy."

"You're crazy. And I know a doctor who can treat that."

"Shut up."

He chuckled. "Call the hospital. See if Mrs. Kensington made it. And if so, whether we can see her."

"You're changing the subject."

"That's because I'm tired of it. Make the call."

While she dialed, they passed a Bentley headed in the opposite direction.

Jim glanced in the rearview mirror. "I know that car. That's Easton Burgess's wife, Paulette. Why would she need marriage counseling when her husband was dead?"

After Chelsea ended the call, she said, "Kensington's going to be fine, but she's not allowed visitors yet. We can call tomorrow. As for Burgess's wife, maybe she's seeing Covington for grief counseling."

"I just find it interesting that one of our potential victims might have been his patient. His wife definitely is. But he didn't tell us."

"Maybe he'll tell you when you have your date."

"Very funny, Sullivan."

"You know, I can't help but think we're making this too complicated."

"How so?"

"What's the first thing that comes to mind when you think about a psychiatric evaluation?"

"Internal Affairs overstepping their bounds."

"Not police-related. In general."

"Lying on a leather couch?"

She sighed. "The old cliché. They always blame a man's problems on his mother or say a woman's got daddy issues. But things become tired and trite because they're so often true."

"So?"

"So, we've already hit a wall asking Speikman about the night Yates died. Financials probably aren't in yet, and if they are, they can wait a bit longer. Davenport's going to make us cut Speikman loose soon if we don't come up with a reason to detain him. Before we do, why don't we talk to him about his childhood? See if we can't uncover some kind of motivation to his current actions?"

"We tried everything else. Might as well."

Chelsea started thinking about where to start and how to best direct their latest line of questioning. But when they finally got back to the precinct, the interrogation room was empty. She brushed past Jim, ran to Davenport's office, then burst in without knocking.

He looked up from his desk. "Can I help you, Detective?"

"Where's Speikman?"

"Had to cut him loose. You just missed him."

"Damn it," Jim said.

She hadn't even realized he'd followed her. "But we weren't done interrogating him."

"And he *confessed*."

Davenport sighed. "And you both told me he was lying. Couldn't keep him any longer. You think he did it, produce the evidence then get a warrant."

"Our best chance of getting evidence on him is talking to him," Chelsea said.

"Then go talk to him."

Jim sighed. "We don't know where he is."

"That's why it's called detective work. Go. Detect. And close my door on your way out."

Chelsea headed back to her desk. McPherson pulled the door closed a little harder than she could have gotten away with. When they were seated across from each other, she said, "Now what?"

"It's been a long fucking day. I'm hungry and tired generally pissed off. Let's say he has mommy issues and call it a night. We'll look for Speikman tomorrow."

She was hungry, too, so she agreed.

Just wished she knew where Speikman was. And whether mommy issues were really behind his lies. Somehow, she suspected they weren't.

Chapter Eleven

32 Years Ago — Age 5
Dressing Room at Pussy Katt's, Downtown Steel City
7:00 p.m.

PRETTY. Everybody was so pretty.

He liked shiny things, and the ladies in the special room always twinkled like stars. Sometimes they sparkled so much, it reminded him of the baby fireworks sticks he got to use last year. They were fun. Until one of the burny bits fell on the couch and made it smoke. Mum said he couldn't ever have them again. And that was too bad, 'cause she was always working when the fireworks went off on the Fourth of July.

Might never get to see them. Now no sparkly sticks, either.

So, alls he got was the glittery ladies in the back room of Mum's work. They smelled nice, too. Well, sometimes. Like candy or flowers. Until after they took their turn up front. That's what they called it — up front. He didn't know what that meant, 'cause he only ever went in one door, and it led right to this special room. And wasn't the door you went in the front door? But they all called this room "the back."

Sometimes, adults didn't make sense.

Anyway, whenever they came from "up front," they didn't smell nice no more. Most of the time he had to breathe real deep to find the scent of candy and flowers again, but he had to sniff past the stink of smoke. And not the good fireworky kind of smoke, but the bad ashtray kind.

He knew that smell real good 'cause Mum always had the ashtrays at home full of butts.

Butts. He giggled.

But then the smile left his face. Butts were funny on cartoons, but not so much on adults. Especially when they weren't covered up. And the ladies here never had theirs covered. Only Miss Katt did. She wore tight skirts and low-cut tops and really high, pointy shoes. Mum said she got to dress that way 'cause she owned the place. But all the other ladies wore different clothes. Actually, kind of almost no clothes at all. They walked around with their underwear giving them wedgies, but they never fixed 'em.

He hated wedgies. Fixed his the second he got 'em. And his were never bunched up as far as theirs were.

If he had to look at the ladies, though, their butts were the safest place. None of 'em wore enough clothes. Made his cheeks burn when they ran around without shirts on. Lucky that some of 'em put sparkly stickers over their private top parts. Maybe a tiny sparkly triangle on the bottom part.

Sparkles sure were nice, but he couldn't look at 'em *there*. So, he spent most of his time looking down.

One night, when Mum was up front, Cherry said,

"Looking at your feet again, Donny? If you're going to stare at 'em so much, we might as well make 'em pretty."

He looked up at her — skipping over her body to meet her gaze. Her eyes had long lashes and super dark lids, but they held a kindness, so he agreed.

She held her hand out to him, and he took it. Her skin was soft, her fingers warm. Cherry walked him to her dressing table, then she lifted him onto her chair. After he scooted back, she took off his shoes and socks.

He was embarrassed 'cause his socks didn't match and one of 'em had a hole in the big toe. Thought she was gonna laugh at him like the kids at school. They always teased him about his clothes being old or dirty or ratty, and that made him feel bad. But Cherry didn't, and he thought that was really nice of her, so he let her do what she wanted.

She painted all his toenails bright cherry red with clear glitter over top. Fingernails, too.

And she was right — they were pretty. He liked looking at them. When the polish dried, Cherry helped him with his socks and shoes and even tried teaching him to tie them. He kind of got it, but sometimes he had trouble tucking the rabbit ears through the holes.

When it was time for him and Mum to walk home, she took his hand. Did a double take. Pulled his arm so hard his shoulder hurt. Then she flung his hand down. "What did you do?"

"Cherry made 'em pretty for me."

Mum wheeled around then stomped over to Cherry's table. "What's the matter with you? Little boys shouldn't wear nail polish."

"Little boys shouldn't hang out with strippers, either, but that doesn't seem to bother you any."

He didn't know what that meant 'cause he didn't know

what strippers were, but Mum didn't seem to like that much. Her face got all splotchy and her nostrils got wide. She was huffing when she stormed back to him. Practically threw him into her chair. He squeaked when he landed and almost bounced back off. But she wheeled around and glared at him.

So, he grabbed the seat of the chair, caught his balance, then scooted back.

And he sat statue-still for her.

Mum scrubbed at his fingers with some stinky liquid from a plastic bottle. The polish came off his fingers, though a little bit stuck in the edges. He wasn't sure if he should tell her or not. Finally decided not. If she was so mad about the red nails, she might get madder that the cleaner didn't work so good.

And he really didn't want to mention his toes.

She didn't say a word to him the whole way home. Didn't make him get a bath, either, even though he knew he smelled like her work and she usually made him wash it off. He was glad she didn't make him that night, mostly because they always got home so late and he had to get up so early and was always super tired. Was used to the smell, so it didn't bug him too much. Even though it was kind of stinky, it was still better than the cigarette smoke and rotting garbage smell of their apartment.

But that night, there was another reason he was happy to skip his bath — because he really didn't think things would go too well if she saw his feet.

Mum never helped him get ready for bed, so she didn't notice the polish. He wiggled his toes and smiled when the streetlight shone through the window and made the polish sparkle. Fell asleep with that same smile on his face.

Next day at school, Miss Harris had a new game to play. They were learning about the five senses, and it was "touch" day. She told them to take off their shoes and socks so they could walk across different things she laid on the floor to see how they felt.

Uh-oh.

He couldn't let his classmates see his toes. Didn't want to take off his shoes and socks. Flat out refused to when Miss Harris insisted.

The more he said no, the more she said yes, until the whole class was staring. Then she crouched and removed his shoes herself. Today, his socks didn't have holes, but they were more gray than white, one of 'em had a brown stain, and they didn't match each other — again.

Donny curled his toes, hoping she wouldn't be able to take them off, but she grabbed the tops then peeled them from his feet.

She stared.

The class stared harder.

She gasped.

The class laughed.

He snatched his socks from her and struggled to slip them back on, but they were inside out and all balled up and it took him too long.

Didn't matter. The damage was done the second she yanked them from his feet.

Miss Harris stood. "Class, I have to go to the office for a quick moment. Everyone return to your seats, cross your arms, and put your heads down. I'll be back after a quick phone call. Hurry up, now. Don't dawdle."

The students slowly shuffled back to their seats. Except for Donny. He scampered across the room and was the first to reach his desk. After dropping into his chair, he buried his head in the crook of his arm. Didn't want anyone to see the tears in his eyes.

"Now, no one is to get up, and no one is to talk. Is that understood?"

"Yes, Miss Harris." The class spoke as one, their voices sing-songy. Happy.

Donny didn't answer at all.

"Count quietly to yourselves. See how far you can get. Anyone who gets to one hundred gets a sticker on their chart. I'm leaving the door open so Mrs. McElroy keep an eye on you."

Donny heard her footsteps disappear down the hall. There were a few murmurs, a few snickers. But he thought they'd die down, too, in a moment. Then he'd have peace. For a little bit, anyway.

Instead, Curtis elbowed him. "Little girl Donny, in a gown."

Crap.

"Skips from the playground, all through town."

Why did Miss Harris have their desks next to each other?

"Holes in his clothes, polish on his toes."

He really hated Curtis.

"Stinks up the place wherever he goes."

Donny bit his lip so no one could hear him snuffle. Hopefully the worst was over.

But his wishes never came true.

The whole class started taunting him with Curtis's stupid chant. They all whispered so Mrs. McElroy didn't hear, but thirty people whispering still felt loud to him.

Then he heard the soft scrape of a chair sliding across the floor followed by the snick of the door closing.

Tears were still falling down his cheeks, but curiosity got the better of him. He wiped off his face before lifting his head to see what was going on. The second he looked up, Curtis punched him.

Donny saw stars — by far his least favorite sparkly thing to date.

Everything was a blur after that.

Classmates cheering.

Curtis punching.

Jamie taunting, egging Curtis on.

Mrs. McElroy yelling.

It all ran together until someone pulled Curtis off him. He didn't even remember falling to the floor.

Then, instead of blows to his face, he felt his cheeks burning. A little from the pain, but a lot from the shame. From the anger. From the confusion.

That happy sing-songy sound from just a few minutes earlier now sounded mean. And was directed right at him, about him. Even Mrs. McElroy scolding everyone didn't make the chants stop.

Dirt-poor Donny.

Dolled-up Donny.

And his new least favorite.

Little girl Donny, in a gown. Skips from school, all through town
...

As much as he dreaded hearing that stupid song every school day from now on, he dreaded something more.

A chill ran through him just thinking about how Mum was gonna react.

Chapter Twelve

JIM SIPPED his double shot Americano as he crossed the parking lot. He'd talked to his parents last night before bed and again this morning. So far, they were well. Nothing on the security system, no weird noises or odd people hanging around. Not even so much as a crank call.

Still didn't set his mind at ease.

Which was why he wasn't sleeping — his thoughts wouldn't stop whirling. If he wasn't sleeping, he wasn't going to be at the top of his game. And if he wasn't at the top of his game, the killer could strike again before they caught him. What if the next target was his parents? They'd die, and it would be his fault.

That thought left him cold. And made his brain kick into overdrive. Which was a feat, considering it was sleep-deprived and sluggish.

He'd roll his eyes at the absurdity of this vicious cycle, but he was too concerned to find the humor in his stupidity.

When he reached the precinct door, he found his way blocked by three officers.

God, he wasn't in the mood. "Thompson. Miller. Berger."

Thompson sneered. "Jackass."

"I tried being cordial. But seeing as how you broke the truce first, I see no reason to continue the charade. Get the fuck out of my way." He started to squeeze through the gap between Miller and Berger.

They closed ranks.

He sighed. "Didn't you learn your lesson in the locker room? You know I can kick all three of your asses. I don't feel like schooling you further today."

"You got IA climbing all over my ass because you jumped me," Thompson said.

"I didn't do shit."

"Says you."

"Says everyone who was there."

"See, that's the thing." Thompson grinned. "The only people IA interviewed were me and my boys. And wouldn't you know it, our stories all synched up and named you as the instigator."

"Well, at least you used the word 'stories' right. Because that's pure, unadulterated fiction."

"Doesn't matter what you call it. It's three against one."

"And yet no one from IA's come after me."

"Yet, McPherson. Yet. You should have been off the force after the shit you pulled in Zone Two."

"Back off, Thompson. You don't know anything about what happened, and you don't want to start with me."

"I don't know how you got away with what you did there, but you won't get away with what you did here."

"I didn't do anything here."

"Me and the boys say otherwise."

Jim rolled his eyes. "If you think anyone's going to take

the words of three troublemaking cops over one decorated detective, you're delusional."

"Mark my words, McPherson. We're going to make sure you pay for what you did."

"Some of us have work to do. We done here? Or you want to throw down with me again? I'd say I could use the workout, but we both know I wouldn't even break a sweat."

Berger and Miller glanced at their buddy. When he nodded, they parted for him like the Red Sea for Moses. As he walked past, each stuck out an elbow and threw their weight into him.

He should have been better prepared, but he was tired and beyond caring about these morons.

Then his cup slipped from his hands, his jolt-juice splattering all over the steps, all over his pants.

The three stooges walked away, their laughter ringing in his ears.

Now he was tired, wet, and pissed off. Fucking hated days that started this way. They never got better as time ticked by. Frequently got worse, but never better.

Jim stormed downstairs to the morgue. Nia was already there. And working on someone. He pulled on gloves as he stepped inside, then he approached the table.

It was Caleb Yates whose ribcage she had cracked open.

"Good morning, Detective."

The few sips of coffee in his stomach sloshed, and he was glad he didn't have more. The metallic stench of blood and the cloying sweetness of decomposition hit him like a wall. But he refused to show his struggle and pasted a smile on his face. "Morning, Doc. You got an early start."

"My backlog's growing instead of shrinking. What's wrong with the world these days?"

"The list is long and varied. Nothing would make me happier than if my job became obsolete."

"Don't think you have to worry about that."

"Truer words never spoken, I'm afraid."

She nodded as she removed an organ, then she placed it on a scale. After noting the weight for her record, she turned back toward him. "I guess it goes without saying, I haven't finished yet. It's going to be a few hours."

"Yeah, I can see that. You find anything of note yet? I mean, I know it's early, but we don't have much to go on."

"Actually, there is a marking of note."

"A birthmark? Scar? Tattoo?"

"A scar. Of sorts."

"I don't follow."

"He's been branded."

"Branded. You mean, like cattle?"

"That's one way to put it."

"Where? Show me."

She reached between the corpse's legs.

"Whoa, Doc. What are you doing?"

"The brand is on his scrotum. I almost missed it."

Jim shivered. "The brand is where?"

"You heard me. The scrotum."

"Was it a sexual sadist kind of thing?"

Nia shrugged. "I can't tell you why. Only that it was done to him. Or by him, I suppose."

"I'd think it's far more likely that it was done to him. I can't think of a single guy I know who would do that to himself."

"I couldn't say. I can only tell you what I discover, not the reason behind it. In this case, I found a brand."

"Do you think it's the killer's calling card?"

She shook her head. "Not unless he marked Mr. Yates years ago then bided his time."

"Years?"

"The wound is fully healed. The scarring old. Come see."

Wonder how many men on the planet had a job where a doctor lifted the balls of a dead man and moved aside the hair so they could analyze the underside of the man's sack. His money was on that number being incredibly small. Like infinitesimally tiny. And lucky him, he was one of the few. He bent down to look at the brand, trying not to notice the "where" and focus on the "what" of it.

"Can you see?"

Too well. "Yeah." She'd shaved a two-inch square section so the brand was more visible. "Are those letters?"

"Yes. I had to take a photo and blow it up to make it out, but—"

"I'm sorry." Jim stood up. "Did you say you already took photos?"

"I did."

"Then why the hell are you making me look at a dead man's junk?"

"Why would you want to see a photo when you could analyze the actual evidence?"

"Because the actual evidence is smaller than the zoomed in photo. And, oh yeah, because then I wouldn't have to look at a dead man's junk!"

She rolled her eyes. "I've already emailed you and Chelsea the photos. I'm pretty sure the letters are C and S. Possibly G and S. Unless it's the number five. Or a backward Z. I'm not really well-versed on local gang names. Sorry I couldn't be more helpful."

"We'll figure it out. The photos are very helpful. Thanks."

"Sure thing." She bent over the body again then reached into the open cavity.

He cringed at the squelching noises and quickly turned around in case he didn't hide it well. Just before he reached the door, he spun toward her. "Hey, Doc?"

Nia looked up. "Yes?"

"Have you seen that brand anywhere else?"

"Funny you should ask."

"Is it, now?" He crossed his arms. "What do you know? And why didn't you mention it sooner?"

"What I know is Detectives Anderson and Paxton are working a case where their victim had a brand on his scrotum. But the scar isn't as defined, so I can't tell you for certain it's letters or numbers or any specific symbol."

"And would that victim happen to be Easton Burgess?"

"It would."

"Why didn't you mention this sooner?"

"Because I can't verify the brands are the same. And the Burgess case isn't yours. Talk to Anderson and Paxton."

"Anything else you think might be relevant?"

"Not at the moment."

"Thanks. Have a good one."

"You, too." But she was already distracted, head bent over the body on her slab. Then she pulled something crimson and shiny from inside Yates's chest.

Jim wheeled around then burst through the door. In the hall, he sucked in a few lungfuls of fresh-ish air. By the time he reached the bullpen, he could smell the Americano on his pants.

If he was going to smell like coffee, he might as well enjoy the perks of a cup. If he worked his imagination overtime, he could almost pretend the sludge in the precinct's pot was actually his caffeinated beverage of choice.

He returned to his desk with a full mug, opened his email, then took a sip.

"Blech." If he wasn't so damn tired, he'd toss it.

"What's the matter?" Chelsea approached from the door to the back staircase.

He held up his mug. "We're cops. Who can we arrest for this crime against humanity?"

"Should have stopped at the cafe if you're that picky."

"I did. Most of my Americano is on the ground outside. What's not on my pants, that is."

"I'd offer you mine, but it's empty." She tossed her cup in the trash.

He sighed. Couldn't catch a break. It was just not going to be a good day. "Open your email. We have a lead. Norm and Charlie in yet?"

"I didn't see them."

"We need to talk to them."

"Why?"

"I think I found the way our cases connect."

"What is it?" Chelsea logged in then started clicking her mouse.

"Nia sent us photos from Yates's autopsy."

"She finished already?"

"No, but she found something."

"What is this? Is — oh, my God. It is." She looked up at him. "Why am I looking at his ... you know."

"Stop worrying about the body part and focus on what's on it."

She arched an eyebrow.

"This isn't inappropriate. It's for real. A lead."

"On his ..." She pointed toward her lap.

Jim sighed. "Sullivan."

Chelsea turned back to her computer, though she kept

staring at him. When he scowled, she averted her gaze to look at the screen. Then she squinted and leaned closer to study the photo. "What is that?"

"It's a scar. He was branded. A long time ago."

"There?"

"Yep."

"Wouldn't that hurt?"

"No. It would tickle and he'd ask for another."

She looked up at him again. "I meant more than just on a regular part of the body, like an arm or leg or something."

"Well, I certainly wouldn't want to experience it."

"Why would he do that?"

"Probably more likely it was done to him."

"Why in God's name would anyone want to do that to someone?"

"The usual," he said. "Sexual sadism. Gang initiation. Someone stoned out of his mind has what he thinks is a brilliant idea. Or a funny one."

"What do you think it is?"

"Could be any of the reasons. Or all. Or something we haven't even considered."

"How high would you have to be to do that?"

"Or how depraved?"

She rubbed her head.

"But that's not even the most important part."

"There's something more important than a brand on his … on him? Down there?"

"Burgess has a similar mark in the same place."

"What?"

"Nia says the scar isn't as clear, but it sure looks similar."

"The link between the cases."

Jim nodded.

"We need to talk to Norm and Charlie."

"That's what I'm telling you."

Chelsea tipped her chin. "Looks like they're just getting in. Let's go see what they know."

Chapter Thirteen

30 YEARS AGO — Age 7
One-Bedroom Apartment in Garrick Neighborhood of Steel City
9:00 p.m.

DONNY WAS GETTING TOO old to sleep in the closet. As far as closets were concerned, it was probably on the bigger side. Except for the kind you walked into, like a little room. He'd heard about those from the ladies Mum worked with. Never seen one, though.

They sure didn't have that kind of closet in their apartment. Not that he was complaining. Well, he was. But not out loud. Mum said he should be grateful for what they had. They lived above a butcher shop owned by Mr. Sylvestri. Their place always smelled like raw meat. Always. And it kind of made him sick. The longer he was there, the less he noticed the odor. But when he came home from school or from Pussy Katt's, the reek hit him harder than a punch from Curtis. Made his eyes water and his stomach flop.

Usually took ten minutes or so before he could ignore it. Never mentioned it to his mother, though. Not again, anyway.

He'd made that mistake once. Just the once. Mum had beat him something awful for not appreciating what she provided then sent him to bed without supper. Well, sent him to closet. Either way, he didn't eat. She left him there when she went to work and didn't even wake him for school the next day.

That part wasn't so bad. Any day without Curtis and the other kids teasing him was a good day.

But she'd slept through breakfast time and lunchtime and dinnertime, too, sprawled on the couch with empty bottles all around her. And since he'd mostly gotten used to the meat smell, his tummy had stopped churning from the odor. Instead, it growled from being empty. Rumbled for hours. When Mum finally woke, she was running late for work and didn't have time to feed him. The whole way to Pussy Katt's, she yelled at him.

To this day, he couldn't figure out how he'd made her late. But she was convinced he did and blamed him every step of the way.

That night, while Mum was working out front, Roxanna and Dominique kept an eye on him. He tried to be both quiet and still — quiet because he didn't want to draw attention to himself and still because he was sore from his punishment — but his stomach growled. Really loud. And they heard it.

Roxanna wrapped a robe around herself then stooped down to look him in the eye. Even though she covered up, he didn't want to look at her, but she turned his head until he did. "What did you have to eat today, Donny?"

He chewed his lip as he tried to figure out how to

answer. If he got his mother in trouble for not feeding him, she might make him wait longer to eat. And his belly already hurt from being so empty. But if he told them, maybe they'd give him a cracker or something. Mum sometimes had a package of crackers or a bag of pretzels in her bag. Not often, but sometimes. He liked it when they shared. It was special to have a treat like that.

Before he decided how to answer, Roxanna stood. She whispered something to Dominique, then they both left the room.

Not even a cracker. Maybe he should have told.

But then Roxanna came back with a bag of chips and a soda from a vending machine. He loved chips. Wanted to take his time and enjoy them, but he was too hungry to munch them slowly. Couldn't even eat them one at a time. Shoved them in his mouth — two, three, sometimes four at once.

As he was licking the last of the crumbs from his fingertip, Dominique returned with a burger and fries for him. Even got him a milkshake. He'd never had one of those before. It was pink and fruity and cold on his tongue. On his first sip, he looked up at her, eyes wide, and grinned. "This is so good!"

"I wasn't sure what flavor to get. Glad I chose strawberry."

"Me, too." It reminded him of Cherry. He really missed her. She left without saying goodbye, which really hurt his feelings. And she never came back to visit. Not once. No one ever told him why she'd left or even where she'd gone. Just got sad and quiet when he asked. Stopped mentioning her all together, though his heart ached to act like she didn't exist.

He'd asked Dominique about her again, one last time.

She got a faraway look in her eye, frowned, and stooped down to talk to him face-to-face. "Your mama still hasn't said nothin' to you about this life, huh?"

"No."

She sighed.

"Okay. It's like this, sugar. There's only a few ways out. The Julia Roberts way, and almost none of us is that lucky."

"What's that?"

"Doesn't matter. Some of us age out. Some of us manage to make something a little more respectable of ourselves. But most buy the farm."

"I wouldn't mind living on a farm. You ever see those fainting goats? They're so cute!"

She smiled and tousled his hair. "I'm hoping for the Julia Roberts option."

"Is that what Cherry got?"

But Dominique's eyes got shiny and she walked away.

Donny sipped his shake. It was a nice reminder of Cherry, even if no one talked about her anymore.

After Mum was done up front, Dominique and Roxanna pulled her aside. Donny didn't know what was said, but he knew it was bad. When they got home that night, she beat him harder than she ever had before. Harder than Curtis ever had, too. So bad, he didn't go to school or Pussy Katt's for a week. Not until the bruises weren't noticeable. Parts of him had still been sore, though he'd been afraid to tell her.

Just kept sleeping in his closet and trying to be grateful for the food she brought him. Meat. Always meat and nothing but. Mum told him she and Mr. Sylvestri downstairs had come to an understanding. Called it a professional quid something or other. Never heard the term before. She said it meant they'd trade favors. That's how she was getting stuff from his butcher shop without having to pay for it.

"What favor do you do for him, Mum?"

But she didn't answer. Just walked into the bathroom then closed the door behind her.

When he heard her crying, he decided not to ask again.

After that, she went from almost never smiling to *never* smiling. And when Mr. Sylvestri would knock, she'd frown or press her hand to her stomach like she couldn't stand the smell of meat, either. But she managed to put a smile on her face for him. Mum would go downstairs for about an hour then come back with food wrapped in butcher paper. Why it took so long to make bundles of ground beef and chicken legs, Donny didn't know, but it would make a lot more sense to him if Mr. Sylvestri spent the hour getting his package ready by himself then just deliver it to them when he was done.

He said that to Mum one time. She burst out laughing even as tears welled in her eyes. "Yeah, kid. I wish he'd deal with his package himself, too."

Donny decided never to bring that up again, either.

Maybe Mum's favor was keeping Mr. Sylvestri company while he worked on his meat. Whatever she was doing for him, she didn't seem to like it. So, he tried to be more grateful for the food she quidded. Or pro-ed. Or whatever she called it. And he was. Much as the smell of meat sickened him and the taste bothered him more each day, he never complained and gagged down what she cooked.

At least they were eating regularly. Almost daily. Mum hadn't cooked last night, and he was hungry.

But she'd be angry if he left his "room." The one time

she'd caught him doing that, he got a beating for it. And not even from her but from some guy she was with. Called him Donny's uncle. Uncle Matt. Mum didn't have any siblings, so it had to be an uncle on his dad's side of the family. And that was exciting, 'cause Mum never talked about his father.

If Uncle Matt was Dad's brother, Donny was glad he didn't know the family. His beatings hurt even more than Mum's.

Now, Donny lay on his mattress, a homemade one made of bundles of old newspapers wrapped in a frayed quilt from the Salvation Army, wondering if one of his other uncles was there — he seemed to have a lot of uncles — or if it was safe to open the door. He'd grown too tall to stretch out or roll over or be comfortable in any way. When his finger snagged in the cuff of a sweater and it fell on his head, he had enough. He scrambled to his feet then burst into the living room.

Nope. No uncle. No Mum, either. He knew she wasn't there because her bedroom door was wide open and when she was in there, company or not, she kept it closed.

Maybe she was in the bathroom.

And now that he thought the word bathroom, he had to go.

Donny padded across the floor to the only other door in the tiny apartment. It was open just a crack, and light spilled from inside. He pushed it open, nudging an empty bottle so that it clattered over the chipped tiles. Inside, he found his mother, naked, resting her head on the toilet. She'd sprayed vomit on the lid and seat and floor before finally getting some in the bowl. The stench was worse than the general raw meat smell he suffered.

He pulled the door closed then walked over to the

window. It wouldn't budge. Then he remembered to flip the lock. Even after turning the latch, it took him a few tries to open it, only managing a few inches with each heave. When it was up high enough, he poked his head out and breathed some fresh air. Some fresh, raw-meat-tinged air.

Still, it was better than the lungful he got in the bathroom.

Donny looked up and down the street. When he was certain no one was around, he peed out the window. Couldn't hold it anymore and couldn't go in the toilet. Didn't have another choice. No options came to mind, anyway. Not unless he traded a favor to Mr. Sylvestri, too. Wonder what he'd have to do in exchange for using a bathroom. Might have to consider it if he had to poop before Mum got out of there.

Bladder emptied, he went to the kitchen. Nothing but a dry piece of meatloaf. His stomach growled, and he rubbed it. Guess he didn't have a choice. He gagged it down then washed the plate. Drank a glass of water, but it didn't take the taste out of his mouth. Maybe some of one of Mum's special juices … the kind she didn't allow him to have even a sip of. She'd never know.

Except she would. The cork was still in the green bottle, and the seal hadn't been broken on the bottle with the brown stuff in it.

Eh, if it made her throw up, he didn't want it, anyway. What he really wanted was a strawberry milkshake. Something cold and sweet. Refreshing but comforting.

Donny went into the living room without even looking for dessert. There would be none. But he was surprised to find a brownie on the coffee table. Only one bite had been taken from it — a small nibble from the corner.

He couldn't believe she hadn't shared. They always shared. But she'd kept this treat for herself. Rage rolled through him, making his stomach clench for a whole new reason. She'd been so selfish!

Oh, well. He'd get his fill now. She probably wouldn't even remember it had been there.

Grinning with anticipation — as much for the treat as for the revenge he was about to take on her for hogging it — he grabbed his pillow from the closet. No way was he going to sleep in there anymore. He stretched out on the couch, picked up the brownie, then took a big bite.

The pure joy of chocolate and sugar couldn't be denied. He moaned with pleasure. There was a weird aftertaste, but that didn't stop him. He devoured the whole thing in two more bites.

Then he sat there, sad it was gone and he hadn't taken more time with it. Sad its deliciousness was going to have to mingle with the nastiness of dry meatloaf in his gut. Sad that he kind of had to pee again and only had the window.

No. That wasn't true. Mum had a bottle. And empty one, right beside her.

She'd be so mad if she woke and found him doing that. But he really had to go.

He couldn't.

Donny danced over to the window, thumbs already hooked in his waistband. But when he looked outside, he saw two guys tying a moose to a maple tree. The people weren't looking at him, but the moose was. And he didn't know what happened if you peed on a moose, but he bet it was nothing good. Then the men would see and they'd climb up the tree, and it would be a whole moose-man-mistake thing, and he'd have to wake Mum, and she'd be mad, and it just wasn't worth it.

Eyeballs practically floating inside his skull, he went

into the bathroom. Mum hadn't moved. The bottle was still on the floor where it had rolled earlier. Looked like it had gone right though some drops of vomit, but they had to be dry by now.

He stepped over her feet.

Picked up the bottle, careful where he held it.

Pulled down his pants.

Lined everything up, best he could.

Emptied his bladder with a satisfied sigh.

Felt like he went for about an hour. So long, the bottle had to be overflowing. That explained why his feet were wet. Donny wiped them on the bathmat in front of the tub, put the bottle down near his mom's hand so she could empty it when she woke — he was thoughtful like that — then went back to the living room.

He was thirsty. So thirsty. But if he drank anything, he'd have to pee again, and the bottle was full and the bathroom was full and if he peed again, the whole apartment would be full. He needed a boat. If he made a boat, he could float on the Pee Sea and anytime he had to go, he could go over the side and it wouldn't matter.

Donny went into the kitchen to get a knife. He needed one to cut a branch from the maple tree. Shouldn't take much to saw it right off. Once he had the branch, he could build his boat. Then he'd sail away and not have to worry about Curtis or the men or the moose or anything.

Men. Moose men. Moosemen. Mooseman. Superhero Mooseman. With a brown suit and a white cape and antlers on his cowl. Like Batman's ears, but antlers.

Bet they'd make good weapons.

Bet they could lop a limb off a tree.

He hurried over to the window to see if he could reach a branch of the maple. His arms were just a little too short. Donny stretched. Stretched some more.

Stretched a little further still. Finally, he reached a leaf. If he didn't pluck it, he might be able to pull the tree to him.

Except, he didn't move the tree. Didn't move the leaf. Didn't even have a leaf. The only thing in his hand was what he'd brought from the kitchen.

Someone had moved the tree. Zapped it and the men and the moose away. He was holding on to nothing but the knife. To nothing at all.

Then he was falling. Falling, falling, falling.

Wasn't going to be any boat for him to escape in. Wasn't going to be a sea of pee or anything else to soften his landing. And there wasn't going to be a Mooseman to catch him before he hit the ground.

Donny didn't stop with a bang. He stopped with a bounce, the surface beneath him soft and spongy. Like the couch cushions.

Because he was on the couch cushions.

Thought for sure he was a goner, but he was still alive. Still in the apartment. Still holding the knife.

Only it was stuck in his side.

Probably should feel that. An ache, a pain. A sting or a stab.

But he felt nothing. Nothing but lightness. Weightlessness. A fat, floaty feeling. More carefree than he ever thought he could be. Would be.

Was that a problem? Maybe he should care that he had a knife in his side. Maybe he should care that he couldn't feel it. Maybe he should care that this could be the end.

But would that be so bad? If it was the end, it meant no more pain.

He wasn't feeling pain now, and that was pretty freaking nice.

Donny closed his eyes. Hovered in the shimmering fog

between awake and asleep. Floated there until a scream woke him.

Eyes popped open.

Head whipped up.

Mum loomed over him, hand cocked back. She swung toward his face, connected with his cheek. The slap, the sting, the lingering burn …

He wiped a tear with one hand and blocked her with the other. "What's wrong? Why are you hitting me? What did I do?"

"What did you do?" Her voice rose to a screech. Her face was purple, her eyes bulging from her head. "I drank urine because of you!" She rained blows on his head, his arms, his legs. Kept swinging and kept hitting until she couldn't raise her hand again, then she collapsed onto the floor.

Every inch of his body hurt. Even his hair felt like it was throbbing.

Why hadn't he just died last night? Why did he think he should have?

Oh.

He looked down at his stomach where the knife had plunged into his side. Except, it hadn't.

It was still there, though.

Donny palmed it. Pushed to his feet. Slowly climbed over his mother.

She didn't move. Just sat there, eyes closed. Panting. Sobbing. Moaning.

He raised the knife above his head, gripping the hilt with both hands. His muscles quivered with the exertion as he moved through the pain. His fingers trembled from the tightness of his grip. His thoughts whirled with visions of possibilities.

Could plunge it into his chest.

Could embed it into her heart.

Could take it to school and slice open the throats of every one of his tormentors.

So many options.

Decided instead to take it back to the kitchen. After putting it back in the drawer, he returned to his closet, closed the door, then curled into a ball on the floor.

Chapter Fourteen

CHELSEA FOLLOWED Jim over to the board Norm and Charlie used to track their cases. Charlie was back at the coffee station, pouring two cups. Norm greeted them with a nod of his head.

"We need everything you've got on Burgess," she said.

"Good morning, Chelsea. Jim. Fine weather we're having, isn't it? Afternoons are a bit hot for my liking, but you can't beat a colorful dawn and bright start to the day. And how are each of you doing?"

"Sorry," she said. "Didn't mean to jump down your throat like that. Just got a little excited."

"So I see."

Charlie approached. He handed one cup to Norm and gestured to them with the other. "I hear you say something about Burgess?"

"They want to know what we've got."

"Why aren't you on his case about not saying good morning?"

"Because I've been with him for the last twenty minutes."

"We haven't."

"Then you can chew his ass out. Later. Now, why do you want to know about Burgess?"

"I was down in the morgue this morning," Jim said. "Nia was starting the autopsy of our latest vic, Caleb Yates. She found scarring on his sa—scrotum. A brand. Said she found a similar mark on your guy, but it wasn't as pristine a mark, so she couldn't make it out. We were hoping to compare the two. If they are connected, then—"

"What do you mean, if?" Charlie said. "You think there's a big population of branded men walking around out there?"

"Didn't she send you pics?" Chelsea asked. "We wanted to compare."

"Yeah, we've got 'em." Norm walked to his desk then started looking through a stack of folders.

"Why don't you have them on your board?"

He looked up at her, brow furrowed. "If it was you, would you want those photos hung up for anyone walking past to see?"

"Good point." She tapped her toe while she waited for him to find the pictures.

Meanwhile, Jim stared at the board. He pointed at a toxicology report hanging under the scrawled word POISON. "Did you suspect poison before the tox screen?"

"No." Charlie took a sip of his drink. "Wife thought he had a heart attack. By the time the ER got the report, Burgess's staff had already cleaned the house. Had to collect and test a mountain of trash before we were sure it wasn't accidental."

"Accidental poisoning?" he asked.

"Sure. It can happen. The wrong plant invades your garden without you realizing it. Took too many painkillers. Mixed something you shouldn't have. Grabbed the wrong bottle from your medicine cabinet. This was definitely intentional, though. Hemlock in the wine."

"And it wasn't one of those cases where the killer didn't care who drank it." Norm handed Jim a file. "Easton Burgess was a wine snob. There were certain bottles in his collection he wouldn't even let his wife near. Whoever did this knew who would be drinking it."

"And had access," Charlie finished.

She stood on her toes to look over Jim's shoulder. Rather, past his arm. He lowered the file so they both could see. "The shape looks right, but the details are impossible to make out."

"Our best guess is the guy moved when he was being branded," Norm said.

"Yeah. Can't imagine why." Charlie took another sip of coffee then put his cup on his desk.

"Come see what we've got." Jim tipped his head toward his desk. "Pretty sure that's the same mark, and our guy didn't move." He handed her the folder.

Chelsea followed the three men back to their workstation. How they could stand to look at the pictures, she couldn't fathom. Other than the obvious privacy violation, there was the pain to consider — pain she couldn't help but feel despite not even having the same anatomy. A shiver ran up her spine just thinking about what the two — and possibly more — victims went through. It was all she could do to not squirm and cross her legs. Yet the three of them, other than sporting identical grim looks on their faces, seemed completely unaffected.

Sometimes she really did wonder if she was cut out for this job.

Then she took heart in the fact that she brought compassion and empathy to bear when her coworkers were often cold and impassive. She knew these people well.

Knew them to be kind, caring men who put family and friends always above themselves. So how did they turn it off for work?

And did she want to learn?

Man, if she could bottle that ability, she'd make a mint.

While the three crowded around Jim's computer, she walked around the desk to her own, then pulled up the photo. Even though Nia had sent several close-ups, she zoomed in to compare the blown-up image with the photo of Burgess. The more she studied the mark, the more she was certain she wasn't looking at a brand.

She was looking at two separate things.

"Hey."

They all looked up at her.

"I don't think the lack of clarity on Burgess was from him squirming or thrashing."

"Can't imagine a guy not squirming or thrashing while suffering through something like that," Charlie said.

"What I mean is, I think this is a cover-up. A rebrand."

Norm leaned on the edge of her desk. "I don't follow."

"What if Burgess received the same mark Yates did. And it looked the same. But he did something to make his clan or gang or family or whatever angry. So angry, they threw him out of the organization. If he had to get a brand to be let in, maybe he had to have it removed when he was tossed out."

"Like someone having his trident taken away when he got booted off the SEALs?" Jim asked.

She had no idea. "Yeah. Look, you can see the outer edge over here is pretty defined. Then there's this bubbly part that could be a brand over a brand. And the raised ridge gets thinner on this edge, like the hot metal or whatever was on pristine skin instead of previously scarred tissue."

He nodded. "Makes sense, Sullivan. I can see that."

Norm leaned over to study the picture on Jim's screen. "So, what does the brand say? Is that a five?"

"I think it's an S," she said.

"There aren't any gangs in the city with an S-word in their names." Charlie absently reached for a cup of coffee, then shook his head and retracted his hand.

"Might be a five," Norm said. "I kind of think it looks like a five."

"We don't have any gangs with the number five in their names, either," she said.

Norm stepped back, tipped his head, and squinted. "Could be new. Maybe it's C-5. Like the explosive C-4, but the next number up."

"There is no Compound-Five," Jim said.

"As a chemical explosive, no. But as a gang name, maybe. Someone might think it sounds ominous."

Chelsea leaned back in her seat. "I still think it's an S."

"There is no Compound-S." Norm sighed.

Charlie clapped him on the shoulder. "You're the only one obsessing over the markings being related to explosives. Could be a C and an S and have nothing to do with blowing anything up."

"What if it's an O?" Jim asked.

Norm's eyebrows arched. "O-5?"

"If the O was a zero," Charlie said, "it could be fifty."

"Or 5-0. Like us."

Jim looked at her. "None of our vics is associated with the police."

"None?" Norm's gaze bounced from Jim to Chelsea then back. "Not neither, but none? You got more dead bodies we don't know about?"

He was wrong about the five, she was sure of it, but even so, his mind was sharp. Agile. Quick. The way and speed with which he saw even the smallest of details were just two of the many reasons she'd hoped to be paired with him when she'd made detective. With the benefit of hindsight, she knew Davenport made the right call putting her with McPherson. Still, she couldn't help being impressed with Norm. She hadn't even noticed the distinction between the two words, and he'd already pounced on it.

"I—"

She shot Jim a look and cleared her throat.

"*We* suspect there is a third victim in Zone Two. Alexander Kensington."

"Wasn't his funeral yesterday?" Charlie asked.

"Yeah. Sullivan and I went. His wife ended up in the hospital."

"She drink poisoned wine, too?" Norm smirked.

"Poisoned wine was Burgess, not Kensington."

All three of them looked at her like she was the butt of a joke. Or simply didn't understand the punchline to one.

"Laugh all you want," Jim said. "You're not far off. Accidental OD. Prescription sedative and too much liquor."

Charlie scratched his chin. "You sure it was accidental?"

"No reason to think otherwise. Yet. Wanted to talk to her yesterday, but the hospital wasn't letting anyone in."

"So, go today," Norm said.

"Yeah." Jim rubbed the back of his neck. "Pretty sure the detective on the Kensington case will be there. I wouldn't mind avoiding her."

"Former fling?" Charlie winked and elbowed his partner. Both of them chuckled.

"No. She just doesn't like me much."

And just like that, they both sobered. Everyone knew Jim had had trouble with Internal Affairs when he worked at Zone Two. *Everyone*. But few knew the details. He'd opened up to Chelsea during their first case, but even she wasn't sure she knew everything. Just that she knew more than most. And believed his version.

Detective Soto did not.

"We don't mind going to see Mrs. Kensington," Norm said.

"No. We'll go. I'm the one who found her, and I want to be sure she's okay. Besides, I kind of know her."

"If you change your mind, let us know." Charlie started back to his desk.

Norm followed, waving as he walked away.

"How about it, Sullivan?" Jim tipped his head toward the door. "Want to go to the hospital with me?"

"You sure know how to sweet talk a girl."

He laughed.

Down in the car, she turned toward him. "If Soto's there, she's going to make your life miserable."

"I know."

"You think she really believes you were having an affair with Mrs. Kensington?"

"It's a crazy theory, but if anyone would think it possible, she would. She'd like nothing better than to throw the book at me."

"Yeah, I noticed."

"Plus, she's accused me of sleeping my way up the ladder more than once."

"Isn't the captain in Zone Two a man?"

Jim chuckled. "Dean? The manliest they come. But one of the instructors in the academy had taken a liking to me."

"A female instructor?"

"Well, they all loved me. But yeah, Soto meant Gina."

"You called your instructor by her first name? No wonder Soto thought there was something going on."

"I call her Gina now because we're colleagues and friends. Then, she was Sergeant Jefferson." A wistful smile crossed his face.

"Did you date her?"

He took a deep breath. "I've seen her socially, two friends going out. But not while I was in the academy. Only after grad. And seriously, we're really *just friends*. That's all we ever were. Marcela didn't believe it, but I can't help that."

"Why did she care?"

"I told you, she thought Gina was padding my scores. I graduated first in my class. Marcela was a close second. But she didn't believe I really beat her. Couldn't accept I did it on merit and ability, anyway. She's always been convinced I had help. And wanted to take me down ever since. When everything happened with Dom and then IA …" He shrugged. "She was convinced I'd broken the rules. Hell, broken the law."

"I don't know." Chelsea shook her head. "I think maybe she has a crush on you."

"Marcela Soto?" Jim scoffed. "The only thing keeping her warm at night is her burning desire for vengeance."

"Maybe if she had a some*one* keeping her warm, she wouldn't need a some*thing* so much."

"Please. Don't make me picture it. Call the hospital. See if we can see Ophelia. Also, find out if Soto's there. And for God's sake, drop this line of questioning."

"I didn't ask a question."

"Just dial."

Chelsea took her phone from her pocket and looked through her recent calls list for the number to the hospital. But she couldn't help but wonder if Marcela Soto's fixation on Jim was grounded in unrequited interest in him and unprocessed jealousy of Gina.

Which made her wonder if the killer's MO was similar. A brand on the genitals could be part of a deviant sex act and not membership in a club. Or maybe it meant membership in a deviant sex club. Doms could be incredibly possessive of their subs.

And jealousy, especially when it came to passion, was a powerful — and all too common — motive.

Chapter Fifteen

29 YEARS AGO — Age 8
One-Bedroom Apartment in Garrick Neighborhood of Steel City
9:00 p.m.

DONNY'S WHOLE LIFE, Mum had told him his father was "not in the picture" and to stop asking. So he did. For months at a time.

But he'd always ask again.

And she'd always say the same thing again.

Then he'd always apologize and promise not to do it again.

But he would. He knew it, and she knew it. Was only a matter of time.

And time was up. Again.

Yesterday, Donny had steeled himself for her refusal then posed the question.

Much to his surprise, she didn't sigh or lecture or press her hand to her stomach. She marched to the phone, turned her back to him, then dialed a number from memory.

He didn't know who she called. The only numbers she knew without looking was Pussy Katt's, Mr. Sylvestri's, the candy man — who, much to his annoyance, she never let him see — and her daddy. That one made him maddest of all because she wouldn't let him meet his dad but she knew hers. And even if she wouldn't let him meet his dad, she could at least let him meet his grandfather. Donny had complained about that to Miss Katt once.

"Your mom told you about her pim—" She cleared her throat. "About her daddy?"

"Yeah. She talks to him all the time but won't let me meet him. He's my granddad, and the only other family I got. How come she won't let me meet him?"

She looked sad when she patted him on the head. "It's too … complicated for you to understand, Donny. But if your mom's *candy man* or *daddy* ever come to the house, don't talk to them."

He heard the stresses on the words but didn't understand what they meant.

"You understand? Do not talk to them. Don't even look at them. In fact, hide before they get there and don't come out until they're gone. It's super important that you do that, okay? Can you do that for me, sweetie?"

"Okay."

But yesterday, Mum dialed a number that wasn't Pussy Katt's or Mr. Sylvestri's or her candy man or her daddy.

She'd called *his* daddy.

Donny tried to hear what she was saying, but she was whispering and crying and moaned a few times. Words were impossible to make out through all that.

And when she hung up, she didn't say a single thing to

him. Just went into the bathroom to throw up, then she went to bed.

Guess she wasn't making dinner or going to work. At least he'd get to sleep at a decent hour. He took two left-over drumsticks from the refrigerator, ate 'em over the sink, then tossed the bones. After washing up, he stretched out on the couch with a thin sheet and fell asleep thinking about his father.

Mum didn't come out of her room in the morning, so he didn't go to school. It was nice not having to see Curtis, but he began to regret it when his stomach started grumbling. It was beef-a-roni day, too. One of his favorites.

He finished the chicken, then frittered the day away on the sofa.

Mum didn't wake until after dinnertime. Donny thought she'd make some food, but she got in the shower instead. Maybe Roxanna and Dominique would get him a burger and fries and chips and a milkshake.

His stomach rumbled again.

When she stepped out of her room, she wasn't dressed for work. But when she stayed home, she wore comfy clothes, tied her hair back in a ponytail, and wiped all the makeup off her face. Now, her hair was a cloud of curls and she had on work makeup, which didn't make sense because she was in a short, silky robe.

"You skipping work again?" That meant no burger.

She sat beside him on the sofa and took his hand. "Doodlebug, I need you to do something for me."

Doodlebug? Mum hadn't called him that in years. He just figured she'd forgotten he'd once been her doodlebug. "What?"

"I have someone coming over here."

"My daddy?"

Mum closed her eyes, took a deep breath, then

breathed it out slowly. When she looked at him, tears welled. But she didn't let them fall. Instead, she grabbed his hands and squeezed them with her cold, bony fingers. "I don't want you to think about that. I want you to go in your old room."

"You mean the closet."

"I'm not going to argue with you about that right now. There isn't time. Go in there. Close the door. And no matter what you see or hear, stay in there and stay quiet. I don't want anyone to even suspect you're home. Understand?"

"But it's cramped in there."

"This isn't up for discussion. Go. Now."

Donny trudged to the closet. Mum had shoved a few boxes in there when he started sleeping on the couch, and he tried to rearrange them to make more room, but she was waving her arms for him to hurry. He plopped on the floor and had just closed the door when a loud knock sounded.

The jackets hanging above him, combined with his mother's whispers, muffled her words. It was impossible to know what was said. He couldn't even make out the tone. Was she glad to see him? Was he happy to see her?

Was it his dad? And did he hope to finally meet his son?

How Donny wished he'd worn his nicest clothes. What kind of impression would he make with a hole in his sock?

He shoved a coat off his head then pressed his ear to the door.

"Let's go in the bedroom," Mum said. "I lit some candles, sprayed the pillows with perfume. Even have music ready to play."

"I'm not here to romance you. The sofa is more than adequate."

Mum *ooofed* as the couch creaked. Did she plop down on the furniture?

Did he throw her?

Dad or not, no one was going to hurt his mother. Not on his watch.

But she said not to come out. No matter what.

Something ripped.

Something unzipped.

The slats of the closet door weren't tipped the right way, so he couldn't see. And he needed to know what was going on before he decided what to do.

Sounded like Mum gagged. Why? He sniffed but didn't smell anything foul.

Donny quietly pretzeled his body until he could peek out the gap at the bottom of the door. All he got for his trouble was a crick in his neck and an eyeful of shoes with pants bunched on top of them.

As he was trying to get up, again without making a sound, his mother yelped. Then she moaned.

He sat straight, shoved a coat off his head, pressed his ear to the door. Mum sounded like she was panting. Her visitor grunted.

Donny grabbed a shoe — the best weapon he could find — then turned the knob without making a sound. Well, maybe a little squeal, but no one could hear that over the noises of their struggling. He briefly thought about going to the kitchen for a knife, but then he looked at the sofa.

At the man assaulting his mother on the sofa.

At the very pants-less man doing very bad things to his mother in her very private places as she struggled under him on the sofa.

Donny raised the shoe over his head, bellowed a war cry, and charged.

The shoe landed on the man's shoulder with a useless *thwap*. It wasn't even enough of an impact to make him turn around.

He did, however, arch his back and let loose a bellow of his own. "Fuuuuuuck!"

The inside of Donny's body turned wintery and watery. His liquid legs barely held him upright as his blood frosted in his veins. But Mum needed him, so he stepped closer, shoe clutched with trembling fingers high above his head.

Should have taken the time to get the knife, but he didn't. Now he had no choice but to continue on. He cocked his arm, ready to strike, when the man lifted his fist then back-handed him with a full swing.

Donny sailed across the room, crashed into the wall, then slumped to the floor.

The man hiked up his pants as he turned around. The closing of the zipper echoed in the stillness of the room. He strode to where Donny lay in a crumpled heap. Didn't bother with his fist this time. Didn't bother speaking, either — not the f-word or any other. Just bent his leg back, then kicked it forward, hard-leather connecting with soft flesh, possibly cracking brittle ribs.

No matter how hard he tried, air refused to inflate his lungs. Donny held his side, curled into a ball. Mum didn't need his help anymore. He needed hers.

But she wasn't coming.

"Stupid runt." The guy kicked him again. This time, his foot landed dead-center on Donny's tailbone.

He cried out, the agony too much to hold in.

Then, Mum yelled, too. But not at the man. At Donny. "What do you think you're doing? I told you to stay in there and not come out!"

Taking a chance, he uncurled to look at her. She'd

gotten up from the couch, though she hadn't dressed. Couldn't, as her clothes hung from her like tattered rags. His cheeks burned as he watched her naked chest heave from her labored breathing.

She stepped forward, but not to comfort him. Mum walked to the man and placed her hand on his arm. "I'm sorry. I'll deal with him."

He flung her hand aside. "Forget it. Deal's off."

"But we already—"

"I said no. You were barely worth it then. Sure as hell aren't worth it now." He shot Donny one last glare, then strode from the apartment.

Didn't even bother closing the door.

Mum screeched and ran after him.

Donny heard her yelling as he lay on the floor, still clutching his ribs. The only words he could make out were the bad ones, but he got the idea. She was mad that he went back on their deal, whatever it was. Given the screaming didn't stop, he figured she didn't change his mind.

Which meant she'd be back upstairs soon. Probably fuming. And that left only one person for her to take her temper out on.

Pounding footsteps got louder as she returned to their apartment. The door slammed.

Donny didn't look up, but her bare feet came into view.

"You stupid, selfish brat!"

Spittle fell on his arm.

"I thought he was hurting you. I was trying to protect you. Look what he did to your clothes. And your …" But he couldn't say the word.

Mum barked a bitter laugh. "I knew what I was doing. Prepared for it. Didn't even mind some of it. Would have been worth it, I suppose. But you couldn't listen. And I debased myself again! For nothing!"

"Debase?"

"Aaaargh!" She gripped her hair, stomped her foot, stormed across the room and back.

Donny pushed to his knees. Hissed and pressed his hand to his side. Taking anything more than the shallowest breath was agony.

Mum strode back toward him. He lifted his hand for help, but she kicked him, knocking him over, stealing his breath. Donny rolled on the floor, gasping, crying. Wheezing. Managed to pant one word. "Why?"

She bent down to look him in the eye. Her complexion was splotchy and mottled. Her eyes glassy and wild. Her nostrils flared, her mouth and brows slanted down at sharp angles. "Why? Because I made one mistake nine years ago and have been paying for it ever since. Because I was too poor to abort and too stupid to sell. And because you don't fucking listen to a damn thing I say!"

There would be no helping him, no caring for him. She left him lying on the floor, wishing he were dead. And probably coming close to it. But not close enough.

The sweet relief of the afterlife stayed just out of his reach. Instead, he lay there for hours. Coughing. Crying. And contriving a plan to better his circumstances.

Chapter Sixteen

JIM DIDN'T HESITATE when Chelsea told him Ophelia Kensington was awake but Marcela Soto was with her. He diverted from the hospital and headed toward his parents' house.

"Why are we going there?" she asked.

"I just want to be sure they're okay."

"I'm sure they're upset after what happened. Okay. We have time to drop in."

He didn't correct her. Technically, she wasn't wrong. They probably were upset after what had happened after the funeral. But he was less concerned about that than he was about their physical safety.

Chelsea didn't need to know that.

Jim wasn't sure why he was keeping that a secret from her. She knew his parents were wealthy and sometimes socialized with the known victims. If she took the time to connect the dots, she'd realize they could also be potential targets. Of course he would be concerned about their safety. That was nothing to be embarrassed about.

So, why was he hiding that fact from her? He had no idea.

But he was.

When they arrived, Jim didn't knock or ring the bell. He simply tried the knob and was not happy to find the door unlocked. After pushing it wide, he led Chelsea into the foyer and called, "Hello?"

No one answered.

"Are they home?" she asked.

"Better be. Door's open." The question wasn't whether they were home. It was whether they were alive.

He strained to hear any sounds of life over the thundering of his racing heart. His hand hovered near his gun as he crept down the hallway. A shadow stretched along the far wall. Jim nodded toward it as he made eye-contact with Chelsea and drew his weapon. Steadying his breath, he flipped the safety, rounded the corner—

And came face to face with his dad.

"I trust you have a good reason for almost killing me in my own home?" Dad put down a basket of produce on the kitchen island like he hadn't a care in the world.

Jim, on the other hand, trembled as he holstered his gun. "Why didn't you answer me when I called you?"

"I didn't hear you. I was emptying the car. We just got back from the farmers' market."

"Then why was the front door unlocked?"

He started unloading vegetables and fruit. "I didn't realize it was."

"I unlocked it." His mother walked in from the mudroom. She planted a kiss on his cheek then leaned over and smiled at Chelsea. "Hello, dear. How are you?"

"Fine, thanks. How are you?"

"I'm well, thank you. Can I get you something cold to

drink? I gather you're on duty. How about some lemonade? It's freshly squeezed."

"Mom! Why'd you leave the door unlocked?"

She turned to face him. Assessed him with a cool stare. "I'd thank you to remember I do not answer to you, James Patrick McPherson."

Chelsea mouthed his middle name at him.

Jim ignored her. "Mom, I'm not trying to pick a fight with you. We talked about this. With everything going on …" He shook his head and shrugged. "Not only should that door have been locked, that alarm should have been set. And you know it."

"We just got home. Dad was unloading the car. I was getting the mail."

"Chelsea and I came in the front door. You weren't out there."

"Because I'd already gotten the mail."

"Then you should have locked the door behind you."

"My hands were full."

"Of what?"

"Mail!"

"Since when do a couple of bougie catalogs and a half dozen envelopes take two hands to carry?"

"Since when did you become a Nosy Nelson?"

He crossed his arms.

She sighed. "It wasn't the stuff in the mailbox that was the problem. It was the package on the porch that kept me from locking the door. I only managed to close it with my elbow."

"Were you expecting a package?"

"No, but it's not addressed to me. It's for your father."

"And the killer is targeting men, Mom. Where is it?"

Her face paled.

"Mom!"

Chelsea laid her hand on his arm. "Jim, there's no reason to scare her like that. I'm sure it's just something he ordered."

He wasn't.

"Jimmy?" Mom's eyes were wide as she looked up at him with both hope and fear on her face.

Dad walked into the room, confusion evident on his by the furrow of his brow and the stutter in his gait. "What's going on?"

"You expecting any packages, Dad?"

After a brief pause, he shook his head. "No. I didn't order anything."

"Where's the box, Mom?" Jim took gloves from his pocket.

"In the study."

"Stay here." He took a few steps, then stopped. Shook his head. Turned. "In fact, go outside. Other side of the house."

"Jim—"

"Dad, it's not up for debate. Take Mom outside now."

When they'd left the room, he once again started for the study. And once again stopped. "What are you doing?"

Chelsea finished putting on her second glove and looked up at him. Her brows drew down until she developed a little wrinkle above her nose, and she cocked her head as she looked up at him. "What does it look like I'm doing? Don't want to contaminate any evidence. Same reason you put on gloves. Same reason we always put on gloves."

"Get your ass outside with my parents."

"Ah, no."

"What do you mean, no? That's an order."

"First of all, I don't take orders from you. We're partners, not boss and subordinate. Thought we cleared that up six months ago. And second, what the heck's wrong with you? It's a box, Jim. People get them all the time. Literally every day. There's a whole industry built around it."

"You forget we've got a serial killer on the loose, Sullivan?"

"No, I haven't forgotten. But do you seriously think your *dad* is a member of a deviant sex club?"

"What? Of course not!"

"Then why do you think he's a target? Our evidence suggests our vics are members of some kind of weird club or gang. That brand means they were involved in some sort of twisted organization. Unless your dad's got one, or it's a coincidence that two of the victims have them, I think your parents are safe."

The tight cords in his neck started to release. He'd been so keyed up for so long, watching friends of his parents being picked off one by one, he'd totally forgotten to eliminate his parents as potential victims once the brand had been discovered.

Then the stress made those muscles tighten right back up again. Until he verified that Kensington had a brand, he couldn't totally relax.

But that wouldn't really mean his dad was in the clear, would it? The only way to truly set his mind at ease would be to know for certain his dad didn't have one, and that was an exam and/or conversation he didn't relish having.

"I'd still feel better if we checked what's in that box."

"That's a federal crime, Jim."

"Only if we don't have Dad's permission."

She frowned.

"We've got three victims of upper-income families that we know of. There could be more. Male, all in the same social circle. Of the three, we know two have matching brands. That's a great lead, but that's not enough. These people were all friends, my parents' friends. That means my parents — my dad — could be in danger. So, yeah, I'm scared for them. And if that means I have to open a box of some weird ass kink shit they got from Doms R Us, then that's what I'm going to do. If you're with me, great. If you want to wait outside, I understand that, too. In fact, I recommended that a moment ago, if you recall. But either way, I'm going to go in there, open that box, and see what they got."

"I thought you said they weren't into Red Room stuff."

"I hope to God they aren't. And why does a Girl Scout like you know anything about Red Room shit?"

"Let's go open that box."

Jim filed that question away for a rainy day and led the way to his father's study. The box wasn't too big, and there wasn't a return address. He grabbed the letter opener from his dad's desk, sliced open the tape, then gently peeled back the flaps of the box. Inside was a brown paper-wrapped package with a note taped to it. With a glance at Chelsea, he picked up the note. "If you don't have bunkers on your mind, you should. By the time you see this, it'll be too late to help you. — GS."

"Jim." Her face was white, her eyes wide. "Run!"

He practically pushed her out of the room. Or she pulled him. No way to tell for sure, as she'd grabbed his wrist at the same time as he'd put his hand on her back. Either way, the second they hit the driveway, she was on the phone with the bomb squad and he made a beeline for his parents on the far side of the house.

His face must have told them everything he was thinking, or at least the highlights, because his mother turned as pale as Chelsea. "What is it?"

But he didn't have time to console her. "We need to keep walking. Get as far from the house as possible."

"What?" Mom said.

Still, he ignored her. The three of them ran toward the property line in silence, Chelsea a few steps behind on the phone. He knew as soon as she was off the phone, his parents would have questions. But he did, too. And his took precedence. So as soon as his partner's call ended, as much as he dreaded it, he turned his attention to his dad. "Can I have a word with you? In private?"

"I have no secrets from your mother."

"This is a father-son conversation."

"Whatever you found inside our house was found in *our* house." Mom was still pale, but she was getting riled up. "You're not shutting me out of this."

"I'm not talking about this in front of you."

"Stop treating me like your mother and start treating me like any other victim. Or … suspect?"

He rubbed the pain that had settled behind his eyes.

Chelsea joined them. "Bomb squad's on their way."

"Bomb squad?" Mom and Dad said in unison.

"Didn't you tell them?"

"No, Chelsea," Mom said. "Apparently my son thinks I have too delicate a constitution for such matters."

"Sometimes he thinks the same of me."

"Then perhaps you'll tell us what's going on?"

Her cheeks pinked and she looked at Jim. "I really think it's more appropriate coming from your son."

His eyebrows shot up. "You think *this* is a topic that should come from their *son*?"

"I demand to know what's going on here," Dad said. "This is my house. That mail was addressed to me. And you've called the bomb squad. If it wasn't for a series of coincidences, I would have opened that package, not you.

So either tell me what's going on, or I'm going in there to see for myself."

Chelsea shook her head. "We can't let you do that. sir."

"Then one of you better start talking."

Jim stared at his partner, silently begging her to take the lead, knowing she wouldn't. Knowing she shouldn't. He heaved a sigh, his last moment of stalling, and closed his eyes — because what else could he do — then muttered the words every child never wanted to know about their parents. "Are you now, or were you ever, involved in any weird sex cults?"

"Excuse me?" his mother asked.

"Or any other kind of freaky sort of club or organization?" His tone was decidedly more hopeful. And his eyes were still closed.

"What's this all about?" Dad's voice held a lot less censure than Mom's. "Would you look at me, please?"

God, he didn't want to. His face had to be about fifty shades of red. And he didn't want to know if his parents' faces were. He managed to open his eyes, though he kept his attention on his feet.

"Jim?" His dad's hand was warm and firm on his shoulder.

Finally, he mustered the courage to meet his father's gaze. "Tell me. No matter how awful, Dad."

"This is about the case?" Mom asked.

He ignored her. Stared at his father. "Go on."

Dad cleared his throat and looked back at the house. "How does my mail relate to your case?"

Jim took a deep breath. Totally pretended his mother wasn't standing right there listening to every word he was about to say about male genitalia, particularly with respect to questioning the condition of his father's. "You seem to have received a package signed from someone with initials that are associated with our case."

Chelsea nudged him.

"We've noticed a commonality between two of the victims and are in the process of trying to ascertain if the third had a similar mark. A brand."

"A brand? You mean, these men were burned? Scarred?"

Jim nodded.

"With what? Like, a cigar or something?"

"No. More like metal. The way you'd brand cattle. I was hoping you'd tell me you'd never been branded as part of a hazing or orientation."

"Don't you think you'd notice if I had?"

He cocked a brow. Sirens sounded in the distance.

"Oh." This time Dad looked at the grass.

"What?" Mom asked.

"I'm going to go to the road to make sure they don't miss the turn." Chelsea jogged toward the end of the long driveway.

"Coward," Jim muttered.

"That's why Jim asked if we were into—" Dad looked at him then leaned over to whisper into Mom's ear. Her cheeks turned scarlet and she looked up at her son. "Who on earth would get pleasure out of burning themselves there?"

"I'm not discussing this with you, Mom." He started walking toward Chelsea, stopped, then turned back toward his parents. "Dad, do you happen to know any groups with the initials G.S.?"

He thought for a moment then shook his head. "Sorry, son. I don't."

"Well, they seem to know you. And you're now on their radar. That's who sent you that package."

Chapter Seventeen

CHELSEA WAVED goodbye to the train of emergency responders — ambulances, firetrucks, several police cars, one armored vehicle that transported the robot, and the K9 unit. Probably looked as moronic as she felt waving, but that dog was gorgeous. And Rafferty waved back, so she was only about ninety-eight percent embarrassed instead of one hundred.

His goodbye, goodwill gesture shaved two points of humiliation off the scale, temporarily anyway, but she heard the not-so-quiet whispers about the Grimm Reaper detectives not knowing the difference between an incendiary device and an inside joke.

They weren't wrong.

Chelsea wasn't sure how it happened. She was reasonably sure she'd been level-headed when she'd arrived at the McPherson residence. Jim hadn't been. He'd been off-kilter since they landed the Yates case, and she hadn't been able to figure out why. Not until Jim connected the dots and decided his parents — his father — was the killer's next target.

But there was a reason connect-the-dots books came with numbers. Five dots arranged equidistantly from each other with no instructions on the page could be connected as a circle, a pentagon, a star … or if Jim was left to do it, some weird jagged scribble that made no sense at all and got the bomb squad called to his parents' house for no good reason whatsoever.

Cheeks flaming, she watched the last of the emergency responders round the corner and disappear from sight. With no other reason to dawdle outside, she walked up the drive then let herself back into the house. Hopefully the McPhersons had had enough time to discuss any private matters.

She walked into the study. The bomb techs had left surprisingly little mess. Just some packing material and a torn box. A VHS tape lay on the desk. "May I?"

Brant nodded.

Her dad had an embarrassingly large collection of VHS tapes, so they weren't unfamiliar to her, though his were mostly all hockey-related. This was a sports-themed tape, though she didn't recognize this athlete. He was the antithesis of what she expected of a pro golfer. "*Dorf on Golf.*" She looked at Jim. "Is he Swedish? I've never heard of him."

He and his father burst out laughing.

Vivian frowned and shook her head. She gently took the video from Chelsea then shoved it into her husband's chest, taking a little of his wind as she did so. "Come along, dear. You can help me get a tray of refreshments for these two buffoons. Not that they deserve it. We'll sit on the veranda and chat."

Chelsea could still hear them laughing as she followed Jim's mother to the kitchen. "How can I help?"

"Just keep me company, dear. I didn't want to leave you with those two imbeciles."

"They're not so bad."

"No, they're not. I'm rather fond of them. Most of the time."

"Most of the time." Chelsea smiled.

Vivian chuckled as she opened the refrigerator.

"So, who is Dorf?"

She put a pitcher of iced tea on the counter, then reached back inside for a few lemons. "Have you ever heard of Tim Conway?"

Chelsea shook her head.

"Did your family watch *The Carol Burnett Show* or was that before your time?" She grabbed a cutting board and a knife, then she started slicing the lemons.

"If it didn't involve a puck or a ball, it probably wasn't on in our house."

"You poor dear. You don't know what you missed."

"Apparently I missed Dorf."

"Well, that's no great loss. But Tim Conway was a comedic genius. Usually."

"So, what was with the tape and the ominous note?"

Vivian put glasses, the pitcher, and a bowl of lemon wedges on a tray. Then she took a canister of cookies from the back counter and a plate from the cabinet. "It wasn't ominous, dear. It was from Gary."

"You say that like it clears everything up."

"Gary Smith. One of Brant's oldest friends. They play against each other in the club's golf outing every year. It was just a joke. 'Bunkers' meaning golf course bunkers, not bomb shelters. And believe me, Dorf's golf advice wouldn't help anyone. It was just the worst possible phrase delivered at the worst possible time. And between you and me, the worst possible movie."

Chelsea chuckled, but she didn't really feel much like laughing. She looked around the room while Vivian plated what looked like decadent chocolate cookies and light lacy tuile. Her gaze landed on a hardcover book on the corner of the island. "*Litigating the Quantum Vow.*"

Vivian's face lit up. "Dr. Van Covington. Are you familiar with him?"

"We've met briefly."

"Don't you just think he's brilliant? He autographed that for us, you know."

"Did he?"

"Go ahead and look."

Chelsea slid the book toward her. When she opened the cover, the spine cracked, and she looked up, eyes wide.

"Don't worry." Vivian chuckled. "The copy we work from is in the library. This is the show copy."

"The *show* copy?"

"We had friends over last night and were bragging about the good Van did for our marriage. Brant trotted out the book."

"You saw Dr. Covington?"

"Saw and still see. Let's take these refreshments to the veranda. You can bring the book. And get the door for me, will you, please?"

"Of course."

"Thank you, dear."

The veranda, thankfully, had three ceiling fans blowing a gentle breeze in what was turning out to be another insufferably humid day. Chelsea sat beside Jim on a cushioned rattan chair and silently passed him the book. She poured herself a glass of tea with a squeeze of lemon, warred with herself over whether to eat a cookie — lost, though she did select the more figure-friendly tuile — and waited for her partner to guide the conversation.

"What do you guys know about this Van Covington?"

"We told you," Vivian said. "He's our marriage counselor."

"No." Jim shook his head. "You were very candid about your problems. You never told me who you saw."

"That's true, Viv," Brant said. "I don't recall ever mentioning Van by name. And why would we? It's not like Jim was involved. Or would know him. Or needed to."

"Maybe we didn't. Is it an issue now?"

"Our paths crossed on a case. This case, actually."

"Is he a potential victim? Oh, no!" She fidgeted with her necklace. "Not Van, too. He's too young, isn't he? Closer to your age than ours, I'd assume."

"Oh, he's older than Jim. Just isn't as old as us."

"He's in no danger, Mom. We're consulting with him."

"Thank goodness. Still, when I see him tonight, I'm giving him an extra tight hug."

"You and Dad have a session tonight?"

Chelsea sipped her tea and tried not to look at the chocolate cookies. Van Covington was something else. He was truly a concierge doctor, this time meeting with Jim's parents at night. And not even for an emergency session, but for maintenance. That was dedication. Maybe she'd judged him too hastily.

"No. It's the annual gala to raise money for research to find a cure for muscular dystrophy. Catherine told me they've renamed the event the Easton Burgess Memorial Annual Muscular Dystrophy Fundraising Gala."

That was a mouthful.

"Easton wasn't a researcher," Brant said. "He didn't even work with patients who have the disease. He was an orthopedist."

"And let me guess," Jim added. "People have shortened

the name to 'the Easton Burgess Memorial' because the rest is just too long to say."

"Well …" Vivian shrugged.

"Who renamed it?" Chelsea asked.

"I'm not sure," she said. "Might have been Catherine or Sally or Tricia. Could have been Laurie or Maeve or Michele. Dana? Tracy? I really couldn't say."

"You pretty much named everyone on the committee, Viv. And everyone we know in the book."

"Your friends are all in the book?" Jim asked.

"We only think they're case studies in the book, dear. We have no actual proof. I was naming the people on the committee. Not the case studies."

"Same thing," Brant muttered.

Vivian nudged him.

"If I didn't hate those events, I'd almost wish I was going." Jim snatched another cookie from the plate.

"Why?" Chelsea eyed the chocolate morsel and tried to concentrate on his words. It was so quiet in his parents' back yard and had been so long since her sad little poached egg that morning, she was just praying her stomach didn't growl before they left. It was already making the pre-growl gurgle, and the tuile, though delicious, had only awakened her hunger.

"To see if we can figure out who the next victim — or victims — might be." He shoved the whole cookie in his mouth and groaned. "This is so good."

"Don't talk with your mouth full." Vivian sighed. "You were raised better than that. But thank you."

"What does this even mean?" Jim tapped the cover of the book. "Litigating the Quantum Vow."

"Have you read it?" Brant asked.

"Uh, no. I don't exactly have a relationship to repair."

"Clearly." Vivian glared at him.

He turned toward his dad. "And if I did, no offense to you and Mom, I don't think he's who I'd go to for advice. The title of his book sounds more like a legal treatise. Or a sci-fi novel."

"Why not take home our copy and read it?"

"Not that copy!" Vivian swiped the hardcover from the table then clutched it to her chest. "This one's autographed. You can have our working copy."

"*That* one has our notes in it, Viv. Give him *this* one."

"*This* one's signed, Brant."

"If I want to read it, I'll buy my own copy, thanks."

"You know, Jim," Vivian said, "Catherine always asks if you'll be coming to our galas. You should come to this one."

"I'm working."

"You don't work nights. And you just said you want to go."

"I don't have an invitation."

"I can call her and have one for you in a heartbeat."

Jim looked at Chelsea.

She was usually good at reading his silent messages, but right now, all she could think was they'd embarrassed themselves in front of the entire department, and now she was starving. Whatever he was trying to tell her couldn't get past the fact that she'd missed lunch and was desperately trying to keep her stomach quiet until they left the McPhersons' lovely veranda. So, she gave him a subtle shrug to say they should discuss it in the car.

"All right. Call her. Get us two tickets for tonight."

Apparently he was as deaf and blind to her silent communication as she was to his.

Vivian bounced in her seat and clapped. Her face radiated joy as a smile split her face. "Wait right here. I'll call right now."

"You made your mother so happy. I'm getting a beer. You two want one?"

"It's one-thirty."

"So?"

"We're still on duty."

"I'm getting one. Excuse me."

The second he was gone, Chelsea smacked Jim in the arm. "Why'd you agree to us going to a gala?"

"You nodded yes."

"I shrugged so we could talk in the car."

"I thought you were saying you didn't care."

She sighed.

"Well, your plus one doesn't have to be me. Take someone else."

"Oh, no. I tell my mom you aren't my plus one, and she's going to want me to go with Alessa."

"You don't have to obey your mother."

"You've known her for six months. Have you ever seen anyone say no to her?"

"Yeah. You. And I've only met her a few times in the last six months."

"I pick my battles. That's one I won't win."

"I can't go. I have nothing to wear. Unless this happens to be a jeans-and-sweatshirt kind of gala."

"Yay! Shopping spree!" Vivian danced onto the veranda with far more energy than a woman of her age should possess.

More energy than Chelsea felt most days. "I'm sorry, Mrs. McPherson—"

"Vivian. I've been telling you that forever."

For literally a few days, max. "I forget sometimes."

"I know, dear. Usually when you're about to tell me something I don't want to hear."

"I simply don't have the money for a ballgown."

"It's my treat."

"I couldn't possibly let you do that."

"Then write it off as a work expense. You are going as part of your investigation, right?"

"I don't think Davenport would agree to this."

"We'll work out the details later. Come with me. We're going to Maeve's."

"Where?" Chelsea asked.

"Holt Couture," Jim said. "Mom's favorite boutique."

"I certainly don't have the personal money for a boutique. And the department would throw a fit. I'll be surprised if they'll cover off the rack."

"Even with your perfect figure, you'll need some alterations. At this late hour, you'll never get that at a department store." Vivian actually blanched when she said those words.

Chelsea blushed at the same time.

"Maeve will take care of us through the whole process. Style, price, fitting, alteration, everything. I promise. This is the best bet. Trust me. Now, time is of the essence. Let's go."

"Mom, we're still on duty. And we've been here too long." He glanced at his watch. "I'll have Chelsea meet you at Maeve's in about an hour."

"We're already cutting it so close."

"We're *working*, Mom."

She sighed.

So did Chelsea. What had she gotten herself into?

"I'll drop her off as soon as I can. We have to go." He rose, kissed her cheek, then grabbed a handful of cookies. "Later."

"Is your tuxedo pressed?" she called.

He was already through the door, and if he heard, he didn't acknowledge her.

"Thanks for the refreshments." Chelsea gave her a wan smile.

"Don't let him dawdle, dear. We'll want as much time as we can get!"

But Chelsea hurried through the house, too.

When she got in his SUV, she slammed the door.

"Hey!" At least he didn't dawdle and immediately started driving.

"Your mother thinks I need all the time I can get. Apparently I'm not pretty enough and am going to take forever to be made presentable."

"That's not what she said."

"That's what she meant!"

"No, it's not. Look, I don't have any idea what women do before these events. And I make no claims to understanding how to sew a dress. But I know my mom buys everything at Maeve's and always looks amazing. And her fittings take hours. I suspect most of that is gossip, but I can't swear to that. So, while you're there, guide the conversation toward our case and away from me."

"I don't want to know anything about you."

"But my mother does."

Chelsea felt a scream welling in the deepest part of her soul. Before she could let it out, her stomach rumbled.

"When was the last time you ate?"

"I had a lemon cookie at your mom's."

"Those are good. But the chocolate are fucking phenomenal. You should have had some of those."

No kidding. "Too heavy for this heat."

"It's never too heavy for chocolate. What did you eat before the one very filling lace cookie?"

"Breakfast."

"Sullivan. I'm losing my patience."

"A poached egg."

He took a deep breath. "It's almost two o'clock and all you've had today is one poached egg and one lemon lace cookie?"

"I've been a little busy. What have you had other than a dozen triple chocolate death cookies?"

"We're grabbing burgers on the way to the hospital."

"How do you eat the way you do and stay so fit?"

"A little gym time and a lot of good genetics."

"I hate you."

"No, you don't. So, burgers?"

She ignored him.

"Burgers, it is."

The last thing she wanted before a formal gown fitting was a burger. But her stomach had other ideas and grumbled with excitement at his proclamation. Chelsea didn't give the ball gown a second thought and ordered hers with double cheese, lettuce, tomato, dill pickle, mayo, and a fried egg. Despite the looming shopping trip, she enjoyed every greasy bite.

When they were done eating, Jim said, "Call the hospital. See if Ophelia can see us. And if Soto is around."

While she placed the call, he was also using his phone. After she hung up, she spun in her seat to face him. "Looks like the coast is clear. Soto's not there, and Kensington's awake."

"Okay. Let's go." He pulled out of the restaurant's parking lot.

"What were you doing?" She pointed at his phone.

Jim frowned. "Downloading that stupid psychologist's book. If we're going to look for victims tonight, I want to have some kind of screening framework."

"But he's not a potential victim."

"No. But he treats the people who are. We might be able to learn something from him. Much as it pains me to say it, learning about his ridiculous legal sci-fi whatever nonsense might actually be helpful tonight." He turned into the hospital parking lot.

Chapter Eighteen

GETTING to Ophelia's room without incident wasn't a problem. Getting inside was going to prove more difficult.

Jim grabbed Chelsea's arm then tugged her to a family waiting room at the far end of the hall.

"Let go of me." She yanked free of his grip. "What's this all about?"

"You told me Soto wasn't here."

"She wasn't." Her mouth formed an O. She looked down the hall then back at him. "Is she here now?"

"No. I thought it would be fun to pretend and see what you'd do."

"We don't have time for this."

"No kidding."

She chewed her bottom lip. "Okay, here's what we'll do. I'll go in there, act like I'm there on my own. I'll get her to go grab a cup of coffee with me. When we're out of the room, you go in. Get what we need from Kensington, then get out of there. Walk to the coffee shop two blocks up."

"What?"

"She might follow me to the garage. Give me your keys."

"No one drives my car."

"You have a better idea? Time's of the essence."

"No one drives my car."

Sullivan held out her hand and raised a brow.

Jim scowled and fished for his keys in his pocket. "You better be able to pull this off. Marcela can spot a con job a mile away."

"I'm not conning her. I really did come to the hospital to get answers from Mrs. Kensington. And I really would like to know anything Soto can tell me about her case. The secret to a good lie is not to be lying." Again, she held out her hand.

He dropped his keys into her palm.

Chelsea grinned her thanks then left the room, headed down the hall practically with a skip to her step.

A few moments later, the coast was clear. His partner was leading Soto to the elevator. And after the bell dinged and the hallway was empty, he headed toward Mrs. Kensington's private room. Her door was open, and instead of the ugly and scratchy hospital johnny, she wore a clingy black satin gown trimmed in lace. Not a hair was out of place, and she'd applied a full face of make up, so it was impossible to tell if she was pale or not. "Looks like you're ready to go home."

When she glanced his way her eyes lit with delight, though she affected a pout. "I really thought you'd have come to visit before now. I could have died."

"From what, exactly? Shame? Boredom?"

Somehow, her blush-tinted cheeks got redder. The pout gave way to a scowl. "I was poisoned, if you recall."

"I was referring to your, ah … outfit." He waved at her nightgown.

"It is a little shameful to be in black in a hospital, isn't it? Normally I'd have gone with lilac or emerald, maybe dusty rose or teal. Those colors do flatter my coloring." She sighed. "But I am in mourning, So … black."

Yeah, that was what he meant. "Are your children around?"

She looked toward the window. "They do have busy lives. They were just here for the funeral. It hit them rather hard. And I'm fine. Nothing they need to be here for."

"Thought you could have died," he muttered.

Her head snapped back toward him. "What was that?"

Jim cleared his throat and perched on the edge of her bed. "I'm glad it's just us. I have a matter that's rather delicate to discuss with you, and I wouldn't want to have to do it in front of them."

A wicked grin lifted her scarlet lips, and she shimmied closer to him on the bed. "Do tell, Jimmy."

He was getting rather tired of talking to people about scars on scrotums. At least this time it wasn't one of his relatives. "Forgive me in advance for insinuating anything about the dearly departed."

"You might be using the term 'dearly' a bit generously, love."

He rubbed his forehead. "Did the two of you belong to a … maybe not the two of you. Perhaps before you were married, did your husband engage in or join a club of an alternative persuasion?"

"Are you asking me if Alex was bisexual?"

He shook his head. "No."

"A cross-dresser?"

"No." Jim closed his eyes and sighed, though he supposed it could be possible. "Not that, either."

"What, then?"

"Did Mr. Kensington happen to have a scar on his

scrotum indicating that he'd been branded earlier in his life? Perhaps as an initiation into a sex club?"

"What makes you ask that?"

"Odd response if he doesn't have one, don't you think?"

"We were adventurous in the sack, Detective. And in all sorts of other places. When you have resources like ours, the sky's the limit. Literally. We've done all kinds of freaky shit. I doubt there's anything you could come up with that we haven't done so much that we grow bored of it and moved on to the next thing. And the next and the next and the next. So, if you were thinking you were going to shock me, you didn't."

"I'm not trying to shock you, Ophelia—"

"That's Mrs. Kensington, if you please."

"Noted." He'd call her the Grand Empress of Venus if she'd give him a straight answer. "Mrs. Kensington, did your husband have a brand?"

"You know, people have been in and out of here, and I was poisoned. On top of being grief-stricken on the day of my late husband's funeral. It's been a very difficult time for me, Detective, and I think I'd like to rest now."

"It's a yes or no question, ma'am."

"Where is that nurse's button?" She patted uselessly in her covers for the remote that was on her side table. "Or a damn aide when you need one? In the middle of the night, they're in here every five minutes. Can't get a moment of beauty sleep. But now? Nowhere to be found."

"Just a yes or a no."

She looked up at him, face suddenly pale under too-dark foundation. Her eyes were open unnaturally wide and darted from his face to the door then back. She whispered, "They'll kill me. They'll kill us all."

"Who?" he whispered back. "And why?"

Mrs. Kensington took a deep breath. "It is a brand. He got it before we were married. And that's all I'll say. I probably already said too much. Now go. And don't come back."

"What does—"

"*Go*." She pointed at the door while turning her head toward the windows.

Jim recognized the end of a witness's willingness to cooperate, so he turned to go, careful to check the hall for Soto before leaving. He thought about taking the elevator but didn't want the doors to open to her smug, satisfied face while he was trapped in the car. Instead, he decided to take the stairs. And just as he reached the bottom floor, the door to the vestibule opened.

Marcela Soto entered the stairwell, blocking the exit. Her eyes lit with unholy glee. Or possibly the fires of hell, he couldn't be sure.

He didn't want to go back up. Didn't want to go through her. Definitely didn't want to deal with her.

"I've been itching to talk to you, McPherson."

"Run out of puppies to kick?"

"I knew if your partner was here, you were, too. No way any cop in this city is that nice."

"Just goes to show how wrong you can be, Soto. Sullivan really is that nice. Doesn't drink, doesn't swear. Always believes the best of people. Actually thinks you're a good cop."

Her eyes narrowed.

"Funny thing is, with the exception of your total distrust of me, I do, too."

"What game are you trying to play now?"

"None, Soto." Jim sighed and took a risk. He grabbed her arms. She bristled so hard under his touch, her animosity traveled in waves through his own body. As soon as he moved her aside, he released her. "I'm sorry, but I don't have time for this. You want to talk? Come to our precinct tomorrow. You can look at both our case files."

"Both?" She started to follow him.

But he was already in a full sprint, and she didn't have a prayer of running him down. In under three minutes, Jim reached the coffee house where he was supposed to meet Chelsea.

"Where were you?" she said when he tapped on the driver's side window. She climbed out. "I could have driven."

He moved back the seat, flipped off someone who honked at him for blocking traffic, then folded himself behind the wheel. Before she was fully inside the car, he was pulling out. "I told you, no one drives my car."

"I thought you'd be waiting here."

"Soto cornered me in the stairwell."

"Sorry. I thought you'd be gone before we'd finished our coffee."

Jim adjusted his side mirror, stomped on the gas pedal, then cut into the left lane. He would apparently be using his middle finger liberally on this drive, as they were running late and his mother would not be happy about it. "Kensington took more persuading than I expected."

"You get anything out of her?"

"She confirmed that her husband had a brand. Wouldn't give me anything else. Said her life was on the line giving us that much."

"Well, it's confirmation, anyway. We didn't have it before, and we weren't going to get an exhumation order."

"Chels, we have to put this discussion on hold. We're almost at Holt's."

"Okay."

"No, you don't understand. I have to prepare you."

"For what?"

"My mother."

"I've met your mother. I've known her for months."

"This is different, Chelsea. This is a social thing. And I'm not there as a buffer."

"I think I can handle it." She looked at him with wide eyes and an indulgent smile.

He wedged between two trucks to get into the right lane to a cacophony of horns. Should have just left his damn finger up for the duration of the drive. "I know you think you know what's about to happen, but you don't. Have you ever watched those nature shows where innocent prey is surrounded on all sides until one alpha predator goes in for the kill? Then they all swoop in for the feast?"

"You're insane."

Jim pulled to the curb in front of a brick storefront. Big glass windows showcased elegant displayscapes featuring mannequins in designer clothing. A sign above double doors read *Holt Couture* in beautiful gold script lettering. "Can I at least ask you to keep me out of it? Leave my social life off limits?"

"The last thing I want to talk about with your mother and her friends — or for that matter, with anyone, ever — is your sex life."

"I thought the last thing you wanted to discuss with anyone ever was branded scrotums, tire irons as dildos, and deviant sex clubs."

"Why? Why, Jim? Why do you have to bring these things up? Especially when I'm about to spend time with a bunch of nice older ladies? One of whom is your mother?"

"Nice older ladies, huh?" He scoffed. "We'll see if you're still whistling that same tune when you're done here today."

His mother bustled through the doors. "You're late. I

didn't think you'd ever get here. So embarrassing, Jim. Maeve is doing me an enormous favor, and you keep us waiting all this time."

"Literally three minutes, Mom. And we were working. We're technically not even off duty yet."

"Well, this is for work, isn't it?"

"Have fun, Chels."

"I'm sorry, Vivian," she said as she got out of the car.

"What time should I come back for her, Mom?"

"I'll take her to our house, then she can ride with us tonight."

"Oh, no. I'll need to go home and freshen up. Do my hair and makeup. Get—"

"No, dear. I've got it all covered. We'll see you at the club tonight, Jim." Mom closed the door and guided Chelsea toward Maeve's shop.

He pulled away before his partner could change her mind.

Give him Soto any day. Sullivan was the one in for the real torture session.

CHELSEA TRIED NOT to balk at the price tags, but she'd have to max out a credit card and live off ramen for a year to afford the mid-range gowns, and Vivian was looking at the higher-range items. There was one in the window that was particularly eye-catching for every reason imaginable — style, beadwork, color, and of course price. Chelsea steered well clear of that one and drifted toward the bargain-basement priced items.

Which would have made her laugh, if she wasn't horrified by the numbers on the tags. The only thing "bargain-basement" about the prices in that section of the store was that they'd been struck through with a marker and the discounts were written beneath them. No, she didn't like the styles quite as well. If the dresses had any adornment, they were appliqués, not hand-stitched. And nothing came close to the gown in the window in terms of shade or material quality, which was probably why it cost what it did.

She refused to look at it and held up a black dress with cap sleeves.

Vivian hurried to her side. She shoved the hanger back onto the rack. "What are you doing?"

"You can't go wrong with black, right?"

"Yes, you can."

"But it's in my price range." Sort of.

"I told you, dear, I'm treating."

"I can't let you do that."

"Well, I can't let you do that." She wrinkled her nose at the black satin as she guided Chelsea toward more extravagantly styled — and priced — gowns. Vivian leaned in so she could whisper a confidence. "Maeve keeps a few things for people who want to say they bought a Holt but really can't afford to. You don't want to be seen *looking* at those racks let alone *buying* off them."

"I'm really not label-conscious, Vivian. I'd rather be comfortable in my clothes and be able to afford my rent than go into debt for five years for a one-night event."

"I thought the department was covering the basics and I was picking up the slack."

"The department isn't going to cover designer prices. Not even off the embarrassing racks." Her face flamed as she glanced at the other corner of the store.

"Then it's all my treat."

"I can't let you do that."

"Why not? I have the money. You're a family friend. Maybe more?" She winked, smiled, cocked an eyebrow.

"What?"

Two women stepped from the fitting rooms, one pitching her voice to whomever was still back there. "No, darling, the mermaid cut doesn't make your ass look fat. I promise. Does it, Felicia?"

"It doesn't," the other lady — Felicia — affirmed.

"If you're sure," came a voice from the back.

"Her ass was fat before she squeezed it into that gown," Felicia muttered.

Vivian cleared her throat. "Maeve?"

"Viv, darling! You're finally here." She walked over to them then air-kissed both of Vivian's cheeks. "And you brought Jim's girlfriend. So nice to meet you, sweetheart. Let me get a look at you." Maeve held Chelsea at arm's length.

"Not Jim's girlfriend. Girl and friend. Separate things."

"Turn around."

"What?"

Vivian spun her.

Chelsea felt both invisible and intensely scrutinized, which was an odd combination, and she didn't much care for either. Also didn't know how to put a stop to it.

"What do you think, Felicity, six?"

"Four. She's hiding under that god-awful boxy man shirt."

Maeve spun her back around. "She needs the upsize for the C-cup. Or is it a D?"

If her cheeks burned any hotter, she'd burst into flames, but she'd be damned if she'd give them the information they were discussing, as they so rudely refused to ask her and just talked about her like she was a piece of meat.

Vivian placed her hand on Maeve's arm to ease her away. "I don't think Chelsea is used to this kind of ... attention."

"If she's going to marry your son, she needs to get used to this kind of thing. There will be fittings for the engagement shoot. The engagement party. The shower. The bachelorette party — don't want to forget that." She winked at Chelsea. "The rehearsal. The rehearsal dinner. Wedding morning prep outfit. Luncheon attire. It's not an afternoon wedding, I assume? The church gown. The reception gown. The after party. Your lingerie." She smiled and waggled her eyebrows. "Then the honeymoon collection. Where will you be going, dear?"

"I'm not marrying Jim!"

"Did you have a spat?" Maeve glanced at Vivian, then back to Chelsea. "I'm sure it's nothing. Cold feet. You'll be back on track in no time. Ooh! A make-up vacation wardrobe! But that's for another time. Now, shall we see to tonight's gown? With your coloring, you could wear practically anything. Maybe not yellow. Although a bright lemon could work. And it is summer. It would make you stand out."

"I really don't want to look like fruit."

"How about this red one? Spaghetti strap, scoop neck."

"So, instead of a fruit, I can look like a tomato."

"Technically, a tomato is a fruit," Felicity said.

Maeve put the dress back and continued rooting through the racks.

"Maybe you could be a little less insulting?" Vivian whispered.

She nodded. "Sorry."

"It's okay." Maeve waved her hand as she rifled through the gowns. "It was a little ... produce-like."

Chelsea tried not to snort.

Vivian smiled.

Maeve glanced at the dressing rooms. "Felicity. The Carmichaels are ready to check out."

While Felicity dealt with the well-endowed Mrs. Carmichael and her bored pre-teen whose attention never left the screen of her cellphone, Maeve went through her inventory with them.

Everything was so form-fitting. Chelsea pressed her hand to her stomach and started to regret the lunch she had so thoroughly enjoyed earlier.

It wasn't long until the woman stopped letting her select dresses and started choosing them for her. But Chelsea still had veto power.

The skirt was too full on the lilac one. The neckline — if you could call it that when it plunged to the navel — was too low on the coral one. The cream one looked too much like a wedding gown. And though her gaze lingered on the black sheath, Vivian refused to let her consider it.

"It's not a funeral, Chelsea. It's a benefit."

"But black is classic. I'm sure dozens of women will be wearing it."

"Which is why you won't be. You need to stand out."

"I really don't."

"We want you to make a statement."

"And what is it I'm trying to say, exactly?"

"You know, if you're trying to win back Jim's heart …" Maeve tapped on her lip and glanced at the gown displayed in the storefront.

"Not trying to win anyone's heart." Or be forced to sell plasma for the next decade.

"It's a size four," Felicia said as she rejoined them.

"But it plunges in the back," Maeve countered, "so she'll have room in the bust, and we won't have to take in the waist. If she wears high enough heels, we might not even have to hem it."

"It's nice," Vivian said, her tone almost dismissive.

Chelsea closed her eyes and sighed. These three women had been playing games for the last half hour. Clearly, Jim's mother thought that by pretending there was nothing special about the signature gown, Maeve would try harder to sell it. Maybe drop the price, hopefully significantly.

She could take a whole zero off the end and it was still more than the department would cover.

"You haven't liked anything else, darling. Obviously only the best will do for you." Maeve took the gown off the mannequin and marched it back to the dressing room. She poked her head out of the middle one in the back labeled "brides" when no one followed her. "Well? Come on."

"Had to be the bridal room," Chelsea muttered. But she followed her down the short hallway.

"Do you need help?"

"No, I can do it."

"We'll be right outside. Just poke your head out if you need assistance."

"Well, I have my weapon, so I really can't let you in here once I remove it."

"Oh. Right." She wrinkled her nose. "We'll wait for you out there, then."

Chelsea locked the door behind her. Once she was alone in the dressing room, she took a moment to just breathe. Jim was right. These ladies weren't like the women she was used to. They had their own sets of rules, almost their own language. No, that wasn't it. She spoke their language, they just didn't listen to her. Because she wasn't one of them. Maeve and Felicity still thought she and Jim were engaged. Or possibly recently broken up.

She sighed.

As she exhaled, her thoughts stilled, and she realized she could hear the women talking. Since Jim had asked her to dig for information, and since no one gave a flying fig what words actually came out of her mouth, this might be the only chance she got to get any inside scoop from them. So, as she started to disrobe, she eavesdropped on their conversation.

"What was I supposed to say when my son asked me who proposed changing the gala's name?"

"Oh, I don't know," Maeve said. "How about the truth?"

"Tori's my best friend. I can't tell Jim she was cheating on her husband with Easton. It would destroy her marriage if that got out."

"I'm sure your son would be discreet."

"I'm sure he'd try. Until he couldn't be. These things have a way of not staying buried in evidence when cases go to court."

"Then maybe Victoria shouldn't have been sleeping around."

"People in glass houses, Maeve."

"What's that supposed to mean?"

"Nothing. Forget I said anything."

"No. You brought it up."

"I think I'm going to go check on Chelsea," Felicity said.

Shoot! She'd been so engrossed in the conversation, she'd dawdled. Now she had to hurry into the dress and possibly miss part of the conversation.

The silk rustled as she stepped into it, making more noise than she expected and drowning out the conversation outside the dressing room.

Then Felicity knocked on the door. "How's it coming?"

"Almost got it." Chelsea pulled the zipper from hip to armpit then stood back to assess her appearance with a critical eye. She didn't believe what she was seeing, so she climbed onto the pedestal by the triple mirror, then turned right, spun left.

The pleated, asymmetrical neckline dipped softly, showing a subtle swell of her breasts before the bodice tapered beneath it. The rest of the dress was form-fitted until it reached her knees, where it flared slightly until it kissed the floor. Every inch was adorned with an intricate pattern of tiny, hand-sewn crystals that accentuated the pattern of the silk brocade.

Vivian rattled the knob. "Chelsea, dear. Is something wrong?"

But she couldn't quite make herself answer.

"I know you said I shouldn't be in here once you removed your weapon, but we're concerned," Maeve said. "I have a key, and we're coming in."

The lock rattled. The door opened. The three ladies rushed inside.

And Chelsea turned to meet them.

Chapter Nineteen

HIS CHEEKS HURT FROM SMILING, but he continued to do so. Because that's what one did when one's recently murdered "friend" had an annual fundraiser named after him.

If Burgess could even spell "muscular dystrophy," he'd throw another thousand dollars into the pot.

Not that the fool was around to answer that question.

At least he didn't have to fake that particular smile. Much.

He swirled the Barolo in his glass. Inhaled the bouquet of berry, anise, spice. Sought the softer notes of licorice, leather, wood. Through all his world travels, he'd never found a wine he liked better. Had told Easton as much.

It was the reason the SOB had started drinking it.

It was also the reason he was incredibly easy to poison.

191

There were certain bottles Burgess had forbidden his family to touch. Then certain shelves. Then a certain rack. Finally, they stopped going near his wine cellar all together. He'd sit there, alone or with a carefully selected friend or two, the lord on his throne, ruling over his grape empire.

A little hemlock. A syringe through the cork. And a personal invitation when the family was away for the evening. Couldn't be simpler.

Hadn't been.

His only regret was that he hadn't been more patient. Now, as he stood there, politely socializing with Steel City's upper crust, he couldn't help but wonder what their reactions would have been if he'd waited for this night. This very public night.

Burgess was shrewd and suspicious, but he was also greedy and jealous. It wouldn't have taken more than a hint that he'd managed to get an exclusive bottle. A Valpolicella. He'd been wanting a DOCG. It would have been so simple to have told him he found him a classico riserva. Too high, it wouldn't have been believable. Too low, he'd want to wait a day to see it. Something around the six-hundred-dollar mark would have been the sweet spot to lure him out. The Giuseppe Quintarelli Amarone from the Veneto. He could have taken him to the car to show him. They'd have argued about cracking it open before he pretended to acquiesce and gave him a little taste. He'd never have seen the tiny hole from the needle.

It was money down the drain and a waste of good grape either way.

By the time they got back to the club, Burgess would have been drooling, sweating, nauseated. His face would have been flushed. He'd have sat on the curb, patted his forehead with his pocket square.

Someone would have stopped to render assistance, but

he would have waved them on, embarrassed to be causing a scene. And just as they walked in the door, he'd have pressed his hand to his stomach, heaved. Futilely covered his mouth with his handkerchief before projectile vomiting all over himself and the road.

Too weak and dizzy to stand, he'd have fallen backward.

Around that time, Burgess would have started to lose consciousness. And control of his bowels. The stench would have been appalling.

Gloriously so.

The guests at the gala would have emptied out of the ballroom, circled around the two of them.

Time to be the doting friend. Call 911. Answer questions — as vaguely as possible while still sounding credible.

Burgess would have been dead before the ambulance arrived.

He'd have been showered with sympathetic attention for days, maybe weeks.

Which was the primary reason the private kill had been necessary. Easton's public humiliation would have been a rapturous delight, but the spotlight wasn't worth the risk.

Watching Burgess die alone had been satisfactory. That had to be enough. For now. Anonymity was crucial until he was finished with his plan.

He swirled his wine, inhaled the bouquet of berry and licorice. Let the Barolo linger on his tongue as he thought about the six-hundred-dollar bottle of Valpolicella he'd never get to taste. Money well spent.

His gaze traveled around the room. When it landed on the newest guests entering the gala, the corners of his mouth lifted in his second genuine smile of the night.

"Let the games begin."

Chapter Twenty

JIM SNUCK in the side entrance then headed straight for the bar. He'd avoided this event — and every other like it — since he'd moved out of his parents' house. If it wasn't for this damn case, he'd be home watching the baseball game. Or if the score was as bad as he predicted, there was probably something on Juke.

At least he wasn't officially on duty. That meant alcohol wasn't prohibited.

But before he ordered the bourbon he was dying for, he decided on a beer. While getting buzzed — or flat-out shit-faced — would make the night more tolerable, it was not conducive to learning about potential victims.

He leaned against the bar, glass in hand, and scanned the room. Same old story. New money rubbing elbows with old money. Old money indulging them in polite chit-chat, then walking away and disparaging them behind their backs. It was tiresome thirty seconds in.

Jim started to take a sip, but Roland Lockwood slapped him on his back. The beer sloshed in his glass, and he only nearly missed spilling it down the front of his shirt. He spun and offered his hand. The shake was returned with a firmer grip than necessary.

"James."

"Ro." He could play the *I know you hate that name so that's the one I'm going to call you* game, too.

Roland grimaced but didn't correct him. "How long has it been? I don't think I've seen you since my fraternity beat yours at the Greek Week Walk for Life senior year. Did you not graduate?"

"No. You're mistaken. You saw me at Spring Carnival when me and my brothers kicked your asses at the derby. And you know damn well I graduated because you were helping distribute honors cords and balked at handing me mine. But I don't remember seeing you with any."

He cleared his throat. "So, I understand you went into law enforcement. What? Your dad didn't trust you with the keys to the family business?"

"Dad still hopes I'll reconsider and join the company. But he also respects my independence and is proud of my service. Didn't I hear your father demoted you to a satellite office?"

"That's not a demotion." Roland turned, tapped his finger on the bar, and demanded a martini. "There are problems in that office. I'm going to straighten them out. It shows how much trust the board has in my abilities."

"Yeah, but you're not going to Europe or Asia. You're going to Michigan, right?"

The bartender placed Roland's drink on the bar.

"Awfully stingy with the olives." He snatched up the glass. "And who is that breath of fresh air? She's got to be someone's date, right? I've never seen her here before. But she's not on anyone's arm."

Jim glanced at the main entrance.

"Say what you want about me, McPherson, but a

woman like that will never go for a cop when she can have an international businessman."

"An international businessman from Detroit?"

"Stand aside. I'll show you how it's done."

The room was filled with adults from eighteen to eighty. Every man sported designer tuxedos, some a bit tight around the middles, but not a rental in the bunch. Even to Jim's disinterested eye, it was evident each woman had spent hours on curls or up-dos, and probably the same amount of time on makeup. Gowns in probably every shade of the rainbow and every style swept the toes of the women and their dance partners as they glided across the ballroom floor.

But no one stood out like the vision in teal descending the staircase and heading for the bar.

Roland managed to not-so-discreetly nudge Jim as he jockeyed for position in front of him. "Hi. I haven't seen you at any of these functions before. First time? Here for Easton? Probably not, as I'm guessing he'd have brought you before. Have a family member with muscular dystrophy? I don't. I just think it's a good cause. My family likes to donate to all the causes. We're very philanthropic. Go to all the events. But then, we have the time and money to do so because we own Lockwood Lumber. We have interests on four continents and are working on deals in Africa as we speak. So, you new in town?"

She looked past him to Jim.

He put down his glass then held out his hand. "Would you like to dance?"

"I'd love to."

Jim led her onto the floor then smirked at Roland over Chelsea's head.

He glowered back.

"Who was that nightmare?" she asked.

"'Nightmare' about sums it up. Just some asshole I graduated with. Always wanted to be Big Man on Campus but never quite was. Still wants to be the hot shot in the room and doesn't measure up. Not sure if it bothers him or his father more. Ro — he hates that nickname, so if he corners you later, be sure to call him that — just confirmed the rumor that he's doing so poorly at headquarters that he's been banished to their Detroit office."

"Do they have a lot of lumber in Detroit?"

"The last time I was there, I didn't see any."

They shared a laugh. More than a few heads turned their way. Once they'd sobered, he looked into her eyes. "At the risk of crossing a professional boundary, I have to tell you, you kind of stole my breath tonight."

Her cheeks pinked, and her exceptionally long lashes fluttered as she looked down and away.

"This color really suits you. And the cut. Like … I don't know. Like …"

"Like I'm a walking waterfall."

"Sort of. Yeah."

"That's what I thought the second I saw it. The gown. The hair. The makeup. Your mom and her friends worked magic."

"They started with magic, Sullivan. They just sprinkled a little fairy dust on it."

She shrugged and smiled. "You look rather handsome yourself."

"I hate monkey suits."

"Why am I a magical waterfall but you're a monkey?"

"X versus Y chromosome. So, you learn anything at the hen house?"

"Just when I think you're not a jerk." She shook her head and lightly smacked him on the back. "Actually, I think maybe I did. Can we get a drink?"

He led her back to the bar, where she ordered a club soda with lime and he asked for another beer. As they headed for the balcony in hopes of fresh air, she caught him up on her overhead conversation.

"Tori, huh? Victoria Waltham. She and Mom have been friends as long as I can remember. I can understand her keeping that confidence." He shook his head, looked up at the moon, and vented a long breath. "Does no one honor marriage vows anymore?"

"I'd like to think it's possible," a man said from the shadows.

Jim whipped around.

Dr. Van Covington stepped into the light. "My apologies. I didn't mean to startle you."

"You could have let us know you were out here."

"Well, you were in the middle of a sentence. I didn't want to interrupt. Fascinating topic, though."

"Not to everyone," Jim muttered.

"I suppose not. As it's the primary focus of my practice, however, you can see why I think it is."

"Do you mind if I ask you a professional question, Doctor?" Chelsea asked. "I mean, I know this is a charity event, and I don't want to mix business with pleasure, but—"

"That's all right. I started it. Ask your question."

"The title of your book sounds a lot more like it would cover physics or law than relationships. Why is that?"

"Have you read my book, Detective?"

"Not yet."

"I have," Jim said.

"Then I suspect you can answer that question."

"More like I skimmed it, really."

"Don't be modest. Tell me what you thought."

"I have a theory. Nothing more. You're the one who wrote it. You can actually tell her why."

"But I'm far more interested in your thoughts, Jim."

He sighed. "Well, it's kind of cheating. Because I know you read Kierkegaard. But I think your premise is that marriage is a contract. And every contract has clauses that parties agree to. The problem is that most couples are so worried about the better-or-worse stuff that they forget the unspoken clause that makes all the difference. The quantum vow."

"Which is?"

"I can be excited with the chase now but not have the contentedness that familiarity brings. Or I can have the comfort that comes from years of shared memories, but only with the sacrifice of the thrill of newness. Never both. Can't have cake and eat it, too. It's Schrödinger's love — what's in the box? You can have exhilaration or you can have companionship, but you can't have both."

"*Schrödinger's Love*! That would have been a much better title for the book than *Litigating the Quantum Vow*! I wish I'd thought of that. Where were you when I needed you and my publisher was nagging me for a title?"

"Probably chasing the Grimm Reaper through the woods."

"And a much better use of your talents than titling this man's drivel." He clapped Jim on the back. "Let's freshen your drink, shall we?"

"Well, Chelsea and I—"

"No, that's all right," she said. "You two go ahead. I'll mingle."

"But Roland—"

"Is a clod. But I've brushed off men before. I'm a cop, Jim. I'll be okay. Go ahead."

He turned to the doctor. "I'll join you inside in a minute, Doc."

"Please. Call me Van. See you inside." Van walked through the door.

Jim wheeled to face Chelsea. "What are you doing?"

"What?" She batted her lashes.

His nostrils flared.

"He likes you."

"We're supposed to be working."

"So, go work."

"That's not funny."

"I'm not laughing. Much. You read his book hoping to learn how to read the room. Now you have the master at your beck and call. He seems to hate me, but he adores you. Pump him for information."

"That's really not funny."

"I honestly didn't mean it as an innuendo. That's all on you."

"If I have to use my charms, then you should, too. If you're going to show up here looking like that, then you should have to work the room."

"I beg your pardon?"

"Flirt with the guys. Not Roland. But just make your-self … accessible. We need to learn as much as we can about who might be next on the list. Go learn who might be next."

"And how am I supposed to learn that?"

"I just told you how. By flirting with people. Get them talking. Loosen their tongues with alcohol. It won't be hard. Everyone drinks to get through these things. See what you can dig up. You know the old saying. You're a detective. Detect."

She sighed.

"I guess I'm going to go talk to *Van*" — he made air

quotes — "to try to learn who he thinks might be next on the list."

"I'll walk in with you."

Jim held the door for her. He looked over her head and spied Van already at the bar. God, he hated these events.

"I'm going to go mingle now." Chelsea sighed.

"I'm going to go get drunk now."

She scowled at him.

"I mean, I'm going to go get professional insights on potential victims now. If you get into trouble, wave frantically."

"If I flipped people off, that's how I'd wave goodbye right now."

"I believe you."

She stuck out her tongue before disappearing into the throng of guests.

He made his way to the bar.

Van smiled when Jim joined him. "I thought maybe you were trying to let me down easy."

"What are you talking about?"

"Well, I was coming on pretty strong, and … you do know I was hitting on you, right?"

"Two guys can't have drinks?"

"So, you are straight. I thought so. It practically radiates off you in waves. You and your partner are … partners?"

"Not romantic partners. Just work partners. But yeah, I'm straight. Still doesn't bother me to have a drink with you, though. Does it bother you?"

"Other than my complete mortification for asking you out and being politely turned down? No."

"Focus on the 'politely' part, Doc. No reason to feel bad."

"Why do you keep calling me Doc instead of my name?"

"Sorry. Do you hate that? I tend to do the nickname-thing. Most cops do, I think. Don't know why."

"Do they? Or just you?"

"I don't know. Never really thought about it. Just feels natural to me. If it's too informal for you, I'll make the effort. Yell at me for it enough times, it'll eventually sink in to this thick skull of mine. Van."

"It's fine. I don't mind it coming from you. It feels … endearing. And I am a doctor, so it's not like you're insulting me by it. So, what are you having? I'd say it's my treat, but …" He shrugged.

"Beer."

Van gestured to the bartender. He poured two for them then placed them on the bar.

Before Jim could sip his, Van raised his glass. "A toast. To new friendships."

"New friendships." The clinking was a little much, but Jim wasn't going to complain. As he sipped the frosty ale, he scanned the crowd for Chelsea. She was talking to his mom and dad and Tori and David. Interesting.

Catherine stepped to the front of the room, where she tapped the microphone to capture everyone's attention. After the ubiquitous feedback screech, the room quieted. "I'd like to thank you all for coming tonight, to the Easton Burgess Memorial Annual Muscular Dystrophy Fundraising Gala."

The crowd applauded.

A tear rolled down her cheek, and she dabbed it with a tissue. "On behalf of his wife, Judith, his daughters, Holly and Trinity, and his son, Beau, we'd want to thank you for making this the most successful gala to date, with ticket sales exceeding last year's total by fourteen thousand dollars."

This second burst of applause was louder than the first.

"Thank you. The doors to the dining room will be opening shortly. There will be a thirty-minute window where you may browse the silent auction offerings and place your bids, then the auction will be closed so the offers can be tallied during dinner. Winners will be announced during dessert and coffee. Ah! And the doors are opening now. Please be generous. It's for a good cause. Thank you!"

But the guests were already filing into the dining room. Catherine returned the microphone to the band then joined the throng.

"You hungry?" Jim asked.

"A little," Van said. "But we still have thirty minutes. And I can fly myself to Tuscany or whatever their prime ticket item is this year. I'd rather get a little more air before dinner."

"Suit yourself." He headed for the balcony again. "But this is a fundraiser."

"Believe me. I'm very generous. Probably would be more so if they didn't rename the event."

Jim laughed. "You know, I feel the same way. Do you know Laurie Rink?"

"The pastry chef who works here?"

"Yep. Her son AJ has muscular dystrophy. She's been baking the club's daily treats, weekly desserts, and wedding cakes for literally decades. I can't tell you how many awards she's won. But they put the name of that putz on the fundraiser instead of her or her boy? It's a joke. And I don't think I'm the only person who feels that way."

"I know you're not. There are a lot of people in my practice who aren't fans of — never mind. I've said too much."

"What? Of Easton?"

Van shook his head. "HIPAA. You know I can't."

"Easton's dead. His records aren't protected anymore. Especially if revealing a detail will help us catch a killer. Do you know something?"

"What do you know about Easton's relationships here?"

"I think you're in a better position to answer that than I am."

Van scowled and raised his eyebrows.

Jim sighed. "I know he was having an affair. And I know who with."

"That's all well and good, but I said his relationships here. At the club."

"I don't follow."

"Don't you think it's a little odd that he'd have an event named after him at a club that threw him out?"

"What?"

"He was barred, Jim. Membership revoked for conduct unbecoming."

"Conduct unbecoming? People here make shady back-room business deals all the time. Practically every one of them cheats on their spouses. What the hell could he have done that would have been labeled 'conduct unbecoming' and gotten him thrown out? And why would the club have hidden that fact and named an event after him?"

"Find that out and you might have the answers you're looking for."

Chelsea stumbled out onto the balcony, Roland on her heels. He had a red splotch on his cheek that looked remarkably like a handprint. His nostrils were flaring, his chest heaving as he panted for breath, and his hands were clenched into fists.

The top of her dress was torn at the seam.

Jim stepped between them, his fingers now curling into fists. He'd waited years for a reason — any reason — to pummel that asshole into the ground. Couldn't think of a better one.

Or a worse one.

"That's the last mistake you're ever going to make, Lockwood."

Chelsea slipped between them. "Go inside, Roland."

Jim stared over her head. "Get out of my way, Sullivan."

She placed her hands softly against his chest but pushed firmly against him. "I need a ride home."

Lockwood glared at Jim, snarled something unintelligible at Chelsea, then spun and stormed inside.

He lunged, but she stood her ground. "Hey. Are you listening to me? Your parents drove me. My car is at the precinct. Either take me to the station for it or take me home. Please."

For a long moment more, he stared after Roland, then he finally looked down at his partner. "Are you all right?"

"Just tired."

"Chelsea? Your dress is ripped. What did he do?"

She shook her head.

"Are you okay?"

"Fine."

"Chels?" His voice softened, but it was raspier. "Your dress—"

"I'm really okay. I do know how to take care of myself, you know."

"Come on. I'll take you home." He took her hand and led her to his car.

As they were driving through the gate, she gasped.

"What?"

She pointed at the logo on the fence. "Gooseberry Strand. GS."

"Shit. The symbols even look similar."

"Could the club be involved?"

"They kicked Burgess out before he died for conduct unbecoming a member."

"But you don't know what that was?"

"In that group? God only knows. You're talking about titans of industry. Athletes. Politicians. Actors. They're all known for bending the rules. Back room deals. Cheating and lying. What could Easton possibly have done that the Gooseberry Strand would have taken exception to?"

"I know."

"How could you possibly know?"

"Because Roland can't shut up."

"Well, that's true. But what could he possibly know?"

"What his father knows. Mr. Lockwood is on the club's board."

"Yeah. So?"

"So, Burgess cheated Lockwood in a deal. More specifically, he cheated Roland in a deal that cost Lockwood Lumber billions. Made your buddy Ro look like a complete fool, though it totally wasn't his fault. He was swindled — his words."

"Of course."

"Anyway, Lockwood Senior lost his shirt, and his mind, over the deal. Went over Burgess's head to the president of his company and said he was going to file a law suit and a complaint with some ethics committee somewhere. I don't know. I think they reached a compromise where neither company was satisfied. Ro got banished to Detroit. Burgess lost his job. And his club membership. And his wife."

"What?"

"Yeah. Seems when the guy lost the money and power

and prestige, he also lost his appeal with the missus. She filed for divorce the same day. Not even the next day. The very same day. According to Lockwood. There's probably some wiggle room in his story, but it's easy enough to confirm."

"Shit. Chels, you know what that means, then?"

She shrugged.

"He might not be a murder victim. He might just be a suicide."

"With a brand?"

"Coincidence?"

"I don't know."

"We need to talk to the guys again. Or maybe Van will have some insights as to — fuck. I just ran off and left him there."

"I'm sure he'll understand. He saw what happened."

"Yeah, but it was rude. And he gave us that lead."

"So, call him tomorrow and apologize."

"Can't. Tomorrow's that stupid golf outing."

"Better be careful, Jim. Gala tonight. Golf tomorrow. Before you know it, your parents are going to have you in the board room and married to Alessa."

He shuddered. "Never gonna happen."

Chapter Twenty-One

27 YEARS AGO — Age 10
Emerson Park, Steel City
4:00 p.m.

DONNY'S MOTHER HAD NEVER, in all the years he'd been alive, taken him to the park. Not that he could remember, anyway. Maybe she'd walked him through one in a stroller when he was a baby. If she did, he'd been too young to remember it, so it didn't count.

Would have required a stroller, anyhow, and he was pretty sure he never had one.

But today was a special day. His tenth birthday! Finally reached double digits. Curtis could suck it — he wouldn't be ten for two more months.

Might not get cake or ice cream or presents or a party or nothin' like that, but Mum took him to a park. Their first time. She made the day special. Forgot to actually say the words "Happy Birthday," but that didn't matter. Actions spoke louder than words.

"Can we go to the playground section instead of sitting on this bench?"

"No."

"Why not? Today's my special day."

Mum sniffled. "Yeah, it is. And it starts right here."

"What happens here?"

She closed her eyes and tipped her head back.

Donny looked up, but he didn't see anything but leaves, and there was nothing special about those. And Mum couldn't even see those, 'cause she had her eyes shut.

A few minutes later, she rubbed her face then looked at him. "Your whole life, kid, you're gonna have questions. When you do, I want you to remember one thing, okay? I tried. I for sure didn't succeed, but I damn well tried. You remember that."

"All right. Can we play now?"

She again wiped her cheeks, like she was wiping away tears, but her eyes were dry. Then she took Donny's hand and pulled him to his feet. A man in mirrored sunglasses was walking toward them.

He looked familiar, but no name came to mind. Couldn't see enough of his face.

"Donny. I want you to meet your father."

The man sucked in a deep breath.

She said, "Owen."

His breath came out in a harsh rush and his head snapped toward Mum. Then he frowned and looked at Donny. "Donald."

"That's not my name!"

"I see."

"Where've you been for ten years?"

He looked at Mum. "Does he always talk to you this way?"

"No. He's usually very agreeable. But he doesn't know much about you. And I told him today was special."

"It's my special day," Donny said.

The man — his *dad* — handed Mum a fat envelope. She started to open it, but he shook his head. "Not here. It's all there."

"It's not like I see you every day. Only makes sense to count it. Could be a bunch of newspaper clippings in there."

"Keep. It. Closed." He wrapped his arm around her wrist.

She whimpered.

"This isn't exactly a legal transaction, Emily. You want to insist the brat is mine, fine. I'm not submitting to a DNA test because then everyone will know."

"Isn't everybody gonna know when you bring him home, anyway?"

He flung her arm away from him. "You got your money. Now you got no say about what happens going forward."

Mum's eyes grew wide. "Maybe this isn't the right deal. We could work something else out. A trade."

"Yeah. We tried that two years ago. Didn't work out for either of us. Or the kid."

Two years ago? The closet! He was the guy who hurt Mum when Donny hid in the closet. And then hurt him when he tried to help her. That's why he looked familiar!

"You!" Donny screamed and jumped to his feet.

"At least the kid can connect the dots. Takes him a hell of a lot of dots, but ..."

Mum caught him mid-air, stopping him from tackling his so-called father to the ground and punching his stupid face in.

Or trying his hardest.

The guy just stood there and laughed.

Donny lay in his mother's arms and sobbed. "What's going on? Why would you take me to meet him on my birthday?"

"Your birthday?"

"Oh, my god!" The guy laughed harder. "You didn't know today was your own son's birthday?"

"Did you?" she countered.

"Well, no." He wiped his eye. "But to be fair, this is only the second time I've seen the kid."

"You didn't know it was my birthday? My *special* day?"

"Of course I know your birthday." She hugged him tighter. "And this is my gift to you. You're going to go live in a big, beautiful mansion. You're going to have lots of food to eat and toys to play with and the nicest clothes to wear. No more Curtis What's-His-Faces of the world to deal with. You're going to become the Curtis to other little boys."

"I don't want to be a Curtis. I want to stay with you."

"No, Donny. You're getting older. Hitting your formative years where a boy needs his dad. Someone good and strong to set an example of the kind of man you want to grow up to be."

"And you pick him?"

"He's your father, Donny. And he has the means to give you a good life. Be grateful. Besides, you know where I am if you need me."

"I do need you."

She gave him one last squeeze, then chucked him under the chin. "Head up, shoulders back. You are smart and strong and there's nothing in this world you can't handle. Now, you go with your daddy and become the best version of you that you can be."

"I don't want to go."

"Hush now. Be brave. And remember what I told you."

"Come on," his father said. "Been here too long already."

Donny approached him, but the man made no effort to take his hand or show any other sign of affection. Which was fine by him. He was too old for that kind of thing. Tears welled in his eyes, but he blinked them away. Too old for that kind of thing, too.

He looked back at his mother.

She mouthed the words, "Happy Birthday, Doodlebug."

Donny waved and mouthed back, "Love you."

"Turn around," his father snapped.

So, he did. "Maybe the three of us could go for pizza or something. You know, like a birthday-slash-goodbye party."

"I've got other plans for you."

"Do they involve food? Mum didn't feed me today, and my stomach's kind of rumbly."

"That happen often? Your mother make you skip meals?"

"I wouldn't say she *made* me. Just that she forgot. Or we didn't have nothin'."

"We're going to have to work on your grammar. I won't have you sounding like a child."

"I am a child."

"And you need to get some muscle tone. I suspect you have the endurance of an asthmatic."

"I don't know what that means."

His dad stopped in front of a car that looked more expensive than the entire building he and Mum lived in. "Get in."

Donny didn't know you could smell or feel wealth until he entered the car. He took a deep breath and

213

rubbed his hands over the soft leather. "Wow, Dad. This is nice."

He grimaced. "Don't call me that."

"What do you want me to call you? Owen?"

"For now, how about you forget you ever heard that? Just call me Sir."

"That's not very personal."

"And that's exactly the point. This isn't personal. You know nothing about me. You don't even know who I am. Should never have seen my face. So the less you ask, the less you remember, the less you know, the better."

"But I'm your son."

"No. You are a contractual obligation and a business transaction that I'm already regretting. But it was long past my turn. So just forget you know anything about me. And for God's sake, never tell anyone you're related to me. Never, you got that?"

"But I'm your—"

"You say 'son' and so help me, I'll pull over and beat you to within an inch of your life."

Donny blinked back tears.

"Do you understand?"

He nodded.

"What's my name?"

"Owen," Donny whispered.

"No!" He pulled over to the side of the road.

"Sir! It's Sir!"

Owen rested his elbows on the steering wheel and held his head in his hands. "Can you do this? I need to know you can do this."

"I can. Sir."

"You better be able to. Because your life and mine depend on it."

Chapter Twenty-Two

IT WAS SATURDAY, but Chelsea had nothing better to do than work. And how sad was that?

Jim would be at his golf tournament, and as badly as she wanted to see him swing a golf club — especially in a foursome with his father, who she suspected took the game much more seriously — she wanted to catch this killer more. So she took the bus to the station. Or close to it. Jim had insisted on seeing her home after the gala, and even walking her to her door, so her car was still in the lot. His gallant gesture last night turned into an inconvenience this morning, but she couldn't fault him, as it came from a place of good-hearted concern.

Chelsea got off a stop before she needed to so she could pop into a cafe for a breakfast sandwich and coffee. And, as it was the weekend and she had a brisk walk ahead of her, she treated herself to a bear claw, too.

Properly fed, sugared, and caffeinated, she refilled her drink then walked to the station, where she was glad, though not remotely caught off guard, to find the bullpen buzzing with activity. Charlie and Norm stood at their case board. They both nodded a greeting to her like it was a regular weekday. Delfino sat at his desk, grumbling over paperwork that he seemed to be weeks, if not months, behind in. As he always procrastinated in filing his reports and as Davenport was always on his case about it, this was not a surprise. He nodded his hello without looking up.

She continued sipping her coffee as she joined the two detectives at their wall of evidence. "Gentlemen. You are aware this is the weekend, right?"

Charlie rubbed his eyes.

Norm glanced at his watch, which she knew did not have a date function on it.

Chelsea took a closer look at both of them — the shadows under their eyes, the uncombed hair, the wrinkled clothes, the unshaved faces. "Did you guys go home last night? Or the night before that?"

Norm yawned.

"What day did you say it was?" Charlie asked.

"I didn't. But it's Saturday. You guys need a break. Go home. Get some sleep." She took a step back. "And a shower. Maybe not in that order."

This time, Charlie yawned. "You here to compare notes?"

"I didn't expect you to be in. I can compare without you."

"But it'll be easier with us."

"It would be easier with alert-and-focused you. Not with asleep-on-your-feet you. Go home."

"Where's your partner?" Norm asked.

"Golf tournament. So this isn't official, anyway."

Charlie rubbed his face. "You're already down a man. No reason to be down two more. We'll leave when you're done."

"I can't ask you to do that."

"You didn't," Norm said. "Now, let's start at the beginning. Who was first?"

Chelsea sighed, both relieved for being helped and frustrated for being ignored. Again. Didn't seem to matter what group she was in — she was talked over and disregarded. In most cases, she'd say she needed to grow a backbone. But in this case, she was grateful. Felt bad for her colleagues, but it was part of the job.

"We landed Burgess before you got Yates," Charlie said.

She shook her head. "Not our timeline. The actual timeline." She grabbed a marker and drew a line on their board. Made a tick mark in the middle, then wrote a K under it. "Kensington died first. In his home. Severe beating."

"Not our jurisdiction." Norm tapped his finger near the letter she's written. "Are we even sure it's the same MO?"

"We confirmed yesterday. Kensington also had a brand."

Charlie let out a low whistle.

Chelsea continued. "He clearly knew his attacker because there was no sign of forced entry. Billiards were his game of choice, so the killer knew him well enough to make the cause of death personal to him."

"That should limit the suspect pool," Norm said.

"Not nearly enough." Charlie shook his head. "The guy gave interviews from his game room. The whole world has seen his pool table. Anyone could have known about his interest in the game, not that it even mattered. He was a public figure. Probably knew half the city. Had global contacts. Could have invited someone from Singapore to his house that night to talk business. Literally could have been anyone."

"So, we don't have anything to narrow our list." Chelsea put another tick on the timeline then wrote a B underneath it. "Then we lost Burgess."

"We got that one," Norm said. "Family said heart attack, but we discovered poison in the wine."

"His family wasn't allowed near his prized wine collection, so unless one of them found a way to get into the locked cellar, it wasn't them."

"That proves it was someone who knew him, too," she said. "And he also had the brand, which links the two."

"But his was marred," Charlie said.

"And I think I know why. Last night, Jim and I found out Burgess was in an unhappy marriage. He was cheating on his wife."

"That's hardly a surprise these days." Norm frowned.

"There's more." She sipped her coffee, which both men eyed with envy. "Want me to brew a pot?"

Charlie shook his head. "Not if I'm going home soon."

Norm waved her off with a half-smile.

"Okay. So, Burgess made some kind of shady deal that cost Lockwood Lumber a mint. Started a behind-the-scenes war. Long story short, Little Lockwood got banished to Detroit, but Burgess lost his job, his membership at the country club, and his wife. When he lost everything, she divorced him."

"Why would a country club care about a job and divorce?" Norm asked.

"Ethics violation, probably because Lockwood is on the board. But get this … the initials of the club? G.S."

"I'm sorry." Charlie rubbed his eyes. "You think the country club is running a secret deviant sex ring, branding its members, then killing the ones that violate their ethics codes?"

"When you say it like that, it sounds ridiculous."

"You think?"

"Finish your timeline, Sullivan." Norm nodded at the board.

She drew her final tick mark then placed a Y under it. "After you got Burgess, we got Yates. The killer was escalating in violence. He wasn't only electrocuted. The lug wrench …"

"We remember." Charlie's jaw ticked.

"This doesn't look right," Norm said.

"What do you mean?" she asked.

"There's not a pattern."

"We've got a locus — kills are confined to the city, even if they're not all in our zone. We have a profile. Wealthy men of great prominence, all of whom are or were friends and belong to the same country club. A club whose initials happen to correspond to the brand found on them. And guys, are you familiar with the logo? Even the shape is similar."

"Similar?" Charlie said. "Or the same?"

"Logos do change over the years. And those brands are really old."

He yawned. "Then the first thing I'd do is look into how Gooseberry's logo has changed over the years."

"I still say it doesn't look right," Norm said. "Usually you see escalation."

"There is clear escalation," she said. "None of the earlier kills ended with a sadistic attack."

"That's not what I mean. Poison is the most passive of the weapons. That should have come before a beating. And take away the sodomy, and I'd have put the electrocution before the beating, too. The crimes aren't getting more violent."

"Maybe they're getting more personal to the killer?" she asked.

He shook his head. "I don't think that's it. I think the point is that they're all personal to the victims."

Charlie nodded. "Most serial killers have a signature MO, but this guy's murdered in three different ways already. That we know of."

"Night Stalker didn't have an MO," she said.

"That freak's an exception, not a rule. We keep saying our victims knew their attackers. Maybe that's the point. The killer's waiting until his vics are the most comfortable, the most vulnerable, before he strikes. He's getting them where they should be safest. Making a point that there's nowhere they can hide from him."

Norm shook his head. "That doesn't quite track. Yates was killed on a back road."

"But he was a gear head, right?"

"What?"

Charlie tapped the board. "Kensington loved pool. He was beaten to death with a sock full of billiard balls. Burgess was a wine snob. He drank poisoned wine. Yates loved cars. Collected them. Went to car shows. Restored a bunch of classics himself. He was on at least three episodes of Jay Leno's show. Then he was electrocuted at his car and violated with a lug wrench? Home isn't where his heart is. His cars are."

"You're right." Chelsea turned to Norm. "He's right. It all fits. Everyone's dying by the thing they love most."

"So, what? Your country club is running some kind of secret cabal, and the people who aren't loyal to them first, who don't love them above all, are being killed by the things they loved instead? Like the Israelites worshipping the golden calf?"

It was her turn to rub her head. "I don't know. I want to talk to Marcela Soto. If I share all this with her, she may have other cases that fit this description."

Charlie shook his head. "Share it with all the zones. If it is what we think, it's not just two zones that are in the killer's radius. It's the whole city."

"Just don't mention the specifics of the secret cabal in the country club," Norm said. "I'm too sleep-deprived to know if I'm thinking clearly, and I don't want to be laughed out of town over something crazy."

"You're lucid enough to know you think it sounds far-fetched."

"Which is why I'm telling you to keep your trap shut about it." Then he smiled. "Just ask all the precincts if they've had any cases in the past year of affluent men dying — even if COD was ruled accidental or natural — by way of one of their hobbies or passions."

"And the brand. We need to ask about the brand."

"Yeah," Norm said, "but I'm guessing a lot of MEs will have missed it. Just be careful with the info you share."

"Will do. Thanks, you guys. Now, go home. Shower. Eat. Sleep. I don't want to see either of you until Monday."

"I might not wake up until Tuesday," Charlie said.

"Call if you need us." Norm waved on his way to the stairs.

"Not likely," Chelsea muttered. She sipped her coffee as she prepared her request for information to the other zones in the city. Once she was satisfied with it, she sent it off, threw her cup in the trash, then headed to the golf course.

Chapter Twenty-Three

JIM COULD DO the social scene as well as anyone who'd grown up in the upper-crust viper pit. He knew how to charm, how to slither. When to hiss and when to strike. Usually he was a master at it, the guy with the flute who left with everyone mesmerized and not a bite on him.

Today he was hemorrhaging and filled with venom. What he didn't know was why.

And because he didn't want to be at this stupid thing to begin with, he'd run late that morning, so he hadn't had a chance to talk to his father. A foursome didn't exactly give them much private time to chat, so he wasn't able to ask what Dad knew. Which had to be more than the nothing he was operating with, based on the disappointed stares he was getting.

As uncomfortable as those were, it beat the oppressive silent treatment from the other two members of their quartet. Even his eagle on the eighth hole didn't so much as earn him a smile.

After turning in their scores at the end of eighteen, no one but Dad shook his hand. The other two members of their foursome — men he'd known his whole life — couldn't walk away fast enough. Even his father was putting a little distance between them as they returned to the clubhouse.

"You've got to be shitting me," Jim said.

Dad stopped but didn't turn around.

"I come to this thing every year for you. I hobnob with these people for you. Now, for some unknown reason, some slight taken out of context or some gesture misconstrued, I've become a pariah among people I don't even like. And you won't even tell me why. Moreover, you — my own father — are barely acknowledging my existence. Are you fucking joking?"

His father wheeled around, grabbed Jim by the arm, then dragged him off the course toward a copse of gooseberry trees for which the club was named. "Misconstrued gestures? Out-of-context slights? Who's the one joking?"

"What are you talking about?"

"When you had all that trouble in Zone Two, your mother and I stood by you. Fought to keep you in this club. Threatened to leave if they kicked you out."

"I couldn't have cared less if they did. Wouldn't have cared if you stayed, but you know this isn't my scene."

"That isn't the point. We're a family. We stand by each other. Support each other. That's what families do, right or wrong."

"I was right."

"In that case, yes."

"And yet last night, I somehow wasn't?"

"No!"

"What the fuck did I do last night that was so wrong? I didn't even stay for dinner. Is that what this is about? I didn't bid on hockey tickets or some shit?"

"Nobody cares about the silent auction, Jim."

"Then I don't get it. I came. I wore a tux — one that fit me a lot better than Old Man Tomlinson's fit him, by the way. I drank, but not enough to embarrass you. I made small talk with everyone's favorite doctor. I danced with a beautiful woman, one who Mom put her seal of approval on, and even rescued said damsel in distress from a wolf in sheep's clothing. What more do you want from me?"

"It's the rescuing that has everyone so upset."

"I admit, calling her a damsel in distress is sexist. She'd already taken care of it. Kind of. Chelsea knows how to handle herself. She was trained in self-defense. But he'd torn her dress."

"I don't care if — what?"

"What did he tell you happened?"

"Just finish your story, Jim."

"There's not much more to tell. She came out on the balcony. Her dress was torn. Roland chased her. He had a red handprint on his face where she'd obviously slapped him. I was out here with Van. We saw the whole thing. I stepped between Chelsea and Roland so he couldn't hurt her further. Ro looked like he was thinking about going through me to get to her anyway, but then she stepped between us and defused the situation. He stormed away, and I drove Chelsea home. I was so worked up by what he'd done to her, I forgot to even say goodbye to Van, but that was my worst offense of the night."

Dad ran his hand through his hair. "The board took a vote on whether to even let you on the premises today. They were tied three to three."

"I don't know why they'd do that. And there are seven board members."

"Three of them wanted to hear your side before judgement."

"My side of what?"

"But the other three were of the 'punish now, ask questions later' mentality. They're loyal to Lockwood."

"What are you talking about? And where's Lockwood?"

"You have to be present to vote. Lockwood had to abstain. He's at the hospital with Roland. He was beaten to within an inch of his life last night. No one's sure if he's going to live or die. And everyone said you were the one who did it."

CHELSEA WAS on her way toward Jim and Brant when she got a text. She stopped to read it. Just what she was hoping for. She hurried toward the McPhersons, who seemed to be in the middle of what looked to be a private, and rather contentious, conversation. She considered backing away before either of them saw her, but when she caught the tail end of their conversation, she had to come forward.

"They're blaming me for kicking his ass?"

"Not 'kicking his ass,' Jim. Nearly killing him. He's in the hospital! Everyone said you threatened to kill him."

"No, I didn't."

"Actually, Jim," Chelsea said as she stepped out from behind the trees, "you did."

"I'd never do that. Do you know how bad that would be for a cop to say that?"

"Yeah. That's why I was stunned when you said it."

He crossed his arms. "And what did I say? Precisely. Do you remember my exact words? Because I do. I chose them very carefully for reasons just like this."

She thought for a moment. "Something about it being the last mistake he'd ever get to make."

Jim nodded. "That's right. I said, verbatim, 'That's the last mistake you're ever going to make, Lockwood.' And I chose those words deliberately."

Brant's eyebrows arched. "That's supposed to exonerate you?"

"Yeah. Because I wasn't talking about beating him senseless, though I'm not losing any sleep over the fact that someone did the deed. That jackass has had it coming since I met him, and probably for a decade more."

"Then what was that statement supposed to mean?" Chelsea asked.

"Come on, Sullivan. You're not only a woman who was sexually assaulted. You're a police officer who was assaulted. There's a laundry list of charges we can slap on that asshole."

"It was nothing. I don't want to get into that."

"See, that's the kind of bullshit that sets me off. You don't want to make a big deal of it because you're one of the guys, right? You're tough. You can take that and a whole lot more, huh? Well, what about the women who can't? And what about when Roland gets out of the hospital and finds one of them? When they're not strong enough to slap him and get away? They could end up with a whole lot more than a torn dress."

She chewed on her lip while she thought about what he said. Then she sighed. "You're right. I was being selfish. But we can't charge him now. It will look like retaliation for his family blaming you for his injuries. Or a preemptive strike to stop them from filing charges against you. We need to talk to Davenport. And a union rep."

"Because that always goes so well."

"You do that," Brant said, "and Mom and I will talk to the club. Tell them your side of the story. And Van. I'm sure he'll be helpful, too, once he understands what really happened."

"Did he think I went after Roland?"

"He was called in as a witness, but he wouldn't tell me what he said. But Kyle Rothschild told me Van said something along the lines of 'a man pushed to his limits is capable of anything.'"

"Why would they ask him to be a witness but not me?" Chelsea asked. "I know more of the story than he does."

"You're not a member," Brant said. "They probably didn't know how to reach you."

Jim shook his head. "That's his polite way of saying you're an outsider and they didn't care what you had to say."

"Oh."

"Come on. We have calls to make."

"I'll call your mother and deal with the club. You take care of things on your end. Good luck."

On the way to the parking lot, they both took out their phones. Jim looked at her, one eyebrow raised. "I'll call Davenport and fill him in. You call the union rep. It'll save time."

"Oh, joy."

She frowned at him.

"I mean, thanks."

Chelsea smiled and dialed the captain. Jim's call was much shorter, as he got voice mail and was forced to leave a message. She was only a few seconds into her discussion with Davenport when he started screaming. Thankfully, her partner held out his hand, and she simply passed him her phone.

Growing up, her family didn't have a lot of money. She wouldn't say she *envied* the rich kids, but she always thought they had it easier. Now that she'd known Jim for a while, she could honestly say money hadn't helped him any. He probably wasn't the stereotypical upper-crust thirty-something, so it wasn't fair to use him as a benchmark, but it wasn't fair to make blanket statements about people, anyway. Money seemed to cause him as many problems as it solved. She couldn't help but think if he didn't come from money, he wouldn't always be in trouble. Back when he worked in Zone Two, IA wouldn't have thought he was dirty because he wouldn't have suddenly had an expensive car on a cop's salary. And now, he wouldn't have made an enemy of Roland Lockwood because he wouldn't know Roland Lockwood. He certainly wouldn't have seen him last night.

Jim ended his call and returned her phone. "Cap said he'll start doing things on his end. Whatever that means. And I'm supposed to stay out of trouble on my end."

"Whatever that means." She laughed.

He joined in, but there was little merriment behind it. "Since we're out, want to do a little work?"

"Actually, that's one of the reasons I came to the course today."

"One of the reasons? What's the other?"

"I wanted to see you swing a club."

"Why?"

"I figured all those business guys live on the course, but you never golf. So, I thought it would be funny to see you in water holes and sand traps while everyone else was sailing down the fairway."

"One, I'm impressed you even know the terms. Two, I actually golf most weekends. When I'm not otherwise occupied."

"Women?"

"Cases. And three, I had the best score of my foursome. This tournament was a shamble. You know what that means?"

"No."

"Everyone hits from the tee. Whoever has the best shot is where all four players take their next stroke from."

"Isn't that cheating?"

"Not in the shamble format. That's the rule. Anyway, in eighteen holes, my shot was used fifteen times. I even shot an eagle once. And had three birdies."

"Two under par and one under par?"

"Very good!"

"Don't be condescending."

"You're the one who came here to laugh at me."

"Let's just get to work."

"The second reason you came?" he asked when they reached his car.

"You know, we could take my car. In fact, we should. I don't have a parking pass to be here."

"Are you in the visitors' lot?"

"Yes."

"Then you're fine. Get in."

She sighed and climbed into the passenger's seat. "So, this morning, Charlie, Norm, and I refined the pattern. It seems the killer is hitting people in a way that is most personal to them."

"Kensington and Burgess were at home, but Yates was on a deserted road."

"No, I don't mean a personal place, necessarily. I mean a hobby. A passion. Kensington had his billiards. Burgess his wine. And Yates—"

"Was a car guy."

"Exactly. So I contacted all the other precincts in the city and asked them to go back a year looking for wealthy males who died while involved in some way with their hobbies, even if their deaths were ruled natural or accidental. Got a hit right before I reached you and your dad. Remember that big blizzard that rolled in last January?"

"Isn't every January one big blizzard?"

"Come on, Jim."

"What about it?"

"Liam Whittaker had gone to his hunting cabin in New Albrecht."

"That's not in the city. That's not even in our county."

"No. But Whittaker is a resident of the city. And he fits the profile."

"Go on."

"While he was up there, the weather got bad. Guess his wife called and asked him to come home, but he said he'd stay and stick it out. Had plenty of propane in the generator if the power went out, as well as a well-stocked kitchen."

"Probably had a mistress up there."

"No, or he might have lived. Crime techs said his purchase history indicated he watched a lot of porn, though."

"I didn't need to know that."

"Anyway, at some point, he went out to the generator."

"Why? A guy with his kind of dough doesn't have the kind of generator that needs priming."

"Power company said his cabin didn't even lose power."

"Then what was he doing out there?"

"Rangers' best guess was he went out for firewood."

"You don't buy it."

She shook her head. "I think something drew him outside. A noise. I don't know. But he walked into a trap. This wasn't a case of someone hitting something they couldn't see in a blizzard. This was a case of a serial killer luring his target out and running him down in cold blood, then letting the snow literally cover his tracks."

"Don't suppose you know if Whittaker had a brand on his scrotum?"

"Family denied an autopsy. COD seemed evident to all parties involved. But I bet the Widow Whittaker would know the answer to the million-dollar question."

Chapter Twenty-Four

Jim pretty much hated all forms of communication, preferring to ignore everyone on principle. It was his experience the vast majority of people he came in contact with would lie to him within minutes of the conversation starting, so he'd rather avoid it all together.

Texting made that easiest of all, but all the shortcuts just pissed him off. To his way of thinking, the first sign a civilization was about to fall was that its people resorted to talking via abbreviations and pictures on devices — even when they were sitting next to one another.

Phone calls would be his second choice in the ease-of-avoidance scale. Whenever someone lied or irritated him, he could just hang up. But they could do the same to him if they didn't like what he had to say.

And what he had to say to Mrs. Whittaker was pretty important. He couldn't have her ending the call then sending him to voice mail for the rest of eternity.

Which meant a face-to-face chat. Couldn't hang up on him then. And bonus, he could read her expression and body language for the tell-tale signs of lies.

The same signs most people exhibited almost immediately.

I got my MBA from Harvard.

I bet you're the bravest cop on the force.

Those drugs aren't mine.

I didn't do it.

He sighed and drove up the winding driveway.

Despite the home being in an exclusive neighborhood, it looked like it was a dean's house on College Row. The lawn was dotted with all kinds of ornamentation in tartan plaid.

"Isn't Mrs. Whittaker around your parents' age?"

"Yeah. They've been friends as long as I can remember."

"So, shouldn't she have left the school-pride thing behind a while ago?"

He pointed to a large cut-out of a football staked into the ground with the number 61 stenciled on it in block letters. "Maybe her grandson plays on the line."

She rang the doorbell.

A woman answered the door, auburn hair pulled back into a low ponytail, the gray at her roots suggesting the reddish-brown he remembered from her younger years was now from a bottle. "Can I help you?"

"Hey, Mrs. Whittaker. Remember me?"

Her brow furrowed. Or the look in her eyes suggested it should have. Her face seemed no more expressive than a department store mannequin's. "Jim? Viv and Brant's boy?"

But her lips didn't move. There was a tinge of brightness in her voice, though.

Jim nodded, maybe a little too much to compensate for her lack of mobility.

"Nice to see you again. This is my part—"

"Heard what you did to the Lockwood boy last night." There was no warmth to her tone now.

"That was all a misunderstanding. I assure you, it wasn't me."

"Right. Just like your parents assured everyone that other incident wasn't you."

"Mrs. Whittaker, we're here about another matter. We have reason to believe your husband's death was not a tragic accident. If we could just have a few moments of your time, we think you could help us find his killer and bring him to justice."

"Get off my property. Now." She started to close the door.

He blocked it a foot before it slammed in his face. "Don't you want justice for your husband?"

"You have the nerve to come here and talk about justice? You, of all people? How is it killers like you always walk free and people like me have to spend every day looking over our shoulders? Where's the justice in that?"

"I'm no killer, Mrs. Whittaker. But I think you know your husband's death wasn't an accident. And if you tell me what you know, I can put the man or men responsible behind bars. I can make sure you don't have to keep looking over your shoulder."

She stared at him a long time. Finally, she said, "You don't know anything. You're fishing."

"Did your husband have a brand, ma'am?" Chelsea asked. "G.S. Somewhere … only you would have seen it?"

Mrs. Whittaker looked at her. Then at Jim. "All this proves is that I need to look over my shoulder twice as often. Don't come back here." This time, she managed to close the door. Then she flipped the locks with sharp finality.

They walked to the car in silence. While they were

heading down the driveway, he took his phone from his pocket and conducted a quick Internet search.

Chelsea turned to him. "Probably as close to confirmation we're going to get regarding Whittaker's brand."

"Unless we get a judge to grant a subpoena for his medical records."

"And even then, there's no guarantee a doctor would have documented it."

"What she said is good enough for us right now to consider him one of our victims. If we have to have her testify to it later, we will."

"Then what's our next step?" she asked.

"We go to campus."

"What for?"

"Talk to number sixty-one."

"Why?"

"Mrs. Whittaker knows something, but she's too scared to talk. Often when one family member knows something, the rest of them do. Even if they don't know everything. But the football player isn't a sixty-something widow who's scared of her own shadow. He's a late-teen/early-twenties. testosterone-fueled, trust-fund-spoiled moron who knows nothing about the real world except that it's round. If we're lucky."

"You do realize you used to be that kid. And sometimes I think you still are that kid. Just older."

"That's why I can say these things and get away with them."

"I don't think you'd get away with them if you said them to anyone but me. You don't even get away with them saying them to me. I just know you don't mean it the way it comes out."

"Yes, I do."

"No, you don't."

"Look. We're here."

She sighed.

The first few weeks of college were always the worst. Everything and everyone was still in summer-mode — temperatures were still high, brains and bodies were still lazy — which made the transition to homework and sports and extracurriculars more difficult. Add in pledge week and parties and parent-free living, and it was a cocktail for chaos.

One Jim was surprised to find he kind of missed.

"Where are you going?" Chelsea asked. "The sports complex is that way." She pointed toward the stadium.

"At this time of day on a Saturday on the first week of school, the first football game will already be over. Assuming it was a home game, the team will already be out of the locker room and let loose on society."

"What's that mean?"

"Number sixty-one will be at his frat."

"He might not even be in a frat."

"He's either in a frat or pledging a frat, depending on his age."

"How can you possibly know that?"

"Because he's a Whittaker. He'll be a legacy, guaranteed to be accepted by the fraternity and expected by his family to join. That's where he'll be."

"And you think they're going to let us in?"

"Well, you're an attractive woman, so they'll let you in. I won't have a problem. And besides, we're cops. We can just flash our badges."

Chelsea grabbed his arm. "Oh. My. God. You were a frat boy."

"Can we go, please?

"Do you have a membership card or a secret handshake or a theme song or something?"

"You know, this unholy glee lighting up your face right now is very unbecoming."

"I just think it's funny that someone who puts down this life so much is such a big part of it."

"Did you ever stop to consider that I *can* put it down so much because I was part of it so long, and that's how I know why it sucks so much?" The music was so loud, he leaned down to speak directly into her ear to finish his sentence. That's why he missed seeing her raise her hand to ring the doorbell. By the time he noticed, it was too late. He shook his head and yelled, "What are you doing?"

"What?"

Maybe no one inside had heard. He certainly hadn't. Jim reached for the knob.

But the door swung open. The frat boy standing there saw Chelsea first. His gaze traveled over her, head to toe and back. He gave a wolf whistle followed by a lascivious grin, then he saw Jim, and his expression soured. "This jam's not for you, old man. Beat it." Then he turned back to Sullivan. "But I've got the perfect room inside for you."

Jim gritted his teeth. "Buddy, there's so much wrong with what you just said, I don't know where to begin. But I'm gonna love explaining it all to you in detail."

Chelsea gave him a wide-eyed, pointed stare. "Let's not give Davenport more to deal with right now."

"Go get Bryce Huntington for us."

"No." The kid, doing his best imitation of John Belushi's Bluto, chugged his drink. Some sloshed on his shirt.

Jim flashed his badge. "Let me see some ID."

He just laughed and belched long and slow in his face. "Dude. This is private property. You can't hassle me unless I come outside."

"Wrong again. If police suspect illegal activity on the

premises, we are within our rights to enter without a warrant and arrest any and all parties breaking the law."

"Gawd. You're such a drag, dude. If you were ever cool enough to be in a frat, you'd know how much guys like you suck."

"He used to belong to this one," Chelsea said.

The kid scoffed. "Right. Like we'd take an asshole like him."

Jim rolled his eyes. "Just go get him."

While the kid went in search of Huntington, Chelsea said, "Where'd you get that name from?"

"Football roster."

She shrugged.

"The Whittakers had a daughter — Cicely, I think, her name was. I vaguely remember her marrying a Huntington, think he was from somewhere north of here. Erie, maybe. Can't remember the guy's name. She died in a horrible wreck about five years ago. Not sure what happened to the husband after that."

"Jim!"

"Anyway, they had a son. And my guess is grandma is filling in for mom, that's why she's got all that shit in her yard. Whittaker had signs for number sixty-one in her yard. When we left her house, I pulled up the roster on my phone. Number sixty-one is Bryce Huntington, Cicely's boy. The reason we're here."

Three frat boys returned. Everyone's favorite doorman — who once again leered at Chelsea, once again burped, and once again glared at Jim — staggered on his feet, clapped his buddy on his back, then ambled away yelling something about beer pong.

It was easy to tell of the two remaining kids which was Bryce. The one who was six foot tall and weighted a buck-eighty was probably a wide receiver. The one towering over him and at least a hundred pounds heavier had to be Whittaker's grandson. "You Huntington?"

"Why?"

"I'm Detective McPherson. This is my partner, Detective Sullivan. We have a few questions to ask you about your grandfather's death."

Bryce shook his head. "My grandmother warned me about you."

Chelsea's eyebrows shot up. "She did?"

But Jim wasn't surprised. That was step one in the playbook. Close ranks.

"Texted about ten minutes ago. Said you're some kind of rogue cop. Didn't I see your name on one of the trophies upstairs?"

Chelsea looked at him, eyebrows raised.

Jim ignored her and addressed Huntington. "You wouldn't happen to know anything about a secret organization your grandfather belonged to, would you? One that might have been loosely related to the cause of his death?"

"Or responsible for it?" Chelsea added.

"Gram told me not to talk to you. You should go."

"At least take my card. One brother to another. If you change your mind." Jim held out a card.

Bryce shook his head and walked away.

His brother took the card, then shut the door.

"Trophy?" Chelsea said as they walked away. "What'd you win a trophy for?"

"Never mind."

"I'm not going to stop asking."

"And I'm not going to tell you."

"I'll ask your parents."

"What makes you think they know? Does your dad know everything you did in school?"

"Yes."

240

"Of course he does."

Jim unlocked the doors. While Chelsea strapped in, he scrolled through his playlist until he found a song she wouldn't object to. Just before putting the car in gear, a text came through.

The fence. Tonight. 3:30. Park on Friar. I have info on GS.

He showed the text to Sullivan.

"Who's it from?"

"I don't know the number."

"We should trace it."

"They want to meet at the fence."

"Where's that?"

"On campus. Which means we don't need to bother with the trace."

"No?" Chelsea's brow wrinkled.

"I can only think of one person who would have this number and would want to meet there."

"The frat kid with Bryce who just took your card."

Chapter Twenty-Five

27 YEARS AGO — Age 10
  The "Spa," Somewhere Outside of Steel City
  5:00 p.m.

IT HAD BEEN two months since Sir had brought Donny to the "spa." He'd arrived on his birthday, and while he'd been really sad to leave Mum, it had been the best celebration of his life. He'd eaten until he was full, the best meal he'd ever had. It wasn't just pizza or mac and cheese or chicken nuggets, either, but real food. Stuff he'd never seen before.

Figured it was a one-time thing. Something Sir had arranged as a Welcome Home Donny party. Or a Welcome to the Family party. But this wasn't Sir's home, and the people there weren't Sir's family.

And it wasn't for Donny's birthday because Sir hadn't known.

Regardless, it would have been foolish to not take

advantage of the surprise, so Donny had tried not to be sad about Mum and instead to enjoy the meal. And he did.

But that wasn't the best part.

The best part was, it happened again the next day. And the next and the next and the next.

And the food wasn't the only treat. It was a spa, after all. They had plenty of luxuries, and he not only had access to all of them, he was practically *forced* to use them.

He got to exercise on all kinds of different machines. Run and jump and skip all across the ground. Someone taught him to swim in a giant, crystal-clear pool, then he got to swim back and forth for an hour every day. After showering — where he got to pick from fifteen different scents of soap and shampoo — they had new clothes for him to wear. Not just new to him, but *brand new*. With tags and everything. Then a really nice lady — Sasha — worked with him on his studies. She not only caught him up but even helped him get ahead in several subjects. Sasha looked like Mum and smelled like her, too. And sometimes she even gave him hugs when nobody was looking. He grew to love her and tried extra hard on his homework to make her proud.

For the first week or two, he kept waiting for the check to come due. He lived in a constant state of paranoia, always looking over his shoulder for the person who was going to question his presence there or throw him out or beat him for trespassing.

No one ever did.

So, eventually, he started to relax and settle into the sameness of his new daily routine. Should have known that the second he got comfortable with a schedule, they'd change it. They served dinner at four that evening. Just something light — broiled fish, a side salad, and a thin broth. Not the usual fare, but he'd eaten well at breakfast and lunch and the whole prior two months, so he wasn't about to complain.

Donny was expected to read every evening after dinner until bedtime. He'd have a few extra hours tonight, so he contemplated starting a new work instead of finishing the biography he'd been reading, which he found rather dry.

Sasha placed her hand on his shoulder. "Would you come with me, please?"

"Sure." Seemed dinner wasn't the only thing that was going to be different that evening.

He liked her. She reminded him of his mother — she was blonde and had blue eyes and always wore her hair in a ponytail, just like Mum did at home. When Sasha walked, it swung back and forth, and if it caught in the breeze just right, he could catch a whiff of cherries, which always made him happy. It reminded him of home. Mum smelled like that sometimes. So did some of her friends at the club.

Donny wondered if they were still there, and if they still thought about him.

As the two of them walked down the hallway, the air circulated in such a way that he caught Sasha's scent. Cherries. He closed his eyes and breathed deeply for a moment, lost in a memory that was both warm and painful. Then he opened them and came back to the present. Back to his location. Back to Sasha. He looked up at her and sighed, content in the knowledge that at least he was safe with her. Well-cared for. Well-fed.

She gave him a sad smile as she led him to a part of the facility he'd never been to before. "We're going to give you a little extra pampering today. Starting with a mani-pedi."

"You mean, like, my nails?"

"Your whole hands and feet, yes, but a focus on your nails."

"Oh, no. I had that before. Mum went nuts."

"Owen insisted."

"Sir won't like it, I'm sure."

"Donny, I have to."

He shook his head then whispered. "Kids at school teased me terribly for having polish on my toes."

"Oh, no, sweetie. Not like that. No color. We're just going to trim everything so the nails aren't rough or chipped. Make sure everything's smooth and buffed. Very masculine. I promise."

"No colors or sparkles?"

"No. I swear. Cross my heart."

"Okay." But he still wasn't sure.

"After that, we'll do a full body polish, followed by a mud wrap. Then, you'll have a Vichy shower."

She'd lost him. He had no idea what that stuff was, let alone what it was supposed to do.

"We'll get you fully moisturized — do you need any waxing?"

"Waxing? Like the floor?"

"Oh. Um. Well." Her cheeks flushed. "We'll figure that out once you disrobe."

"What?" He knew what that meant!

"Well, you can't have your body worked on if we don't have access to your body."

"I don't want anyone having access to my body."

There was no mistaking the sadness in her eyes this time. But he didn't know why it was there.

"Donny, everyone has to play the game. And very few of us like the hand we're dealt in this world. When you're all in and finally show your cards, the best you can hope for is that there are one or two friendly faces at the table, maybe a kind waitress or dealer."

"I don't know what you're talking about."

"I have to think about my own kids," she whispered. Tears welled in her eyes, then spilled down her cheeks.

"Okay."

"Okay, then." She dried her face. "Let's start with the manicure." Sasha led him to a completely empty room except for a white leather salon chair. When he sat in it, it reclined back. A nail technician entered, wheeling a cart. Before he knew it, his socks and shoes had been removed and his feet and hands were soaking in sweet smelling liquid.

"What's this for?"

But this lady wasn't friendly like Sasha and didn't answer him. She just busied herself with the items she'd brought with her.

Donny's anxiety levels grew as the time passed, but Sasha hadn't lied so far. After the soak, his hands and feet were thoroughly dried. Then his nails were trimmed, filed, and buffed until they shined almost like they had clear polish on them. But there was no color and no sparkle, so … promises kept. "Can I go back to my room now?"

The technician didn't answer.

Instead, Sasha returned. And she had a robe in her hands. "Time for your body polish."

He stared at the robe. His knees started to tremble.

She sighed, and her shoulders slumped. "You know what? We're running a little ahead of schedule. Why don't we get your hair cut first?"

"My hair?"

She ran her fingers through it. The bangs were nearly at his eyebrows and the back touching his collar. "It's a little long, don't you think?"

"No." Mum almost never got his hair cut. It usually brushed his shoulders before she remembered. And if he pulled it into a ponytail like hers, she didn't notice sometimes until it was longer than most of the girls at school. Didn't bother him much. Not unless Curtis pulled it, which he didn't like. Or called him a girl, which he hated. But Curtis did that anyway, so it didn't much matter. Donny liked his hair long. It kept his head warm in the winter. And he didn't like scissors or razors near his face or ears or neck … none of the sensitive places. The barber nicked him once, and it really hurt. More than a regular cut on his finger or knee or something.

"Well, it's on the list. Might as well do it now."

So, he got his hair cut. And shorter than his mother ever insisted he get it done. At least it postponed the disrobing. But with every tuft of hair that fell onto the floor, the knot in his stomach got tighter.

Maybe it would have been better to keep the longer hair for a bit more time and get the nakedness over with. How bad could it be? Sasha said people paid to have these things done to them, so it must feel good. Right?

Nails smooth and shiny — and based on the hair on the floor, head nearly the same — he followed Sasha to yet another room he'd never been to. She handed him his robe and showed him where he could change.

In the locker room, he gazed into a mirror — the first he'd seen in two months. Initially, he thought it was a doorway to another part of the facility and not a looking glass. He didn't recognize the boy staring back at him.

The added calories, as well as the quality of them, had caused him to grow several inches taller. And all those healthy meals, combined with the constant exercise, had filled him out. Not only couldn't he see his ribs or his hip bones, he'd started to develop some muscles. More than any of the other boys in his grade, anyway. And his head wasn't shaved bald as he feared. The hair was actually cut into a rather flattering style — short on the back and sides, just a little longer on top. The shadows under his eyes were long gone, and the time he spent outside had replaced his sickly pallor with a pretty nice tan.

"You ready?" Sasha called from the hallway.

"One second!" Donny had to trust her. If his appearance was any indication, she'd never done anything to hurt him. He stripped out of his clothes, wrapped the robe around him, then stepped back into the slippers the nail technician had given him. "Coming!"

She gave him another sad smile when he met her in the hall, but he tried not to think about it. He just followed her to the next room. Still another he'd never seen. "How big is this place?"

"You'd be surprised."

Inside, she explained what exfoliating meant then gently took his robe from him. He was embarrassed, though far less than he thought he'd be. And what she called sloughing actually felt kind of nice. Afterward, he had a mud bath, which he made her swear to never tell anyone about. Last thing he needed was for Curtis — or anyone else — to start calling him a pig. Then she rubbed him down with all kinds of sweet-smelling moisturizers.

"Am I done now?"

"No. Now you get a massage. Need you nice and … loose for tonight."

"Why?"

"It's … a special night."

He'd heard that before. Wonder what was in store for him this time?

Sasha lit a bunch of candles. She put on soft music with a hypnotic beat, then had him lie on a table, where she began to rub all his muscles. Her hands were warm and slippery because she used scented oils. He was kind of getting dizzy from all the heat and smells and stuff to relax him.

His head swam. His limbs grew heavy. So heavy. His heart kept time to the music until his pulse was the song and his thoughts floated away on the currents of incense in the room.

Donny must have fallen asleep because he was startled when he heard a male voice. He looked up, rubbed his eyes. Jumped to his feet. Owen was back. And he wasn't alone.

Two dozen men were with him, every one of them in black hooded cloaks. Not even Owen's face was revealed, but he'd know that voice anywhere.

"Sir!" Donny snatched his robe from where Sasha had laid it on the bench at the foot of the massage table and hurried into it. Humiliation and betrayal rolled through him, fast and hot, and his gaze darted around the room. He clutched the lapel, the belt. Turned toward the door and tried to run away.

Two large men stood there, barring his escape. Sasha waited next to them, tears in her eyes.

"Sasha? Help me, please!"

"You gotta just play the hand you're dealt, kid. Even if you only got deuces."

"I don't know what that means!"

The men ripped the robe from him while restraining him. But unlike the kids in his school, they didn't laugh. No one in the room laughed at him. They were taking this seriously. Very seriously.

Sasha walked to the back of the room. A few seconds

later, a squeak of a wheel preceded a wave of heat. He struggled and bucked, but the men only held him tighter.

And the heat got hotter.

Then he saw why.

When Sasha returned, she was pushing a cart, on top of which was a pile burning rocks. And he didn't think it was another kind of spa therapy.

"What is that?"

Owen stepped forward until he stood toe-to-toe with Donny. "You will speak when spoken to, Donald."

"That's not my name."

The men holding Donny jerked him up so they were closer to — though not nearly — eye-to-eye.

"It is, now."

Donny spat on him.

And Owen backhanded him across the face.

Stars burst in Donny's vision as pain exploded in his cheek. The only ally he had in the room was Sasha, and she'd already proven she would not stand with him. And while he'd put on some weight in the last two months, it wasn't nearly enough to fight his way past twenty-four full grown gorillas.

"To answer your question, Donald—"

"That's not my name!"

Owen turned around. Even though his face wasn't visible, his anger was. "Do not make me silence you again." He returned his attention to the object radiating heat. "This is a firebox. It is used to heat these." He picked up one of two sticks with some kind of swirly symbol on the end. "This is a brand. One has uppercase letters, one has lowercase letters. Do you know what brands do?"

Donny shook his head.

"Do you have a favorite brand of cereal? Or jeans? Or sneaker?"

Again, he shook his head. He was always just happy to have food or clothes or shoes.

"How do you not have—" Owen sighed. "Never mind. The point is, a brand defines what something is. It signifies what makes something different from all other things. In some cases, more special than all the rest. Or, in other cases, and you'll want to take note of this, it denotes ownership."

"I'm going to own something?"

For the first time that evening, the people in the room laughed. It was a tone he knew well.

They weren't laughing with him — he wasn't laughing.

They weren't laughing because of him — he didn't tell a joke.

They were laughing at him — he *was* the joke. And he didn't like it.

Owen turned away from him. "Sasha."

Sasha hurried forward. She took Donny's hand then led him to the corner of the room. The men who had been restraining him stepped to the foot of the massage table. All the other men surrounded it.

A man Donny hadn't noticed earlier appeared from the shadows. He was draped in a scarlet cloak and carried a thick, ancient book.

"Who's he?" Donny whispered.

"It's better you don't know anyone here," Sasha answered in a hushed tone.

"What's going on?"

"Initiation."

"I'm not sure what that means."

"The two men who held you are about to join this exclusive club."

The man in the red robe started chanting.

Donny didn't understand what he was saying. "What language is that?"

"I don't think it's spoken anymore. It's from a long time ago."

"Then how did they learn it?"

"Please don't ask any more questions."

"How do you become a member of this club?"

"I don't. Only men do."

"Men like me?"

"Men like them."

"Owen said—"

"Don't say his name!" She shook her head.

"Fine. Sir said tonight was membership night."

"Yes, he did."

"So, what happens?"

"Come here." She wrapped him in a hug, made sure his face was pressed against her body.

A horrible burning funk wafted through the room, but she kept his head held tightly to her. It was confusing to him, being held by Sasha. On one hand, she was motherly, and he'd missed that over the last two months. Then again, it kind of felt like he was betraying Mum. But was it really a betrayal when she'd sent him away? And how motherly was Sasha, when she'd led him to this freak show?

The fact that he was naked was so far down on his list, it barely registered.

There was another increase in the stench of something charring, and this time, someone grunted.

"What's going on?" He tried to pull away. Fear made his palms clammy, his legs liquid.

She held him tighter. "It'll be over soon."

"Are they setting the place on fire?"

"No."

"Are they setting *someone* on fire?"

When she didn't answer, his bladder nearly released. "Sasha? Let me go."

"I can't."

"Are they going to hurt me?"

"You'll live through this. You're strong."

"You can't let them. It's wrong!" His voice was barely above a whisper.

"They'll kill my kids."

"They'll kill *me*."

"No." Tears streamed down her face and dropped on his head and shoulders. "No. They want you. They need you."

"No!" This time, he screamed. He thrashed. Whether he overpowered Sasha or took her by surprise, he didn't know, but he pulled free of her grip and ran for the door.

One of the robed men grabbed him. Yanked his arm so hard, his shoulder nearly pulled out of its socket. Started dragging him toward the massage table.

Two of the men were naked. One was holding an ice pack to his private parts. The other was grimacing and holding his hand out, waiting for an ice pack of his own.

He had a blistering burn on one of his testicles.

Donny's head whipped toward the firebox. The two brands.

One uppercase. One lowercase.

More special than the rest. Or owned by someone else.

He wheeled around. But he was too slow.

Hands were all over him. His arms. His torso. His legs. His feet.

Donny was lifted into the air, placed on the table, limbs stretched as wide as they could make them go. Someone lifted his head, and someone else held his eyes open like he'd want to watch the horrors about to be visited upon him.

The man in the scarlet robe read again from his ancient book, then he selected a brand from the firebox. Donny had no doubt it was the one with the lowercase letters. The one labeling him a slave.

And unlike the "special" men who were initiated into an elite club, when he was branded, he screamed.

Chapter Twenty-Six

At two-thirty in the morning, Chelsea met Jim in her apartment's parking lot, then he drove to campus to meet their contact. A reverse lookup on the phone number proved Jim right — it was the kid who had been with Bryce at the frat house. Chad Redding. Wide receiver, Bryce's roommate, and apparently their latest confidential informant.

"Why the fence?"

"Students have been painting messages on the fence overnight forever. It's a long-standing tradition. Groups stake their claim first thing in the morning sometimes just so they can paint it that night."

"So, we could be walking up to a bunch of fence-painters, and this is just a big joke on us?"

As they approached the fence, Jim nudged her and nodded toward the tennis courts. All the way across them, near the football stadium, was a flashing light. It was blinking a pattern, almost like morse code, but not. If it was a message, she couldn't read it.

"I don't recognize any of the kids at the fence," he said.

"What do you say we try our luck with twinkle-twinkle over there?"

"It's as good a plan as any."

They made their way toward the field. Chad Redding stepped out of the shadows by the ticket stand.

"Why didn't you just tell us to meet you here?" Jim asked.

"Because if anyone was following you, I was going to bail."

"And how would you know if anyone followed us?"

"I watched you since you walked past the library. No one's tailing you. I had to know it was safe. Relatively."

"You could have just texted or talked to us on the phone if you were afraid to be seen with us."

He shook his head. "You don't get it, man. Nowhere's safe. Your phones are probably bugged. Your cars are probably being tracked. Unless they're old clunkers, the GS can hack into the computers and run you off the road if you get too close to them."

"I don't think a country club is going to wreck our cars for solving a couple of murders," Chelsea said.

"Country club?" Chad looked at her like she was stupid then back at Jim. He tipped his head toward her. "Girlfriend or quota hire?"

"Excuse me?" she said.

Jim scowled "Neither. My partner happens to be a talented and highly qualified detective who has captured several murderers, including the Grimm Reaper."

Chad looked at her again, this time with a little less derision, a little more interest. "You really busted that guy?"

"Is that so hard to believe?"

"If you think a country club is behind this current spate of killings, yeah."

"Then what does 'GS' stand for, if not 'Gooseberry Strand'?"

He scoffed and shook his head. "Man, you two really are clueless. The Gomorran Society."

"The what?" Chelsea asked.

"The Gomorran Society? Sodom and Gomorrah?" Chad looked at Jim. "Seriously? You and your dad were Alpha Tau Betas, right? You never heard the rumors?"

"I guess not. Fill me in."

"You know the Skull and Bones at Yale?"

"Yeah?"

"This makes them look like an all-are-welcome club. Two seniors are selected a year. Two. That's it. If you're selected, you don't say no. They apparently make you an offer you can't refuse. To become initiated, there's some kind of ritual involved — I don't know the details, but the end result's not pretty. I also can't tell you what's asked of the members once they're in. What I do know is everyone who's ever been a member has become top of his field. Once you're in, you're in for life. And there's only one way out."

"How do you know all this, Chad?" Chelsea asked.

He shrugged. "I'm in the frat. You hear things."

"No," Jim said. "I was in the frat. So was my dad. We never heard things like that. What aren't you telling us?"

"I told you all I can. Probably more than I should have."

"Were you invited to join?"

Chad shook his head. "I'm not a senior."

"We can help you if you tell us the rest." She lay her hand on his arm.

He flinched then pulled away from her. His gaze darted around the campus. "I've told you all I can. We really shouldn't be out in the open like this any longer."

"I don't think you did tell us everything." Her heart hurt for him. He might be a big college football player, but at the moment, he seemed like a scared little boy. "Who do you know that's involved in this?"

"Levi Jameson." Chad started backing away from them. "Look into him. He's the one who's behind all of this."

"Levi Jameson?" Jim asked.

He kept backing up.

And Jim kept talking. "Of Xanastia Pharmaceuticals? He's been dead for almost twenty years."

"Just look into him." Then Chad turned and ran.

"Well, what the hell are we supposed to make of that? Jameson's been dead since ... 2002, 2003. Somewhere around there," Jim said.

"Not sure what to make of that. But the kid's scared. Someone he knows is involved."

"This case keeps getting more tangled. I thought for sure the club was involved."

"We can't rule out some of its members. Not yet." She yawned. "It's the middle of the night. Or super early in the morning. Nothing we can do right now. Let's get some sleep. Figure out our next steps in a more decent hour of the day."

"Agreed."

They started back toward Jim's car, this time at a much slower pace. The fence painters had finished their masterpiece in red on black.

Once you label me, you negate me.

"Your school is ... different."

"Is that from Shakespeare? I remember my freshman year, no — sophomore year. The drama department hogged the fence for a whole month with quotes from plays they were putting on. The Greeks and athletes were not happy. A lot of people thought it was going to come to blows."

"What happened?"

"The CFA professors held a midnight showing of some interactive movie where you throw cards and toilet paper or something."

"*The Rocky Horror Picture Show?*"

"I have no idea. All the drama students left the fence unattended to go to the screening, and some sorority moved in. The regular rotation took over after that." They reached his SUV. There was a ticket under his wiper. "Damn it! In the middle of the night? For a cop?"

"In all fairness, you don't drive a department vehicle. They had no way of knowing."

"It's the middle of the fucking night, Sullivan." Jim ripped the ticket off the windshield then tossed it into the backseat.

She climbed inside. Unlike the middle of day, the street was clear, and it was easy to back out. As he drove past Beaver Hollow Park, he said, "You know, we're not far from Beaver Hollow Road."

"Where we found Yates."

"We should follow up with Speikman."

"We'll put that on the list for tomorrow." She yawned. "Or Monday."

"Probably should talk to Covington, too."

"Why?"

"Well, I still need to apologize to him for running off without a word the other night. But I meant for our case. He may be able to shed some light on secret societies."

"Add that to the list, too. At this point, I might not even remember what Chad said. I'm wiped out."

He pulled up to her apartment. "Need me to walk you up?"

"No, thanks. I can make it." She hoped. "Goodnight."

"Night."

Chelsea barely had the energy to smile her farewell as she let herself into the building. She could hear his car idling out front until she turned on her apartment light. Jim was a good guy.

Man, she was tired. Too tired to do anything but the barest of necessities. She was in bed in under three minutes, and not even the disturbing thoughts of the Gomorran Society and the depraved activities they might be involved in could keep her eyes open.

It didn't stop them from invading her dreams, though.

Chapter Twenty-Seven

CHELSEA TEXTED Jim on Sunday morning — okay, afternoon — and begged for a work-from-home day. It was technically their day off, so she wasn't out of line. Besides, she needed to shop for groceries, as the sad lime and lone container of yogurt in her refrigerator weren't going to get her through the week, assuming she made it home in time to prepare a meal. And she doubted Davenport would appreciate her going to work in yoga pants or duckie jammies, so laundry was a must. Also, she hadn't checked in with Dad in too long, and though he no longer needed her visits, they both enjoyed them.

It was no surprise that Jim didn't return her text until almost ninety minutes later. He claimed he was working out and then in the shower, but she figured he'd just slept through her message. Not that she'd challenge him on his excuse. But he also didn't outright agree with her. He asked her to call when she was free. As she was folding the sock load — the undisputed worst load of laundry — she dialed, put the phone on hands-free mode, then set it on the table.

"Hey, Sullivan. How'd you sleep?"

"All right. You?"

"I didn't."

"What? Why?"

"Listen, we have some things we need to address that can't wait. Want to grab a bite to eat then swing by Confluence House?"

"What's that?"

"I talked with Helen Cespedes, Don Speikman's case worker."

"I didn't know he had a case worker."

"There's a lot we don't know."

"Is Speikman really our priority right now? Given everything—"

"Speikman is our top priority. Like I said, a lot has happened. He's in a halfway house. Confluence. Cespedes placed him there. I'll fill you in on all of it the way."

"When?"

"I'm in my car. I'll be at your place … well, I'm pulling into your parking lot now, actually."

"Come on up, then. I need a few minutes. Door's unlocked."

"Shouldn't be."

"It's not currently. I'm unlocking it for you now. Bye."

"Sull—"

Chelsea threw the rest of the unfolded socks in the laundry basket. It was obvious there were some without matches and she scowled at them. She was certain she'd put only complete pairs in the wash — where had the errant ones gone? The load was the bane of her chore list.

She carried the basket into her bedroom, closed the door, then begrudgingly stepped out of her pajama bottoms. One day. It would be nice to spend just one day in comfy pants. When she heard Jim come in, she called out to him. "I just need a few minutes to get dressed. Make yourself at home."

He didn't answer, but that wasn't unusual. Her hand hovered over her usual dress slacks, but she figured it was the weekend, so she opted for a pair of jeans. The tee she had on wasn't going to cut it, though, so she traded it for a lightweight short-sleeved sweater. While she was strapping on her service weapon, Jim yelled, "Sullivan!"

"Yeah?" She finished fastening it as she opened her bedroom door.

"Are you okay?" He was out of breath, like he'd just run the stairs.

"Of course. Did you not hear me tell you to make yourself at home when you came in?"

"Chels, I just got in here now."

The blood drained from her face. "No. Someone was in here. I thought it was you."

He shook his head and held up the ticket he got last night. Then he nodded toward her coffee table, where an identical citation sat.

"I don't understand," she said.

Jim flipped over the paper in his hand. A familiar marking was emblazoned on it. "I didn't get a ticket last night. I got a warning. And I'm pretty sure you just got the same."

She crossed the room, hand outstretched toward the page on her table.

"Wait," he said. "My prints are already all over mine. It's unlikely, but we might be able to get trace off yours. Don't touch it without gloves."

While she took a pair from her bag, she asked, "What does yours say? Exactly?"

Jim read from his card. "Your investigation, while initially helpful, has now crossed a line into avenues those of your station are not meant to pursue. Cease and desist all further inquiry following this trajectory or definitive measures will be taken. This is your final notice."

"'Those of your station?'" Chelsea snapped on her gloves as she stood over the table, then she picked up her own message. "Mine's identical to yours."

He offered her a bag. "Seal it up. We'll give it to the crime techs. Maybe they'll get lucky and be able to pull something from it."

"Right. Because these snotty rich frat guys who are now bajillionaires have their prints in the system."

"You have a better idea?"

"Are we really going to see Speikman, or were you just saying that in case our phones are bugged?"

"Both, actually."

"Then let's go. You can tell me what I missed in the car."

On the way to Confluence House, Chelsea had Jim catch her up, and she did her very best to avoid interrupting.

"Speikman's financials finally came in. I gave them a quick once over, just to clear him. When he first showed up at the station, I knew it was too good to be true. Don't get me wrong, I badly wanted it to be him because I wanted this killer off the streets. I was worried about my parents and hoped this was a crime of opportunity. Figured a homeless guy came along and found a rich guy broken down, beat him for his wallet. Things got out of hand. But he didn't take the car. Not the stereo or even his phone or money. Which was why I had a bad feeling his confession was bogus. After listening to it, we both knew it was. But I thought maybe he'd been paid to do it. Couldn't work out how he'd rigged the car to stop there in the middle of the night in the rain, but if he'd managed it, it was the perfect place for a hit."

"Financials didn't bear out that hunch?"

"Worse. He's not the deadbeat I thought he was."

"I don't understand."

"He was US Navy. Served overseas. Three tours in Iraq. Injury ended his career, brought him home. But he had no one to come home to. He's on disability. Gets a check every month. But after that money lands in his account, he donates it to a wounded warriors' charity. Every last penny of it."

"You're kidding? He doesn't even save enough to eat? To rent cheap studio apartment?"

"Nothing. Gives it all back. Government takes its cut in taxes, of course, but he gives the rest of it back. Must be feeling survivor's guilt or something."

"Stories like that always gut me. I can't imagine what he's going through."

"I know. It's … I know."

"So, why do you want to talk to him?"

"I still think he saw something he hasn't told us. And I want to know why he confessed."

"That makes sense to me now. He was used to a regimen, right? Roof over his head, three square meals a day."

"Which he could have had with his disability pay."

"He needed to give to charity. Besides, he also needed to be told what to do, when to do it."

"Both of which he could have managed if he got a job."

"Right. Because those are so easy to come by for disabled vets with PTSD."

"There's my bleeding-heart partner. It's not that simple, Sullivan. You don't just confess to a crime because you're looking for structure and you feel guilty for having life, liberty, and freedom when some part of your unit wasn't so lucky."

"So many of our vets commit suicide for that very reason. What makes you think he wouldn't want to punish himself via prison for the same thing?"

Jim shrugged. "I don't know. It doesn't feel the same."

"If you don't believe me after talking with him, ask Covington. I bet he'll concur."

"Fine. Let's see what Speikman has to say first."

They pulled up to Confluence House. When they got to the door, both of them paused. Chelsea looked at him. "Do you ring the bell at a halfway house or just enter?"

"It's still someone's home." He knocked on the door.

A man answered, a somber look on his face, eyes dry but red.

Chelsea glanced at Jim. "Hello, sir. I'm Detective Sullivan. This is my partner, Detective McPherson. We're here for Donald Speikman."

"Detectives. I'm Paul Friedman. Thank you for coming so quickly. They said it could be a little while."

"They?" Jim asked.

"Yes. The dispatcher."

"I'm sorry." Chelsea said. "I think there must be some mistake. We're here to talk to a resident of yours. Mr. Donald Speikman?"

"Talk to him?"

"Yes. Is he available?"

He stared at her. Opened his mouth. Closed it. Cleared his throat.

"Sir?"

"Ma'am, I'm sorry. I thought you were responding to the call I placed to 911 about fifteen minutes ago when I

went to Don's room. He's … it seems … I found … well
…"

"What is it, Mr. Friedman?" But she already knew what
he was going to say.

"Donald Speikman is dead."

Chapter Twenty-Eight

22 Years Ago — Age 15
Jamison Manor, Birch Hill
2:23 a.m.

DONNY, who had long ago grown used to answering to "slave" or simply a snap of someone's fingers, stood naked in the corner. He and the other Gomorran slaves had already served their masters — five years later, the term still nauseated him — in every painful and debasing manner possible. Once the depraved lunatics had had their fill and their fun, they'd gotten down to business.

And the slaves had stood there, in silence, waiting until they were beckoned again. All of them were.

Some were used as servants to fetch refreshments.

Some were forced to perform other sexual acts on members of the Society, or on other slaves or themselves while the voyeurs watched.

Still others were subjected to random torture, just for the sake of someone's amusement.

Donny was in the second of the three groups.

Kevin ended the evening with one broken arm and two broken fingers, but that seemed preferable to the electro-shock wand and five golden showers Donny was subjected to.

After the debauchery was over their business was concluded, the slaves knew their jobs without being told. They put away the food, washed all the dishes, scrubbed the kitchen, and left the meeting area — wherever they were — cleaner than they found it. Then all the masters left with the slave they brought, unless a trade or purchase was made.

That's why Donny was nervous as he stood in the corner. Naked and alone.

Ethan, the Grand Master's slave, had aged out of the system. No one knew what happened to slaves who aged out. They'd been told if they behaved, they'd be set free with a generous stipend to live on. That's why slaves were educated. Not only did it make them more agreeable around the home if a master chose to hold a conversation with them, but it made them easier to assimilate into society later.

But Donny wasn't stupid. It would only take one freed slave going to the cops and the Gomorran Society would be toppled. It made a lot more sense to him that slaves who "aged out" also got "rubbed out."

And now Owen — his biological father, or Sir, as he'd been calling him since Mum had sold him — was having financial issues. Donny probably wasn't supposed to know, but he paid attention. And he could easily do that math. The Grand Master was loaded and needed a slave. Why risk procuring his own when he could buy one from an underling who needed cash?

He glanced at the door. Wondered what would happen if he ran.

"Slave, come here." Owen snapped his fingers.

Donny stepped forward. He'd long ago lost the shame that made him cross his hands in front of his genitals. In fact, he'd been taught to hold them behind his back and to look submissively at the floor.

He only managed one of those things.

"Is he always so insolent?"

Owen slapped him on the back of his head. "How dare you make eye contact with the Grand Master?"

Donny looked down.

"I believe your master asked you a question, slave."

"I don't know," he growled through clenched teeth.

Another blow came, this time to this side of his face. He didn't see it coming because his head was down, and after the impact, he had to force himself not to retaliate.

"I thought you said he was trained."

"He was, Sir. I mean, he is. He's never responded with such impudence before. Not since right after his initiation."

The Grand Master approached. His cloak was still off, but he had a gold mask on his face. He'd been one of the men who'd been particularly vile that night. Probably testing Donny.

And the guy wondered why he wasn't docile? After the night he'd endured? The months? The *years*? Bastard.

"I haven't had a good challenge in quite a while. I'll take him. Fifty thousand less than we agreed since he needs so much work."

"But Grand Master—"

"He's defective."

Donny bristled.

"You promised me a well-trained slave. He's insubordinate. Talks back. Doesn't submit to the cane. Yelps at a little shock treatment. Is squeamish when you piss on him. What would he have done if I took I shit in his mouth?"

"I'd like to see you try."

The Grand Master whirled toward Donny. "You dare speak to me?"

"Donald!" Owen yelled.

"That's not my name, Owen!" he screamed back.

"And you call each other by name? My god, man. No wonder he's so disobedient. I think you need a few lessons, as well." He walked to his desk, opened a drawer, stabbed at a keypad. A locking mechanism released with a beep, then he bent down. When he rose, he tossed bundles of money onto the desk. "This slave is now mine. Do you agree?"

Owen walked to the desk, looked at the cash. "That's seventy-five less, not fifty less."

"You incurred another twenty-five-thousand-dollar penalty for your weakness."

"He's my son, Grand Master," Owen whispered.

"Then you deserve this all the more. Remove your robe and bend over the desk."

"But … I'm not a slave."

"A father should teach his son, not sell him. And you clearly need to be taught a lesson. More than a few."

"Grand Master, I—"

"I am not in the habit of repeating myself. Remove your robe and bend over this desk."

Owen removed his robe and stood naked before his master. He'd been naked in front of him countless times at countless hedonistic parties indulging in countless hedonistic pleasures, but this was the first time he was to suffer a hedonistic pain since his branding when he was initiated into the Society, and his face flushed crimson.

The Grand Master removed a whip from a different

desk drawer. "I want you to count these strokes." His voice was calm, deep. His words slow, deliberate. "And with each one, I want you to think about how you failed your son. And how you failed *me*."

"Yes, Grand Master."

Donny knew from practical experience that the man was a genius with a whip. He could make it tickle, he could make it sting, or he could make it burn like the fires of hell. The first couple were designed to lull Owen into a false sense of relaxation. His ass cheeks weren't even as pink as his face yet. When the word "three" came out in a relieved sigh, the Grand Master's mouth curved up in a sadistic grin.

That was all it took for Donny to clench his whole body in anticipation of what was about to come, and it wasn't even his body that was about to feel the lash. The whip moved so fast, he couldn't track it. But he sure as hell heard it when it connected with flesh.

Owen howled as the sound reverberated through the room, and the welt formed instantly on his skin. Plump and pink and just a little bit puckered.

"You didn't give that one a number. I guess it didn't count." The Grand Master let the whip fly again, just a bit harder this time.

Owen screamed and wailed, "Four!" This continued until he was slick with sweat. Tears, snot, and saliva smeared on his face. "Twenty" was more of an unintelligible sob than an actual word. And his backside had more stripes than the US flag.

Then the Grand Master did something Donny never expected. He handed him the whip.

He looked up at the masked man, one eyebrow raised. How badly he wanted to do it. And how badly he feared it was a test — one he'd fail and pay for dearly.

"He let you down just as he let me down. He deserves to be punished for it. And punishment should always be meted out by the person who was wronged."

Donny held it, tested its weight. It was heavier than he expected. Longer than it looked. Much more unwieldy and impossible to control. He tried flicking it toward his father — who was still braced against the desk and still blubbering, though starting to calm down — but he only managed to flop it gently on the back of his thighs.

"Better than I expected from you, slave."

Slave. Even in their shared quest to make Owen atone, he didn't get the courtesy of a proper name.

The Grand Master took a paddle from his drawer. "Try this. It has holes in it, so it'll hurt more. Especially now that I've tenderized his flesh for you."

Owen whimpered.

Donny hefted the paddle. This he could wield with no problem. And wield it, he did. With reckless abandon and breathless fury. The first blow might have been a bit hesitant, as he'd expected Owen or the Grand Master to stop him, but when neither did, he let loose all his anger and frustration and sadness. He made his father bear it all. All the humiliation and rejection and fear. Everything. And more.

A power surged through him. Something primal and visceral. Primordial. Something foretold by forces incomprehensible by human minds. Coded into the very first atom that exploded into existence in the cosmos and had been developing into something darker and deeper and more dangerous with each iteration of split atom and cellular generation and genetic mutation until Donny was conceived. That same nature had nurtured him as he'd grown and developed into the tortured and tormented soul that at that very second had the paddle clutched in his sweat-slicked grip, blood pouring into his trembling, twitching muscles, giving him the strength to exact the revenge he so desperately needed and richly deserved and—

The Grand Master stopped him. "That's enough."

But it wasn't. He'd gotten a taste for revenge. And it was sweet.

"Now bend over, slave. Because you're mine now, and you also have some lessons to learn tonight."

Donny bent for his punishment. But he barely felt it. He was enraptured with his first taste of vengeance. And planning for more.

Chapter Twenty-Nine

THE EMTS SHOWED up almost before Paul Friedman was done talking to them about Donald Speikman's death. Jim drew the virtual short straw — which was only fair, as he needed to know what was going on with his potential IA problem, anyway. So he stepped outside to call Davenport with the latest developments while Chelsea hung back to see what else she could learn.

He answered on the first ring like he'd been waiting for Jim to call.

"Hey, Captain."

"If you're calling with more good news, like you ran over an old lady or shot some poor kid's dog, I don't want to hear it. Just give me your badge and gun and start running, because I can't and won't protect you from those charges."

Jim just sighed.

"No witty retort? It's that bad? What the fuck did you do now?"

"I didn't do anything. But it's bad."

"It's pretty fucking bad here, too."

"IA coming after me?"

"Not yet. I have them on hold."

"Then what?"

"You first."

It took a few healthy minutes to fill Davenport in on the Gomorran Society, the notes they left on his car and in Chelsea's apartment, and Speikman's death.

"Was it suicide?"

"Sullivan's finding out now. My guess is it's been made to look like a suicide even if it wasn't, so the initial word will be yes."

"Make sure they send the body to Nia."

"Will do. So, what's the nightmare on your end?"

"You been talking to Whittaker's grandkid?"

"Bryce Huntington? Only in the briefest sense. One time, and he told me to get the hell away from him and not look back. Why?"

"His name struck a chord with me."

"Why would it?"

"It seems Alpha Tau Betas had some kind of reunion gathering last night. Some of the alumni were there talking with the boys. A small handful went down to some room in the basement when the rest went to bed. Supposed to be quiet down there."

"Yeah, I know the room. They call it the crypt."

"Three of the current brothers and two of the alumni ended up dead. Poison in the food or drink. Everything's being tested."

"Are you fucking kidding me? Poison? Like Kensington?"

"Different than Kensington."

"But definitely poison?"

"Yes. And Bryce was one of them."

"Of course he was."

"Another of them had your card in his pocket."

"Let me guess — Chad Redding."

"That's right. Want to tell me why he had your card?"

"I tried to give it to Huntington when I went to the frat to talk to him about his grandfather. He wouldn't take it. Redding was with him. He took it."

"And you happen to know his name."

"Who was the third kid?"

"Theo Brenneman."

"You have a description of him?"

Papers rustled. "Caucasian. Dark, curly hair. Big."

Shit.

"You know him."

"Know of him."

"What's going on, Jim?"

"Who were the alumni who died in the crypt?"

"Redding's older brother, Joel. And David Channing."

"I don't know him."

"CEO of Natrumark."

"An adult?"

"Did I stutter?"

"Text me and Sullivan everything you have."

"I will, but I think the two of you should come in. We need to go over all of this face to face. You need to turn over the evidence you have to the techs. And we should bring in Anderson and Paxton. Hopefully they haven't received threats, too."

"We will come in, but I want to stop by Covington's first."

"Why?"

"See what his take on all this is."

"Fine. But there's one more thing you should know."

"What's that?"

"There's been another victim."

"Talk about burying the lede. Who? Where? Are you sure it's one of ours?"

"Yeah, we're sure. Sebastian Brentwood."

"Brentwood? He was in my foursome yesterday. Didn't say a word to me the entire day. And I mean not a single word. Because of the misunderstanding with Roland. Or so I thought."

"Well, he was obviously having a conflict with someone else. Whether he knew it or not. Some time between the banquet after the outing and rounds this morning, he met a violent end on the eighteenth hole. Groundskeeper found him. Head had been bashed in. Ball marker had removed both his eyes. Club had been used the way the lug wrench had been used on Yates. And the flag had been jammed right through his back. Just waving in the breeze."

"It's not like those are on the end of a spear. Even if you unscrew the cup, it would take a considerable amount of force to ram one through someone's spine."

"Or a pre-made hole."

Jim thought about that for a moment. "So, the killer planned on making that statement."

"He's planned everything else."

"You're not wrong."

"I want you and Chelsea in here. I'm calling Norm and Charlie, too."

"You know they've practically been living at the station. It's already close to dinner. Let them have the evening. We'll all touch base in the morning."

"Yeah. You're right. They can have until morning. But I want you and Sullivan in here tonight."

"As soon as we wrap up here. Then talk to the doc. And grab something to eat."

"By the time you do all that, it'll be nighttime."

"So, might as well wait until morning for us, too."

"McPherson, you're trying my patience. That society knows your vehicle. They've been in her home. Get your asses in here."

"Looks like she's done. Gotta go. Later, Captain."

Chelsea approached. "They're saying he killed himself. Doesn't track for me, though. He … I don't want to say *thrived* on the self-punishment, but that's what kept him going. Don wasn't a quitter."

"I agree." Jim jogged over to the crew wheeling the body out of Confluence House. "We need you to take the body to our morgue. Our ME, Nia Washington, knows he's coming. It's part of an ongoing investigation."

"He's a suicide," one of them said.

"My captain specifically requested it." Jim handed her a card and smiled. "You can call him, if you'd like."

She looked at the card, at him, then at her partner. They finished loading Don Speikman's body.

After she closed the doors of the van, Jim nodded his thanks. "I appreciate it."

"Don't be too proud of yourself, hot shot. I'm calling your captain from the van before I decide where to take the body."

He walked back to Chelsea.

"Losing your touch?"

"A, I wasn't turning on the charm. B, I'm tired. And C, she turned left, so she's going where we asked. Now, get in the car. I have a lot to catch you up on."

They were in front of Mamani's before he'd finished telling her everything Davenport had told him. "Well, I don't know what's more surprising. That none of this shocks me anymore or that we're at this restaurant."

"Alessa never works Sundays. Her whole family takes the day off, so it's safe to come here. And I'm in the mood for ceviche and lomo saltado. "

"You can order for me. Every Peruvian dish you've let me try of your mother's has been delicious, but we've only been here that one time."

"Get the blackened chicken. Pollo a la brasa. It's Sunday, so they'll definitely have it. It comes with fries and an aji amarillo sauce."

"I'd rather have rice."

"Must you change everything?"

"Rice is lighter."

"Get both. I'll eat the fries. I'm starving."

As luck would have it, the Mamani family wasn't there, so there were no hassles through dinner, and he was able to enjoy his meal while telling her everything else Davenport had revealed.

Jim had missed Peruvian food. His mother didn't make it often, and he ate with his parents even less often. Unless Mom dropped off a care package at his house, he didn't have the pleasure. And since he'd started avoiding Mamani's because of Alessa, he almost never got to eat some of his favorite dishes. If he wasn't going to the station, he'd have ordered a couple more meals to take home to enjoy over the next few days. And maybe a few more for the freezer.

When they'd finished eating, there wasn't a scrap of food left on the table, his stomach was uncomfortably full, and he was ready for a nap. Or about eighteen hours of uninterrupted sleep.

"Shit." He stifled a yawn.

"What?"

"I wanted to go to Van's tonight. Davenport wants us to go to the station. He doesn't think it's safe to go home when the Society knows where we live."

"Is this how it's going to be? Every big case, we can't go home?"

"Just gives us incentive to solve it faster."

"Our suspect pool just got a lot bigger again. We went from a vagrant to the board of directors of a country club to all current and former members of the Alpha Tau Beta fraternity. The list grew exponentially. Like that." She snapped her fingers.

"That's not true. Not all members. Just the two members from every class who were recruited into the society."

"It's a secret society, Jim. How are we supposed to figure out who those men are? Have a reunion and ask if we can examine everyone's genitals?"

The elderly couple at the next table both looked at her with wide-eyed disgust.

Her cheeks turned pink, and she offered what was probably a mumbled apology but she didn't quite form intelligible words.

"Redding gave us a name, remember? Levi Jameson. We start there."

"He's dead."

"We'll figure that out tomorrow. Tonight, I'm out of gas. I need to sleep."

"Then let's go home."

"No. We go to the station. We've got cots."

"Which we only got because of the last impossible case we had."

"At least we have them." Jim gave her a wan smile.

"I want my own bed."

"They know where you live."

"A hotel, then."

"Sullivan, they know what cars we drive. No."

"By that logic, they could be the old couple right next to us."

Again, the people at the table beside them shot her a look of disdain.

"I am so sorry," Chelsea said. "We haven't slept, and it's been a terrible day."

Jim flagged down their server. "Can you bring the bill, please? And I'd like to pay for that table, as well."

The gentleman started to wave off the gesture, and the server tapped her pen, unsure what to do.

"I insist." Jim handed her his credit card.

She walked toward the kitchen before the argument could continue.

"You didn't need to do that," the man said.

"I wanted to. It's the first nice thing we've been able to do all day."

His expression softened at that. "I'm sorry it's been a rough one for you."

"Sometimes you just have days like that." Jim shrugged.

The server came back with his card and the slips to sign.

"Might I at least get the tip?" the man asked.

"That's all right."

"Can I?" Chelsea muttered.

He just smirked at her, finished scrawling his name, then set his pen on the table. "You ready?"

She nodded.

"You folks have a lovely evening." Jim threw his napkin on the table and rose.

Chelsea gave them each a nod, smile, and another apology, then she led the way out of the restaurant.

Jim walked slightly behind her, head on a swivel. He was too tired to feel confident that he'd pick up on a threat before it was too late, and even once he was in the car, he couldn't breathe a sigh of relief.

It wasn't until they were in the station that the knots in his neck started to loosen. As they made their way toward the locker rooms, they ran into Davenport, who was just heading out.

"What did Covington say?"

"Never made it there. Going first thing in the morning. Decided to crash here tonight."

"Good. No safer place than a building full of cops. But listen, you two. We have a lot to go over in the morning. We've got bodies stacking up in the freezers downstairs and no leads."

"We have one lead, sir," Jim said.

Chelsea scowled. "Our lead is also dead."

"Who?"

"Levi Jameson."

"Jameson?"

"Yeah," Jim said. "Why?"

"I was the detective on his case."

Chapter Thirty

In the morning, Chelsea woke on a lumpy cot with bed-head, a knot in her neck, wrinkled clothes, and a nasty disposition — none of which was going to get the case solved or even make Covington more amenable to their cause. He didn't seem very fond of her, and Jim owed him an apology. It was an understandable situation, one the doctor shouldn't really even be angry about, but in those social circles, an apology was in order, nonetheless.

On the other hand, in the neighborhood she grew up in, the Van Covingtons of the world would be apologizing to the Jim McPhersons for not jumping in to help defend the honor and safety of the Chelsea Sullivans.

She rubbed her head. It was a weird day, indeed, when she was not only referring to herself by name but also in plural form.

Chelsea went to the locker room for a quick shower. Without a blow dryer or makeup at work, she resigned herself to looking rough and, tired as she was, she didn't much care. More often than not, she pulled her hair into a ponytail, anyway. She'd never replaced her spare outfit from the last time she'd needed it — the coffee-spill-before-court debacle in June — so it was back into her jeans — and if Davenport had an issue with it, well, she didn't much care about that, either. Her contacts were so dry, they were practically falling out of her eyes as she blinked, and she didn't have spares with her, nor did she have solution. She tossed them in the trash and put on her glasses.

A glance in the mirror before leaving the room confirmed her worst fears.

She looked like a nineteen-year-old, not a twenty-nine-year-old.

With a sigh, she made her way to her desk. Jim was already at his. He nodded toward a cup he'd put on her blotter. "Morning. Coffee's as wonderful as it usually is. But it's fresh. Got you one before everyone drained the pot."

"Morning? And thanks?"

He looked up at her. "What?"

"That's what I was wondering."

"I don't get it."

"Me either."

Jim leaned back in his chair, stretching and finally succumbing to a yawn. "I'm too tired to play this game. Just ask whatever you're hinting at."

"Aren't you going to make some kind of snide comment about my glasses or lack of makeup or how young I look?"

"I've seen you exactly like this before, and I don't think I made the comments then. Would it speed our day along if I called you Katniss or something?"

"Why?"

He sighed. "What do you want me to say?"

"Nothing, I guess."

"Fine. Are you ready to go see Van?"

"Does Davenport need us first?"

"Probably, but he's not in yet. Chelsea, it's only six-thirty."

"Oh. Then let's go back to sleep."

"No. Let's get out of here before the captain gets in. I'd rather avoid him before he grounds us."

"But don't you want to know more about Brentwood? Maybe we should at least go see Nia. She's usually here by seven. Earlier if she's got a lot of work. And it's a good guess this qualifies as a lot."

"She won't have autopsies done on Speikman or Brentwood yet. I say we leave before we get stuck here."

"Fine. Call Covington and find out if he'll see us. If he will, then we'll sneak out before Davenport gets here."

Jim grabbed his phone.

"What are you doing? I was kidding. You can't call someone this early."

But he did. And much to her surprise, Covington not only answered, he agreed to meet them. Then they were in the car and on the road before she could come up with another reason not to go.

As usual, Steel City traffic was abysmal. Even at six-thirty a.m. So when Jim took a turn Chelsea didn't expect, she assumed he was trying an alternate route to avoid congestion. But when he made a second turn that took them even further out of their way, she said, "What are you doing?"

"Going to the cafe."

"We just had coffee."

"Shitty coffee."

"It's in the opposite direction of where we're going."

"I know that."

She closed her eyes and prayed for patience. "It's bad enough you probably woke the poor man—"

"I wouldn't have called him if I thought I'd have woken him."

"How could you possibly have known he was up?"

"You're his super fan. How do you not know?"

"I'm not a super fan."

He rolled his eyes.

"I'm not. Especially since I met him."

"I like him more now that we met him. A celebrity is a celebrity. Now, he's a guy we know."

"Yeah, a guy who's kind of rude."

"He's not rude. He's just different than the kinds of people you went to school with."

"So, it's okay that he's rude to me because he's rich?"

"That's not what I said. That's also not what I mean. And he isn't rude to you. He's just aloof."

"Aloof is a rich person's word for rude."

"Roland is rude."

"No, Roland is flat-out mean."

Jim sighed. "Which is it, Sullivan? I'm rude because I'm calling on 'the poor man' at an unsociable hour or he's rude because he discusses philosophers you're not familiar with when we're together? Or did I miss some other unforgivable slight because I was born with a silver spoon in my mouth, too?"

She crossed her arms. "I just find it interesting that you've been agonizing over apologizing to him for a couple of days now because you think you somehow wronged him."

"Don't you think it was rude of me to run off and leave him there all alone without even saying goodbye?"

"Under the circumstances? No. If you recall, Roland had just attacked me. You rushed to my aid. If anyone is owed an apology, it's me and you. He should have been by your side, defending me, assisting you. Instead, you're—"

Jim shushed her and held up a finger. He rolled down his window as he pulled up to the speaker at the drive-thru window. "Can I get a box of assorted pastries, please? Make sure you've got at least three bear claws in there. Thanks." Then he turned back to Chelsea. "What were you saying?"

She shook her head and turned away from him.

"What?"

But she wouldn't answer.

He inched forward until it was his turn. Then he exchanged money for the box of goodies. "Don't suppose you'd hold these for me until we get there?"

She entertained visions of smearing them all over his stupid face, but instead, she held the box on her lap as they rode to Covington's house.

Jim, probably in a gesture of good will, tuned into an episode of *Steel City Special*, which she knew he hated. But that wasn't the good will she wanted. The simple courtesy of acknowledging her feelings before Covington's was all she asked. Yet it was too difficult for him. Maybe if she'd been born with a "silver spoon" in her mouth, he'd have made more of an effort.

Instead of talking things out, she brooded in silence and tried to listen to the show. But she couldn't concentrate on it. Kingston Kane was in rare form that morning, overly boisterous for the early hour. Chelsea usually loved his antics, but she hadn't slept much, and what little sleep she did get hadn't been restful, so she was grumpy, and Kane's chipper tone was annoying even her. It had to be driving Jim nuts. It was the only thing she found enjoyable about the episode.

By the time they got to Covington's, she couldn't say

who the guest had been. But she knew with absolutely certainty Jim was ready to explode. And she took a perverse sense of satisfaction in that fact.

Usually, Jim waited for her when they got out of the car, but today, he couldn't get away from her fast enough. She hadn't rounded the bumper when he was already ringing the bell. By the time she'd joined him, Covington had just opened the door.

"Good morning, Detective."

"Van. Thank you for seeing me on such short notice. I've been meaning to call, but I've been busy with work. I just wanted to apologize for running off on you the other night without an explanation."

"I admit, I wondered what happened. I thought perhaps I'd offended you, after all."

"What? Of course not. When Roland came out on the balcony—"

"Roland? You mean Chelsea."

Chelsea was still standing behind Jim, and she had gone from impatient to irritated to angry. Were they just going to pretend like she wasn't there? And keep talking about the details of that night — that painful, embarrassing night — like it had no more relevance than getting the time wrong for a movie showing?

"No. Chelsea came out first, but Roland chased after her."

"Ah. I see where we might have gotten our signals crossed. When your friend came after you on the balcony, I went back inside. It seemed like a private discussion, and I didn't want to eavesdrop. When you didn't come find me afterward, I assumed I had made you uncomfortable and you had used her as an excuse to slip away without making things awkward."

"So, you don't know anything that's happened?"

"If you mean about the fight between you and Roland, I did hear about that. I must admit, I was rather surprised to hear a man in your position would succumb to your baser urges. The club called me in to give testimony, but I hadn't witnessed the fight, or apparently what came before it, so there was little I could say on either party's behalf."

"Van, none of that happened. My department and my family are working to get my name cleared. I can explain everything. If you could let us in for a few minutes, I promise, I can answer any questions you have."

"Us?" He leaned to the side, finally noticing Jim wasn't the only detective on his stoop.

Chelsea gave him a tight-lipped smile and held up the box of pastries.

Van's eyes widened as he recoiled a bit. Then he recovered and opened his door wider. "Please. Come in."

She may have shoved the bakery box into the doctor's chest a bit harder than necessary, but that's how those "no-mannered, lower-class" kids got their points across.

When Jim took a seat on the right side of the sofa, she chose the far left. He rolled his eyes at her and whispered, "What are you, a toddler?"

"Takes one to know one." Chelsea stopped short of sticking her tongue out at him. Maybe — okay, definitely — she was acting childish. If she were to be brutally honest with herself, this case had left her feeling overly sensitive to her upbringing and her lack of money, which was never a problem between her and Jim.

No. Which was *usually* never a problem between her and Jim. But then his mother paid for her gown and accessories. And he paid off the couple beside them last night that she managed to offend twice in a matter of minutes.

Her! She never said mean things like that. Of course, she'd been tired and frustrated and sad. Felt poor and uncouth. Not that that was an excuse. Somehow, though, she'd managed to prove she was exactly those things.

So, maybe that's why she was so touchy about it today. But Jim didn't have to go and make it worse.

Van returned with a gorgeous tray loaded with Jim's pastries — artfully arranged — as well as fruit, fresh roses, coffee, cups, plates, and even red linen napkins rolled and folded into freaking flowers that perfectly coordinated with the arrangement in the vase. The whole thing could have graced the cover of a magazine. "My apologies. I didn't have time for presentation."

She thought about the yogurt in her refrigerator and the paper napkins — well, paper towel squares she ripped from the roll as necessary — and blushed.

"No worries, Doc. Looks great."

"Help yourself." He gestured to the tray.

"Don't mind if I do. We missed breakfast."

Instead of his usual attention on Jim, Covington turned his attention on Chelsea. "So, the two of you spent the night together? Detective McPherson led me to believe you were only partners in the business sense."

Detective McPherson? "We are. We've hit a snag in our case. We discovered who is behind the killings."

"Did you?" He poured himself a cup of coffee, took a "rose" napkin from the tray, opened it with a flick of his wrist, then smoothed it over his lap. "Have you caught him yet?"

"Well," Jim said as he plated a bear claw, "that's kind of why we're here."

Covington sipped his drink. "How can I help?"

Three times the two of them tried to talk over each

other before he put his ring down, raised his hands, and whistled.

He actually whistled.

Chelsea was mortified. Her cheeks burned. Her chest heaved as she tried to catch her breath — and there was no reason to be winded, other than frustration. She glanced at Jim, who mirrored her response in every way. Then they both looked at Covington.

"In my book—"

"We're not married," she said.

"We're not even dating," Jim countered.

Covington shook his head. "It doesn't matter. You're a couple." He held up his hand. "Don't object. You are a couple. Not a romantic one, but a professional one. You have your own language. You have shared memories. When you first paired up, there was an excitement in the newness — would it work out, would it be an epic partnership? As you make a name for yourselves, you can rely on each other against outside threats and even stand united against bosses, coworkers, union problems. Whatever. It's a marriage. A work marriage, but a marriage nonetheless."

"We don't need professional counseling, Doc," Jim said.

"Really? Because you two looked ready to sign divorce papers since you got here."

"This isn't a lover's spat, Dr. Covington," she said.

"Van."

"Van." She took a deep breath. "It's just a difference of opinion between coworkers."

"We're not *coworkers*."

Jim used that tone she hated. The one suggesting he'd clarify something once she left the room. She jumped to her feet, stomped over to where he was sitting, then loomed over him. "Did I not specify it properly? Would you like the doctor to better understand? How would you phrase it, exactly, Jim? Would you say mentor/mentee? Supervisor/supervisee? Why not just call it grand poobah/lowly peon? You're as bad as Roland, you know that? Nothing more than a pompous, egotistical jerk!" Then she stormed out of the room.

His voice was soft behind her as he explained to Covington. "I was going to say 'partners.' I don't know what's gotten into her today. I better go after her."

But she was now thoroughly mortified and couldn't bear to see either of them. So, she ran and hid from them. Once Jim was gone, she'd apologize to Van then call a ride share and go to her apartment. It didn't matter to her if the whole Gomorran Society was waiting in her living room. She needed some sleep.

Chelsea darted into a thicket of bushes, crouched low, then turned her cell to silent. And just in time. Jim and Van burst outside, and when Jim didn't see her, he took his phone from his pocket. When she didn't answer, the two of them started walking the property. Then they expanded their search.

At least two, maybe three times, she was certain Covington saw her, but he never walked her way. In fact, at one point, it seemed he directed Jim away from her. But Jim wouldn't give up the search. He continued walking and calling her for what felt like forever. Kept it up for so long, in fact, that she fell asleep behind the shrubbery.

Chelsea didn't know how much time had passed before she woke, but she was really warm, and the sun had crept high into the sky. She'd probably still be asleep, but something in the bushes rustled, and she prayed it was her partner. And she was mortified. What an immature brat she'd been. Had she really hidden from him in shrubbery? What he must think of her. What Dr. Covington must think! She was positively irrational when she was exhausted.

"Jim?" Her voice was scratchy from sleep. Clearing it, she tried to sit up, but something pinched her. Bit her?

Oh, no!

She bolted upright. What was in the bushes with her?

But she never had a chance to find out. She slipped back into the black of unconsciousness.

Chapter Thirty-One

JIM DROVE BACK to the precinct, each mile adding to his anger. Yeah, Chelsea was younger than him, but not by much. And no matter how much she looked like it that morning, she wasn't a child. Nothing excused behavior like that. He'd seen more mature preschoolers.

When he got back to the station, they were having words.

Except, when he got back to the station, she wasn't there.

Davenport called him into his office. "Where the hell have you been? And where's Sullivan?"

He'd love nothing more than to throw her under the bus right now. But that would be a dick move. "Long story. Fill you in later. You want to bring me up to speed on Jameson now?"

"Sure you don't want to wait for your partner?"

Yeah, he would. "No. I'll catch her up. What do you remember?"

He leaned back in his chair. It groaned under his weight, protesting the strain as much as the captain seemed to regret reliving the story. "It was seventeen years ago, but I see the scene as clearly as if it was last night."

"Some of them stick with you."

"I'm telling you, Jim, I had a bad feeling when you landed the Yates case. But when you said the name 'Jameson,' I had no doubt."

"About what."

"The cases are related."

"You're telling me my killer started seventeen years ago?"

"Is that so far-fetched if it's a society and not one man?"

"What happened that night?"

"That morning, actually. You know anything about the guy?"

Jim shook his head. "Not much. More about his company than him. He founded TerraKind BioChemical before people were even talking about protecting the environment. Had those family-friendly companies long before Silicon Valley did — onsite daycare, flex schedules, adult playgrounds."

"Sounds like a great guy to work for, right?"

"Everyone said he was a great guy, period. Came out hard to support family-values candidates. Adopted some kid when he was seventeen."

"Who adopts a seventeen-year-old?"

"Said it wasn't enough that he felt familial love. He wanted the boy to know that legally, he belonged somewhere."

"Okay. The guy was a saint. Who would want him dead? Well, I guess you're telling me the Gomorran Society did. But why?"

Davenport sighed. "That's the thing. The guy wasn't a saint. His kid called us when his dad didn't come down for breakfast. He went to check on him, thought maybe his date had stayed late, was going to ask if he should cook Eggs Benedict for three."

"A teenager who cooks Eggs Benedict? I don't even cook eggs over easy, and I'm twice his age."

"Plus a little."

"You want to compare notes, Captain?"

"Not especially. Anyway, yeah, that detail stuck with me, too, but I didn't pick at it too much then. The kid said when he knocked on his old man's bedroom door, no one answered. He hemmed and hawed for a while, unsure what to do. Didn't want to interrupt if they were … busy. Finally, because it was so quiet, he decided to go in. His dad's date was gone. And the old man was still there. Naked, spread-eagle. Wrists and ankles cuffed to the bedposts. Collar around his neck. Ball-gag in his mouth and some kind of … electrical device on his johnson."

"Why would a guy … forget it. I don't want to know."

"No, you don't. Anyway, there was remnants of coke on the nightstand. Safe was empty. Jewelry gone."

"All around, good guy, family man, huh? The kid know about this?"

"He fumbled with his answers. At the time, I thought he knew most, if not all, of what the guy was into and was trying to protect his image. My fear was …"

"He was subjected to some of it."

Davenport leaned forward and rubbed his face. "I've tried not to think about it over the years."

"But some of the cases stick with you."

He nodded. "Some of them do."

The two of them shared a long look. Then Jim stood and walked to the door.

Before he left, Davenport said, "Now what?"

"I'm going to see if we have any autopsy results yet."

"Jim?"

"Yeah?"

"I missed something in the Jameson case."

"The brand."

He took a deep breath. "Hair. The device. No one was looking for it, and there were no comps. I don't think that's it."

"Then what?"

"The kid. He didn't tell me everything."

"Maybe he was involved with the drugs and was afraid you were going to bust him."

Davenport shrugged.

"You want me to talk to him."

"Hell, I want to talk to him again."

"What's his name? We'll find him."

"Don. Donald Jameson."

"You know what happened to him?"

"No."

"Happen to know his name before the adoption?"

He shook his head.

"I'll track him down."

Jim tapped the doorframe on his way out. He thought about going down to the morgue, but if Nia was in the middle of an autopsy, he'd only slow her down. Instead, he checked his email. No reports from her yet. So he called her. When she didn't answer, he left her a voice mail.

Since his phone was still out, he tried Chelsea again. Also no answer. Left her another voice mail. His anger had fizzled. Their argument had been ridiculous, sure, but there was no way she was still mad. Hopefully she was in the embarrassed/sulking stage and would soon take his calls. Or maybe she was sleeping off the crazy. Otherwise, she was in trouble. And he was wasting time.

And God help that freakshow society and anybody else

if they had her.

Thoughts of Roland briefly flashed through his head, and he sighed. If anything else landed on his plate, he was going to have to make a list so he could keep it all straight.

Jim started researching Levi Jameson's son, Donald. The adoption record seemed to be on the up-and-up, but that's where it all started to fall apart. The agency that only handled five adoptions, and they were all for Levi Jameson. All for boys who seemed to disappear around their eighteenth birthdays, none of whom seemed to have legitimate birth certificates to begin with.

The social worker responsible for every case was Eli Weitzman, but no social worker by that name ever worked in the office. The attorney who supposedly represented all the birth parents was Susan Lovitz, and Jameson's attorney was always Marlon Wilson. But there was no record of any attorneys by those names ever being able to practice law in the state.

He did another quick search. No records of the adoption agency or the lawyers of record were found. So, he called the judge, who was, of course, in court. Jim left a message for him to return his call and told him what it was in regard to. If he didn't hear back, he'd know the guy was dirty.

Another way to tell would be if the Society came after him again. That would be a good sign.

The adoption records were a bust and Sullivan was a no-show, so Jim did a search for the news coverage of Levi Jameson's death. Maybe Davenport forgot a detail that would show up in a news article.

He hit the jackpot on the second link he clicked. The article wasn't helpful, but the picture spoke a thousand words. And he only needed two — the new identity of Levi Jameson's adopted son.

Chapter Thirty-Two

20 YEARS AGO — Age 17
   Jamison Manor, Birch Hill
   9:27 a.m.

DONNY KNEELED at Levi Jameson's side while he sat at the head of the large dining table. Both of them were naked. The Grand Master no longer wore his mask, as he'd had to reveal his identity at court to get the sham adoption to go through. The one chink in the Gomorran Society's armor was that no sitting judges were members, and he didn't want to risk paying one off in this matter.

Not for something so important.

Besides, they weren't master/slave any longer. They were father and son.

When the Grand Master told him about the adoption, Donny laughed in his face. Which, of course, earned him a beating. Right after that, three members of the Society came in. Two of them restrained him while the third fitted a device around his genitals. Then, for the first time since his branding, he was given clothes.

"Get dressed."

He barely remembered how. As he did, he was struck by how uncomfortable the fabric felt against his skin. How it constricted his movement, particularly with whatever was around his penis and testicles. Donny looked down and tried to adjust himself, wondering what twisted game the Grand Master intended to play this time.

"I told you, we're going to court today. I am adopting you. And before you have another one of your oh-so-charming outbursts, consider this." He held up a remote control and pushed a button.

An agonizing shock ran through his scrotum, into his stomach. Maybe into his soul. He fell to the floor, his muscles spasming. He lost control of his bladder but didn't notice he was lying in a puddle of his urine until the twitching stopped.

When he pushed to his feet, he glared at the Grand Master.

"Fuck. Someone get him a clean pair of pants. And a damn diaper. Just in case." The Grand Master showed him the controller again. "I turned the dial to one. It goes up to twenty. If I want, I can burn off your flaccid little prick. Sizzle your balls until they look like raisins. Hell, for all I know, your heart turns to a prune at fifteen. So don't fuck with me. Or I crank this bitch to critical and watch you fry in court. You understand?"

Donny thought for a moment as he stood there, dick limp and tingling, piss dripping down his legs. Would it be so bad if this was the end? Did he want this for the rest of his life?

"I could turn this to two, if you're unsure."

Someone returned with a towel and new clothes. And

an actual diaper. He didn't even want to know why they had those on hand. Donny began cleaning himself off. "I understand."

"So, you'll behave in court." It wasn't a question.

"Yes, Grand Master."

"Good." He tapped his chin as he watched Donny dress. "You know, I kind of like this toy. We might have to use it again after the adoption is final. You know, to celebrate our … familial union. Now, let's go."

They went. And Donny, ever-aware of the device strapped to his body, played the part of the grateful ward-turned-adoptee.

That's right. It wasn't enough that the sick fuck had spent decades buying young boys to use as both domestic slaves and sex slaves. No, his end game was making them part of his family before they turned eighteen. Not releasing them as they'd been told. Not killing them as Donny had suspected. Adopting them. The question was why.

But then, Donny figured it out.

Bully a boy and it'll hurt, but it won't break him.

Give a boy away and it'll hurt, but it won't break him.

Make him willingly sacrifice himself to such a life?

That will destroy him.

That was Levi Jameson's ultimate goal.

Donny's clothes had been ripped from his body the second they'd returned from court and walked in the door. The device, of course, had remained in place. And he went about his life as Levi Jameson's son, which somehow was even worse than being the Gomorran Society's Grand Master's slave.

It wasn't until three days after Donny was back at the manor, three days after the adoption certificate for

"Donald Jameson" was hung on the wall, when he finally snapped.

Jameson now insisted on being called "Daddy" at meals, bedtime, and bath time.

He'd endured countless unspeakable tortures and humiliations, but that was the final straw. It was then that Donny realized, he had *asked* for this. Actually *requested* a judge grant him this "benefit."

And that fact, that one small difference, was too much to bear.

He had a choice to make. And really, it wasn't a difficult one.

"I think I'll take the wine and cheese course in bed, Donald."

"That's not my name."

Levi slammed his napkin on the table then jabbed his fork toward the wall. "That's what your adoption certificate says, boy! Now, why do you have to go and ruin a nice family dinner?"

"Nice family dinner? I'm naked on my knees at your feet."

"Where you should be, slave. Or would you like me to turn the dial to remind you?" He grabbed his new favorite toy then waved it under Donny's nose.

"No."

"No, what?"

"No, Grand Master."

He sighed. "We're at dinner, Donald."

Donny gritted his teeth. "No. *Daddy*."

"Now, then." He pushed back from the table, rose, dropped his napkin casually to the floor. "I'll have the wine and cheese course in bed. I think I'd like brie and fresh figs."

"We don't have any fresh figs."

"That's not my problem. Figs or the whip, your choice. And honey. I'd like you to lick it off me. I believe there's a nice Barolo in the wine cellar. I'll be upstairs. I expect you in three minutes."

"It takes longer than that to heat the brie."

"Then I guess you'll definitely be getting the whip tonight." He left for the master bedroom.

Donny left for the kitchen. It took a bit of time to get everything just right, but he was getting whipped anyway, and that would be a small price to pay for his freedom. All his years of servitude had taught him to be a whiz in the kitchen, so he knew just what he had to do. By the time Levi caught on, it would be too late for him.

Assuming Levi didn't use the torture device on Donny — or if he did, that it didn't kill him — in a few hours, he'd be free.

As expected, "Daddy" kept the wine all to himself, laughing as he indulged while Donny gagged on honey-dipped testicles.

But somewhere around glass three, his laughter started to fade. "What are you smirking about."

"Just enjoying the evening. Daddy."

"I clearly didn't whip you hard enough."

Oh, he had. Every lash of the leather bit into his skin, welting his flesh, sometimes ripping it off so that even the cool air stung and the salt of sweat burned as it rolled down his body. But he refused to utter even a gasp or grunt of displeasure. No, that whipping wasn't a punishment — it was a release. A scourging of freedom. A rending through which he would finally be made whole.

"Donald!"

"That's not my name!"

Jameson reached for the remote control, but his fingers fumbled for it. He wheezed, coughed, tried again. Swiped his mouth with the back of his trembling hand to get rid of a few drops of errant spittle. Pointed at his glass on the nightstand. "My wine."

Donny helped him hold it then bring it to his lips. "Here you go. Drink up." When the glass was empty, he started to refill it. The bottle was nearly drained.

"Something's … wrong. Call … for help. 9 … 11."

"This will help." He held the glass to Jameson's lips. The fool drank it.

"No." He shook his head. "Call."

"Your hubris was your downfall." Donny walked to the man's nightstand, opened the top drawer, then removed four sets of handcuffs and a ball gag. "You always wanted more, but you never thought about the cost."

"Call … help."

Donny pushed him onto his back and cuffed his right hand to the headboard. "Do you remember what you told me the night you whipped my father?"

"What did … you do … to … me?"

"Poisoned your wine. Hemlock. Like Socrates. Bet you wish you didn't educate me now, huh?" He cuffed Jameson's ankle to the footboard.

"Hos … pit … al."

"Why would I go to all this trouble just to get you help? Don't be ridiculous. No, you'll die here tonight." Donny cuffed Jameson's other ankle to the footboard. "Anyway, do you remember what you said the night you let me beat Owen?"

"9 … 1 … 1." Jameson sucked in a rattling breath.

"Terrible guess." Donny secured Levi's free wrist to the headboard with the remaining pair of handcuffs. "You said, 'He let you down. He deserves to be punished for it. And punishment should always be meted out by the person who was wronged.' Well, guess what, *Daddy*. You let me down. You and your precious Gomorran Society. And you all deserve to be punished for it. So, tonight, your punishment begins."

"You can … still fix this." He wheezed between words.

"I am fixing this."

Jamison pulled on his restraints, but his efforts were weak.

Donny pressed on his arm. "Oooh. That's not good. The cuffs are already tight. That means your body is retaining water. Do you know what that means, Daddy?"

"Let me go. We" — he panted for breath — "can talk about this."

"That means renal failure. Your kidneys are shutting down. Already. It's only been about sixty … maybe ninety minutes since your first dose of hemlock. You're fading fast. I'd hoped to torture you longer."

"You'll never … get away with … this."

"Oh, I absolutely will."

"Cops … blame you."

Donny shook his head. "Wrong again, Daddy. After you die, I will set a beautiful scene depicting you as the sexual deviant you are. I will then be calling a professional who will be paid handsomely to disappear. The twelve-hour head start will be more than enough time to guarantee she is never found. It's a win-win scenario. The escort will be blamed for robbing and killing you, getting her permanently out of the life. The Julia Roberts plan. And I, your beloved and grieving *son* and only heir, will inherit everything. Meanwhile, I'll make sure the photos are leaked to the press, so your reputation will be destroyed. You lose your life, your money, your reputation, your legacy. Everything. Hubris ruined you, old man. You. *Lose*."

Jameson's eyes widened.

"Donald—"

"That's not my name! That's never been my name! My mother named me Donovan!"

He shoved the ball-gag into Jameson's mouth then sat there, watching until the life left his eyes.

Chapter Thirty-Three

CHELSEA WOKE IN UNFAMILIAR SURROUNDINGS — a small, squalid apartment that smelled disturbingly like raw meat.

Hopefully, that was meat.

Trying not to breathe through her nose, she surveyed her surroundings. It didn't seem like anything had been cleaned in decades. The sofa had broken springs and plenty of stains, the origins of which she refused to think about. To her left was a bedroom and probably a bathroom, and beside that, a small kitchenette. Across from her was what she assumed was a closet. The door next to it was sturdier, though not by much, so that had to be the exit. Behind her was the only window she had access to. It faced the street, but she couldn't see enough to know what section of the city she was in. Or even if she was still in the city at all.

A toilet flushed, water ran. In a few seconds, she'd know exactly what she was dealing with.

The bathroom door opened with a squeak, then Dr. Covington exited. "Oh, good. You're up. How'd you sleep?"

"Sleep?"

"You were out a long time."

"Out? I … where are we?"

"Where are we? Home, silly."

Her eyebrows shot up. "Home?"

"Yes."

"What are you talking about?"

"Is this a new game? I don't get it."

"Game? Van, I—"

"Van? Since when do you call me that? You always call me Donny. Unless you get mad. Then it's Donovan Jacob Covington. But I didn't do anything bad today. Not really, anyway." He scuffed the toe of his shoe on the carpet, disturbing a puff of dust. A blade of unfiltered sunlight slicing through the window highlighted the motes in their frenetic flight.

Pieces of a disturbing puzzle were starting to click into place. Chelsea had no idea where her service weapon was, no idea where her phone was. No idea where she was. Her best course of action was to keep him calm and to keep him talking until she could figure some things out. "Donny, I have a headache, and it's making me a little confused. So, maybe we can play a little game until I feel better. Would that be okay?"

"Okay, Mum."

Mum. That's what she was afraid of.

"Let's pretend I'm a reporter and you're an eyewitness to a … news event. I'll ask questions and you tell my audience what happened. Okay?"

"Okay."

"Great." She picked up a remote control for a television that wasn't there and talked into it like it was a microphone. "Thanks, Krista."

"Who's Krista?"

"I was pretending she was the anchor who was talking to me from the news desk. I'm the field reporter."

"Oh. Okay."

"Do you have a name you'd rather I use?"

"No. Krista's fine. Anything but Curtis."

"Krista it is, then." Chelsea cleared her throat. "Thanks, Krista. This is Nicole Moyer for Channel—"

"That's not your name."

The blood drained from her face. Her hands grew clammy, and she nearly dropped the remote control. "I know that. But we're using our pretend names for the pretend game, right?"

"Then use your pretend name."

"This is my pretend name. It's called a stage name."

"I know all about stage names, Mum. You have one. And this isn't it."

"I told you, Van—"

"Donny! Why can't anyone get my name right?"

"I'm sorry! Donny. I told you, I'm a little confused right now. I thought the game might help. Tell me what name you want me to use, and I'll use it."

"I want you to use the name you went by at Pussy Katt's. I want you to recognize our little apartment in Garrick. I want you to know my name. I want my mother to know my fucking birthday!"

"Is today your birthday?"

He backhanded her across the face.

Chelsea dropped the remote and clutched her cheek. Before she lowered her hand to look at him, something sharp pinched her neck. Her vision blurred, then the world went black again.

❦

JIM BURST into Davenport's office. "Captain! We have a problem."

He was on the phone and held his finger to his lips. "No. He's in the field. … He's not answering his calls right now. … Well, when they're in the middle of something life-or-death, they tend not to return calls from their union reps or Internal Affairs. … No, not even their captain if they're, oh, I don't know, protecting and serving the city. When I hear from him, I'll let you know." He hung up the phone and looked at Jim. "You're about out of time. The Lockwoods want blood. Your blood."

"I don't give a lemur's left nut right now. Look at this." He showed Davenport his phone.

"This is an article from the Jameson investigation. Why am I looking at it? I was there. I told you about it."

"Don't worry about the article. Look at the picture."

"I am."

"Who does that look like to you?"

"Levi Jameson."

"Not the picture of the dead guy. The one of his kid."

Davenport barely gave it a second glance. "It looks like his kid. What are you getting at?"

"Age it twenty years. Tell me that doesn't look like Dr. Van Covington to you."

The captain stared at it. Squinted at it. Held it away from him. "Maybe. Different haircut. Nicer clothes. Why?"

"I might have neglected to mention this earlier, but Chelsea went missing today."

Davenport's eyes narrowed.

"When we were at Covington's house."

"Damn it, Jim. This is the kind of shit that pisses me off." He strode around his desk, flung open his door, then bellowed into the bullpen, "Paxton! Anderson! Get in here!" He stormed back to his chair as Charlie and Norm rushed in.

They looked from the captain to Jim then back.

"Before you read them the riot act, I didn't tell them, either."

"Tell us what?" Charlie asked.

"Sullivan's missing," Davenport growled as he glared at Jim.

Both detectives added their hostile stares.

"And I think I know who has her."

"Who?" Norm took a few steps closer.

"Our killer."

"Well, that's just great." Charlie flung his arms in the air. "We've only been looking for him for weeks with no idea who it is."

"Oh, no," Norm corrected him. "We narrowed it down to a secret society."

"Wrong again." Jim stood. "It's Dr. Van Covington."

"What?" The two detectives said in unison.

Davenport dropped into his seat and squeezed the bridge of his nose. "I want an APB put out on him. Charlie, take a few units, go to his house. Norm, take a few more and go to his office."

They both darted out of the room.

"You know Covington's too smart for that."

"I'm going to send a few units to the club, too."

"He won't be there, either."

"What'll you have me do, Jim? Sit here, twiddle my thumbs, and hope he lets Chelsea go? I promised her dad she'd be safe with me."

"I'll find her."

"You're the one that lost her!"

"Thanks for that."

Davenport vented a breath. "Sorry. That was uncalled for."

"You had every right."

"No. I didn't. I'm just pissed because you didn't tell me sooner."

"I thought I was covering for her. I thought she ran off because we were fighting."

"Again?"

He shrugged.

"We'll deal with that later. I am sending units to the club."

"You don't have a warrant."

"I'll get one. Meanwhile, you have any ideas?"

"Now that we know who he is, I need to find out more about him."

Jim went back to his desk. He spent hours on every research site he knew to try. He even asked the gossip grapevine — his mother — what she might have heard, but other than promising to keep her ear to the ground, he came up empty.

That left him with the one source he didn't think he'd ever have to tap.

He glanced across their shared desks to Chelsea's empty chair. "The things I do for you, Sullivan."

Shaking his head, he searched his contacts for a number he never thought he'd call, then dialed. Didn't even get through one complete ring.

"Son of a bitch. After I helped Roland get back at you senior year, you said you'd never talk to me again."

"Desperate times call for desperate measures."

"He's in the hospital because of you."

"No, he's not."

"I figured he wasn't. And if he was, he probably deserved it."

"No one deserves a beating like that."

"Okay, we're friends again.

"No, we're not."

"Come on, Jim. You know you missed me. Say it. Say it. You know you want to. Come on. Saaaay it."

"Cut the shit, Kingston. I need a favor."

"For you, Jimbo, anything. As long as I get a favor in return."

Chapter Thirty-Four

PRESENT DAY
  Holt Family Stables
  2:27 a.m.

IT WAS ALMOST the witching hour. Things had nearly come full circle. Mum had told him he was born at three in the morning. On the nose, she used to say.

She was dead now. He knew that.

After he punished Levi Jameson, he found her and punished her for years of neglect and for forgetting his tenth birthday and for selling him to his father.

She'd let him down. She'd deserved to be punished for it. And punishment should always be meted out by the person who'd been wronged.

He'd also punished the members of the Gomorran Society whose identities he knew. Men who were evil, vile creatures who loved power and prestige more than people.

People like little Donny, who needed their help.

He'd been working his way through the Society for

nearly two decades, administering his own brand of justice. Sure, they'd been adding to their ranks as fast as he'd been eliminating them, but the real power was gone. The real depravity was over. The real horrors had already been visited on him and returned in full.

Now, there was only one name left. One more debt to be collected. One more price to be paid. One more life sentence to be carried out.

He was judge. He was jury. He was executioner.

The charges? Negligence. Abuse. Bondage. Slavery. Trafficking.

The finding? Guilty.

The sentence? Death.

The criminal? His father, Owen Holt.

Owen had let Donny down. He'd deserved to be punished for it. And punishment should always be meted out by the person who'd been wronged.

Donny inhaled deeply then breathed out in a sigh. Microscopic bits of hay and grass tickled his nose, threatening to make him sneeze. The sweet smell of horse feed and soap mingled with the richer musk of leather and manure. One of the horses nickered in its stall, drawing his attention.

Owen, Maeve, and Chelsea were tied with reins to posts in front of the stalls.

After drawing in another deep breath, Donny looked at them. "Do you smell that?"

Maeve sniffled. She'd stopped crying a while ago, but it looked like she might start again any moment. Or she could launch into another tirade. It was anybody's guess.

Donny wasn't in the mood for either. "Before you take a shot in the dark, I'll just tell you. It's horse shit, folks. And you know what? I've seen some nasty things done with excrement in my day. In fact, I've had some nasty things *done* to me with it in my day." He reached down, grabbed a steaming pile, then smeared it across Owen's cheeks and lips.

He gagged and spat.

So did Maeve.

"Want to explain to the wife, *Dad*?"

"Owen?" Her voice was high and bordered on hysterical. "What's he talking about?"

"Did you never wonder what the brand on his ball sack was all about, Maeve? Or do you only do the nasty in the dark so you don't know?"

"Don't talk to her. If you have an issue with me, you take it up with me."

"If? Did you honestly just say 'if' to me, *Dad*?"

"You know what I mean."

"Fine. Yeah, *Dad*, I have a problem with you."

"And if you recall, Jameson let you get your revenge for it seventeen years ago."

Donny scoffed. Smirked. Then he burst into gales of laughter. He laughed until his eyes watered and his stomach hurt. Laughed until he was dizzy from lack of air to his brain and had to struggle to calm down. Finally, when he caught his breath, he wiped away the tears, stood toe to toe with his father, then he punched him in the face.

Maeve screamed.

Owen flinched. "What was that for?"

"Are you kidding? You denied me for a decade. You raped my mother. Twice. You bought me from her to sell me to a cult. I was then branded, gang-raped, tortured, and forced to work as a slave. For years. And you take exception to a punch?"

"I did not rape your mother. Once was consensual. Mostly. And the other time, I paid her."

"Oh, that's much better."

"I think I'm going to be sick," Maeve said.

"And we never did a DNA test. We don't even know if you're mine."

"Does it even matter at this point? Look what you did to me. This is what you made me. I think this solves the nature versus nurture debate."

"Van," Chelsea said.

"Donny, Mum," he corrected her. "Why do you keep calling … but you're not Mum." He rubbed his head. "You look so much like her with your hair pulled back and no makeup on. I've struggled with that since I first saw you."

"What happened to her?"

Van pulled her gun from his waistband. "I don't want to shoot you, Detective. You haven't disappointed me. Yet. Just let me finish my job, then I'll let you go."

"Your job, Van?"

"Owen let me down. He deserves to be punished for it. And punishment should always be meted out by the person who's been wronged."

"But he said you already punished him."

"Jameson let me paddle Owen the night he sold me. That hardly makes up for what he did to me. Does that sound like an eye for an eye to you?"

"Is that what Kierkegaard believed in? An eye for an eye?"

He whipped toward her. "Did you read my book?"

"I skimmed it. Jim had more time to read it than I did. And he's the one with the fancy degree."

"Yeah? Owen went to the same school. Doesn't make him a nice person."

"A lot of great people graduated from that school. Have you met Jim's parents? They're wonderful people."

"Of course I met them. His dad cheated on his mother."

"I know. But they got over that. You helped them heal from that."

"Don't HIPAA laws prohibit you from revealing that information?" Maeve asked.

Every head in the room turned toward her.

"What are you doing?" Owen whispered.

"Asks the philandering criminal with manure on his face." She looked away from him.

Donny glanced at his watch. It was nearly the witching hour. There were four horses in the stables. He still had some hemlock and the detective's gun. Come three o'clock, his father would be drawn and quartered, the women — unfortunately — would be poisoned, and justice would finally be served.

The slave, at last, would be freed.

Chapter Thirty-Five

JIM CLIMBED into his car for the third time, then dialed
Kingston back. Again, he answered on the first ring.
"Kane, I owe you nothing."

"What are you talking about? You asked for dirt on
Covington that no one else had, and I delivered with his
mother. Didn't I?"

"I asked for a lead that would help me find my partner.
I've been to her apartment in Garrick. I've been to her
parents' house in Chesterfield. They informed me I could
find her in Memorial Grove Cemetery."

"I told you the name on his birth certificate — his real
birth certificate, not the fake one his adoptive father forged
— is Owen Holt."

"Yeah, I'm at the Holt residence. No one's here. The
house is dark."

"You check where they work?"

"I'm one man, Kane, and I'm running out of time. I
don't think Covington would be at Maeve's boutique, and
Owen's pharmaceutical plants all run around the clock.
Someone would have seen them."

"Is anyone looking for them?"

"Of course. I have APBs on my partner, Covington, and Holt."

"Well, I don't know where else to look. That's all I have on Covington, which was more than you had. If they aren't at home, and they aren't at work, try someplace fun."

"Where would a serial killer go for fun?"

"You're the detective. Go detect. And you still owe me." He ended the call.

Shit. Jim nearly threw his phone. Where the fuck would a serial killer go for fun? He'd been everywhere, chased every lead. They were all dead ends.

Poor choice of words.

Now, here he was, in the middle of the night in the middle of fucking nowhere. The Holts had twenty-six mostly forested acres in Willow Run, where their five-thou-sand-square-foot chalet-style home was dark. No fire burned in the outdoor pit, no one swam in the infinity pool. The tennis courts and putting green — unsurpris-ingly, at the late hour — showed no signs of activity. Other than the burble of the winding creek, the nightsong of crickets and owls, and the occasional rustle of leaves in the breeze, the only sound Jim could make out were the nickers and neighs of agitated horses.

The Holts loved to ride. They had stables somewhere on their property.

And horses weren't nocturnal animals.

Jim got out of his car, then set off through the thicket of trees. He hoped to find what upset the horses before what upset the horses found him.

~

CHELSEA HAD NEVER WITNESSED anything so depraved in her life. She chastised herself for not expecting it. If the Gomorran Society would put branding irons to their genitals, why not … whatever that apparatus was.

Van held the gun, so he had all the power. He repositioned the two women on either side of the double doors. "Prime viewing location."

"For what?" Maeve asked.

But he just smiled and made Owen walk to the center of the paddock, strip, then attach that device to himself. "I trust you know what happens when I turn the dial to one?"

"Of course." His face was still smeared with manure, but even so, the fear in his expression was evident.

"I'm not sure you do." Van turned the knob.

Owen's body convulsed and flopped to the ground. The moonlight wasn't very bright, but it was bright enough to see he lost control of his bowels.

"Messy, messy." Van shook his head. "Hard to tell if that's your shit or the horses'. Well, soon it's not going to matter much, anyway."

"Leave him alone!" Tears ran freely down Maeve's cheeks.

Owen's too, for that matter. But he was in too much pain to protest and lay moaning in his own filth, pawing uselessly at the device that was the source of so much agony.

"Why, Stepmother?"

"Don't call me that."

He stepped closer to her.

Chelsea pulled at her restraints, desperate to help the woman who had played Fairy Godmother to her Cinderella such a short time ago. As she did, the leather reins around her wrists caught on a bent nail in the door frame. She started to slowly, silently, saw at the bindings, keeping her attention on Covington.

"Why not? That's what you are to me."

"I'm nothing to you. And you're nothing to me. Nothing but an abductor and a murderer."

"No. I'm the one who was wronged here, not you. Your husband — my birth father — should have loved me. Should have been kind to me. At the very least, he should have mentored me. He and his cronies inducted me into their club, after all." He unzipped his pants then let them fall. When she tried to turn her head, he grabbed her chin and pulled her face forward. "Look and see what he did to me. I got a brand, too." Van lifted his testicles.

The movement was anything but gentle. Both Maeve and Chelsea winced at how hard and high the movement was.

But he just laughed and released himself. Pulled his pants back on. "If that made you squeamish, I can't even begin to tell you the rest." He glanced behind him.

Chelsea followed his gaze. Owen was on his knees. Then he was quaking and howling.

"That was only a two, motherfucker. Don't move again."

Once again, he lay sobbing in the corral.

Chelsea went back to scraping at her restraints.

Van turned back to her and Maeve. "In case you didn't notice, my induction to the club was different. Dear Old Dad got capital letters on his brand. I got lowers. He was a master. I was a slave. So I didn't get mentored. I got molested."

"No." Maeve sobbed and shook her head. "Owen is a good man."

"Owen is a monster. He cared more about his horses

than his own son. And now he's going to meet his end by them."

"What are you talking about?"

Chelsea sawed faster. She was afraid she knew.

Van walked into the stables. He came out with a stallion. "I'm going to use his own horses as my weapon of choice."

"Versace would never hurt any of us."

He led the horse to the middle of the paddock then began fastening a long set of reins to Owen's leg.

Maeve turned to Chelsea. "What is he doing?"

She scraped harder against the nail.

Van walked into the stables. He came out with another horse.

"Oh, please, no." She sobbed. "Gucci's even sweeter than Versace."

Chelsea wasn't sure what Maeve thought was happening. She seemed more worried about the horses than her husband, and it wasn't the horses that were about to be split into four pieces.

Then again, it wasn't the horses that had been sleeping with children and trafficking in sex and who knew what else since college. She couldn't say she wouldn't be more worried about the animals had their situations been reversed.

But their situations weren't reversed. She was a detective with the Steel City PD, and she was sworn to protect and serve everyone. Even the Owen Holts of the world who sold their sons into sex slavery rings.

Van made his third trip to the stables. He came back with a beautiful brown mare.

"Prada." Maeve sniffled.

Chelsea's bindings were looser. She was able to slide her hand out to her thumb knuckle, but couldn't quite get her hand free. At least it kept the leather strap tight, which made the scraping easier to do.

"He only has Armani left," Maeve whispered.

"Let me guess. He's a pussy cat."

"Not exactly."

"Okay. Good. Well, I'm almost free."

"Then what?"

That was a good question. She had no weapon. Van had her gun, the torture device on Owen, and three of the four horses already attached. "One problem at a time."

Van headed back toward the stable again. But Chelsea caught movement in the paddock beyond the horses. She squinted, trying to make out the shadowy blur in the distance.

Hope bloomed in her chest, though she was afraid to feel it. Then she embraced it as it closed in, got larger, came into focus.

Jim.

∼

WHAT. The. Fuck?

It took forever to find the stables, and when he finally did, it was to discover Owen Holt lying naked in the middle of the corral, three of his four limbs tied to horses.

Apparently it was going to be some kind of show because his wife and Chelsea were positioned to witness it from either side of the stable doors.

He headed toward her, but she shook her head.

So he dropped to one knee and started to free Owen, but she again shook her head.

Muttering under his breath, he looked at her and shrugged.

Chelsea tipped her head toward the fence.

Jim darted to the edge of the corral, flipped over the rails, then waited in the shadows.

"Damn it, you vicious glue bag!"

"That's a $300,000 stallion!" Maeve yelled.

Van pulled the horse forward until his head and shoulders were through the doors. The whites of his eyes were visible even from as far back as Jim was. The horse snorted and reared up, pulling the reins out of the killer's hands, then it wheeled around and retreated back into the stable. Van chased after it.

Jim darted back to the corral and started working on the bindings on Owen's wrist. Snorts and neighs sounded from the stable, followed by shouts and swearing.

Owen was still out cold and didn't show signs of coming to. Jim slapped his cheek as he untied his ankle. If he got up, he could help with the bindings. But he wasn't moving. Chelsea broke free as Jim moved to Owen's other ankle. Before he made substantial headway, Sullivan waved him off. He worked faster at the knots. When his partner started to panic, he ran back to the fence and she took her original spot by the door.

Van dragged Armani, bucking and snorting, from the stable.

Maeve cringed and yelled, "Watch out! Armani's never been broken!"

Chelsea didn't move.

Fuck. She was trying not to blow her cover, and it was going to get her killed.

Jim drew his weapon and charged. If he revealed himself, all bets were off, and Sullivan was safe to run.

Van saw him and dropped the reins. He turned and raised a gun.

Double fuck. Didn't know the crazy SOB had a piece.

"Don't shoot!" Chelsea yelled.

"No!" Maeve screamed

The horse began stomping, its giant hooves getting closer to Van each time they landed.

Jim hesitated to squeeze the trigger because of Sullivan.

Covington didn't. He grinned as he fired.

All four horses spooked and ran.

Van turned, face lit with rapt anticipation, to watch Owen's limbs ripped from his body. Instead, the horses ran clear of him, reins trailing behind them.

But Armani reared up onto his hind legs. His forelegs came down onto Van, knocking him down. As he galloped into the paddock, his hooves crushed the man's ribs and his skull, and he trampled Covington into the ground.

"Owen!" Maeve shrieked.

But the stallion didn't go near him. He galloped a few laps in the paddock, then it stood alone at the far end, cloaked in shadow by the fence. Prada ventured near him, then the other horses gathered there.

Chelsea quickly released Maeve, who raced to the center of the corral.

Jim was on the phone with dispatch, asking for a bus and other units, when Sullivan joined him. She looked down, but he shook his head.

"Why'd you tell me not to fire? Or were you telling Covington not to?"

"Both, I guess. I didn't want to spook the horses. Van wanted Holt to die by quartering. I knew the gunshot would spook them. But when you fired—"

"I didn't fire. Covington did."

She looked away. "Doesn't matter. I was wrong."

"I'd already untied Holt. It was safe to shoot."

"No, I meant I was wrong to say it. I shouldn't have

told you not to fire. Your life is more important than Holt's."

"We're supposed to protect the innocent, Chels."

"He's not innocent."

"Maeve and you could have been hurt."

"And I could have gotten you killed." Chelsea took a shuddering breath. "Oh, my God, Jim. I made a bad call, and you could have died because of it." She turned to face him, tears welling in her eyes. "I am so, so sorry."

"I'm fine, Sullivan. It was my decision not to fire. Not yours."

"But I told you not to."

"And I decided not to."

"I made the call!" She buried her face in her hands.

He sighed and pulled at her fingers until she looked at him. "Chels, listen to me. You were worried about Holt and shouted an opinion, but I made the call. Guess what. Covington made a call, too. He didn't aim at me. I was never in danger."

"What?"

"He didn't aim at me. I was never on his list. Holt was. He just wanted to spook the horses and kill his final target."

Flashing lights cut through the trees in the distance.

She took a shuddering breath. "Given everything these bastards did to him, I'm almost sorry he didn't finish his list."

"Sullivan. I can't believe you said that."

"I know. I didn't mean it."

"Well, if you didn't say it, I would have."

Her eyebrows arched.

"And I do mean it."

"Do you? Really?"

He sighed. "On some level, anyway."

Chapter Thirty-Six

CHELSEA PUSHED AWAY from her keyboard and rubbed her eyes. "I don't care how many names Holt gave the DA—"

"All of them, Sullivan," Jim said. "He gave up everyone."

"I don't care. He still doesn't deserve this kind of deal."

"It's not immunity. It's still fifteen years."

"In a white-collar country club. Not a life sentence in a super-max."

"We got 'em all. That's what counts."

They both continued typing for another fifteen minutes. The bullpen was oddly silent that day. Even the phones didn't seem to be ringing. Delfino wasn't in. Charlie and Norm were out on the streets. Davenport's door was closed.

The scent of stale coffee was starting to churn her stomach. She slid her cup aside and sighed. "I wish Dad had told me how much paperwork was involved with police work. And how awful it was."

Jim looked at her over his screen. "Then you wouldn't have become a cop."

"I don't think he wanted me to become a cop, so that's just another reason he should have warned me."

"You can always tell the DA you're not interested in taking down the rest of the Gomorran Society and their child slavery ring. I'm sure they'd be happy to put Soto in charge of the city-wide task force."

She scowled. "You're the one who doesn't get along with her, not me. I have no beef with her."

He reached for his phone. "Then I'll call her and ask if she wants to take point."

"No!" Chelsea lunged across the desk.

Jim grinned.

"I mean, I want to see this through. For the kids."

"Not the glory?"

"God, no. Not at all. You know I hate that." She looked up at him. "That's not why you do this, is it?"

"I do this because the thought of making a living sitting behind my dad's desk in his board room every day makes my skin itch. And because someone needs to do the right thing for this city. Look at what these so-called 'pillars of the community' did. People I've known my whole life. Friends of my parents. Alumni of the university I went to."

"Same frat. They could have selected you instead of Roland."

"Can you believe he's one of them? And his dad?"

"Made the charges against you go away pretty fast. Everyone was distancing themselves from the Lockwoods."

"The security footage of Covington jumping him in the parking lot didn't hurt, either."

She chuckled. "No, it didn't. Wonder why he did it."

"Wonder why the club didn't have the recording before, then all of a sudden they mysteriously found it."

"Yeah, Jim. It's a real puzzle."

"Speaking of people I went to school with, there's someone I want to introduce you to."

"That's not at all ominous."

"He saw you at the benefit and was — I can't believe I'm saying this — enchanted. That was his word, not mine."

"*Enchanted*? Give me a break. Another country club snob who's going to tear my dress in a shadowy corner of the ballroom? No thanks."

"Well, you have the 'country club snob' part right," he muttered.

"Then why would you think I'd be interested?"

"I owe him a favor."

"And I'm the prize? Nice."

"It's not like that. Exactly."

"Please, Jim. Tell me how it's not."

"You know how you always tune into *Steel City Special* and talk about how you would love to meet this celebrity or that celebrity?"

She scoffed. "You've got to be joking. I've met one of Kingston Kane's guests, and the old adage 'don't meet your heroes' turned out to be true. He was a serial killer who had a psychotic break, thought I was his mother, drugged me, tied me up, nearly got me trampled to death by a horse, and I'm still not sure if he was going to murder me."

"Yeah, jury's out on that one."

"Nice you can be so cavalier about it."

"This guy's different."

"What is he? Actor? Musician? Athlete? Has he been on Kane's show?"

"Yeah, you could say that."

"And he went to your school?"

"We gonna play Twenty Questions, or do you just want to know who it is?"

She stared at him for a moment, then she shook her head. "I don't want to know. Because I'm not going to meet this guy. I don't fit in your world."

"That's bullshit. You're just scared."

"Okay, fine. Then how about this? I'm no one's prize. And I'm certainly not yours to auction off. You're no better than the Gomorran Society, selling me like chattel."

His eyes narrowed. "That's a low fucking blow, Sullivan."

Chelsea covered her face and took a deep breath. When she lowered her hands and looked at him, he was still staring at her. "You're right. It was. And I'm sorry. That was way out of line. I don't think I realized how much Roland affected me. I was so focused on catching Covington, I compartmentalized what happened that night. Now, I think I'm conflating the two and associating anyone Roland knows with anyone in the Society. It's all a jumbled mess in my head."

"You never filed the charges against Lockwood, did you?"

She shook her head. "And it's too late now. He's being indicted with the rest of the Gomorrans."

"Being guilty of one crime doesn't mean he can't be guilty of another."

"Everything he did as a Gomorran constitutes bigger charges than what he did to me."

"It doesn't matter. He's guilty of both."

"I was only going to file the assault charge because I wanted to keep him from hurting someone else. He can't do that now."

"Chelsea, I think you need to do this for you. It'll be cathartic."

"I'm fine."

"You're not. You're lashing out at me. You're prejudging people you haven't met, which isn't like you. Especially when a celebrity is concerned."

She frowned at him, but it turned into a half-smile.

"If you won't file charges—"

"It's just more paperwork at this point."

"Then talk to someone."

"Ugh." She rolled her eyes. "So IA can get involved? No thanks."

"Do it privately."

Chelsea sighed.

"I'm worried about you."

"I'm fine."

"Fine enough to meet a celebrity?"

"You just won't stop." But she laughed. "I kind of do want to know."

"I know you do."

"Curiosity's killing me. Who is it?"

"Kingston Kane."

She squealed. "Really?"

Jim rolled his eyes and sighed. "Yes."

"He wants to meet me?"

"Yes."

"When? Where? Are you going to introduce us? Are we going today?"

"I'll set something up. And no, I'm not going."

"Why?"

"Because I already know him. And I don't want to spend time with him."

"Jiiiiimm."

"I liked it better when you were insulting me."

"I'll happily insult you if you come with me to meet Kingston."

"You don't need me there. And I don't want to." He got up to get more coffee.

She trailed after him. "What if the conversation lulls?"

"It won't. He'll talk enough for both of you."

"What if he finds me boring?"

"Then you'll never have to see him again, and it'll be your lucky day."

"Are you going to call him now?"

Jim offered to pour her a cup.

"I can't drink any. I'll jump right out of my shoes."

"You're worse than a junior high school girl."

"I'm excited."

"I can see that."

"Just call him."

"What did I get myself into?" He headed back to his desk, cup in hand, Chelsea at his heels.

"You know, if this works out, we could end up spending a lot more time together."

"How?"

"You and Kingston are friends."

Jim put his cup down. "Let's get something straight, Sullivan. Kingston and I have a lot of history. But we are not friends."

"You say that about a lot of people, Jim. Do you have any friends?"

"Sometimes I wonder."

She gave him a sad smile. "Well, you have me."

He shook his head and dialed the phone.

Chelsea didn't know why he kept so many people at arm's length, but she was determined to work her way closer. She'd already made more inroads than most had. But for now, she did a little happy dance to herself. She was going to meet Kingston Kane!

And even better, she and Jim had just taken down the

Gomorran Society. The streets were safer, the captain was happier, her social life was improving, and she was once again safe in her own apartment. She changed her mind. This was definitely a coffee moment.

"Where you going?"

"To get coffee."

"I just offered to get you some."

"You know what? This is cause for a celebration. Let's go out for real coffee."

"Kingston Kane is *not* cause for a celebration."

"But closing our case is. Come on, I'm buying."

"Well, that *is* cause for celebrating." He laughed and grabbed his keys. "But I'm driving."

"Of course you are." And the banter continued as she led the way out of the bullpen.

∼

The End

A Quick Favor...

If you enjoyed this book, please take a moment to write a short review on your favorite online bookstore so other readers can enjoy it, too.

Thanks so much!

About the Author

Nolon King writes fast-paced psychological thrillers set in the glitzy world of entertainment's power players with a bold, insightful voice. He's not afraid to explore the darker side of human nature through stories featuring families torn apart by secrets and lies.

Nolon loves to write about big questions and moral quandaries. How far would you go to cover up an honest mistake? Would you destroy your career to protect your family? How much of your soul would you sell to get the life of your dreams? Would you cheat on your husband to keep your children safe? Would you give in to a stalker's demands to save your marriage?